an
honest
man

simon michael

urbanepublications.com

First published in Great Britain in 2016 by Urbane Publications Ltd
Suite 3, Brown Europe House, 33/34 Gleaming Wood Drive, Chatham, Kent ME5 8RZ
Copyright © Simon Michael, 2016

A CIP catalogue record for this book is available from the British Library.

ISBN 978-1-911129-39-4
EPUB 978-1-911129-40-0
MOBI 978-1-911129-41-7

Design and Typeset by Julie Martin
Cover by Julie Martin

Printed and bound by CPI Group (UK) Ltd,
Croydon, CR0 4YY

urbanepublications.com

"...An Honest Man *drops you into the murky depths of gangland London when the Krays and Richardsons were in their prime. The criminal trial at the Old Bailey is gripping and utterly compelling, as well as thought provoking. The author keeps us guessing with clever, authentic twist and turns as Charles Holborne seeks justice for his client. Brilliant! ... a must read ... a rare treat of an insight into a trial.*"

RC Bridgestock, husband and wife writing team, Bob and Carol Bridgestock, authors of the bestselling D.I. Dylan series of books and consultants on the BBC's *Happy Valley* and ITV's *Scott & Bailey* series.

"*If I lose mine honour, I lose myself*"
Act III, Scene IV, Antony and Cleopatra

prologue

On the last morning of her life, Hilary Prentice rose feeling unaccountably happy. It was just another day, a Monday; Bob had to be packed off to work as usual and she had to clean the house and do some Christmas cooking, but for some reason the good humour of the weekend had remained with her. They'd hosted a dinner party on the Saturday night, their first for years, and had such a lovely time. She'd enjoyed three or four sherries and got quite tipsy. The snow storm had become so bad that after helping to clear up, her brother and sister-in-law, Peter and Anne, had decided against driving home, so they stayed and slept on the put-you-up. And on the Sunday morning, rather than heading off straight away, they'd all gone to the pub for lunch.

Hilary pulled on her dressing gown and gave Bob a shove to re-awaken him.

'It's twenty to six. You'll miss your train,' she said. He had a business meeting in Northampton that day, hence the early start. He didn't respond, so she shoved him harder.

'Bob!' she hissed, keeping her voice down, forgetting momentarily that the twins, whose term had ended last week, had spent the night at the Bells' and were not due home until that afternoon.

Her husband groaned but he did eventually turn over, opening a bleary eye.

'How can you be so perky at this ungodly hour?' he demanded, his voice hoarse.

She grinned. 'Don't know.' She sat on the edge of the bed next to him, and smoothed the thinning greying hair out of his eyes. 'It was a lovely weekend, wasn't it?'

'Hmm?' Bob opened his eyes again with an effort. 'What? Yes, it was.'

'Can we do it again?'

'Sure. But with less alcohol.' He sat up and swung his legs out of bed. 'You've completely made up with Anne, then?'

'Oh, that was just silly. Families and Christmas – always stressful.' She rose again. 'I'll put the kettle on.'

•

A small convoy of vehicles travelled into Coulsdon up the Brighton Road from the south, two Gas Board vans and two expensive saloons. It was still dark, and they travelled with headlights on. The snow covering the carriageway had been cleared into the gutters but the road surface sparkled with frost. The convoy passed shops decked out in Christmas finery – ablaze with coloured lights with only three more shopping days to go – and slowed. The driver of the leading vehicle, a Wolsey, peered ahead into the dark, looking for a landmark. Apparently satisfied, he pulled swiftly over to the kerb where the Brighton Road met a side road, The Avenue, causing a wave of dirty snow and slush to be displaced onto the pavement. He opened the driver's door and leaned out from his seat. Illuminated by the glare of the lights from the following vehicles, he waved urgently to those behind to pull in. The first Gas Board van stopped immediately behind the Wolsey; the second continued past it and stopped in front. The yellow hazard lights on top of each vehicle began to revolve. The last car, a Ford Zephyr, turned round neatly and came to a halt on the far side of the road, pointing in the direction from which the convoy had come.

Men decamped from all the vehicles and immediately set about their tasks. There was a sense of controlled urgency as they worked efficiently – a well-trained, almost military team. One man wearing Gas Board overalls lifted a manhole cover in the centre of the road and unfolded a red and white striped screen around the opening. A second, also in Gas Board overalls, ran back down the road and placed metal paraffin lanterns at two-pace intervals so the road was gradually closed off into one lane. Another man followed him, carrying a large double-sided "Stop-Go" traffic sign. He stood on the northbound carriageway where the paraffin lanterns ended and watched a colleague stoop to light their wicks in turn. Two men simultaneously carried out the same procedure in relation to the southbound carriageway. They had been fortunate, as no traffic had passed in either direction. A line of cars did then approach from the south, and the man standing in the road turned his sign to "Go" and waved them through.

The driver of the Ford Zephyr was the last to emerge onto the road. As he did so he reached back into the car and took something off the passenger seat. It was about two feet long and wrapped in oilskin. He placed the object under his arm and walked to the rear of the second van, climbed into the back and pulled the doors closed behind him. The two men already inside the van stood, waiting for orders.

Bob Prentice saw flashing yellow lights through the obscured glass of the bathroom window as he shaved, half his attention on the Home Service blaring from the kitchen as he waited for the weather report. He tried to open the window with one hand, his razor in the other, but his fingers were foamy and he couldn't get a good grip on the handle. He grunted and continued with his shaving. He could see from his watch, propped on top of the cabinet against the tooth mug, that he had only twelve minutes to leave the house or he'd miss his train to London, and thus his connection at Euston. The smell of toast reached him from the kitchen, but he doubted he'd have time to eat.

The volume of traffic on the Brighton Road was increasing. A small queue of vehicles was by now accumulating in each direction when faced with a "Stop" sign, particularly in the northbound direction, as early commuters attempted to beat the rush hour. They watched the activities of the Gas Board employees, who appeared intent on the leak or whatever it was in the middle of the road, with irritation.

Bob Prentice took a bite of toast and struggled into his

coat, his briefcase in hand. Hilary handed him his gloves, and stood by the front door. He took another bite and placed the last of the uneaten slice on the hall table.

'Sorry,' he said with a grin, spraying crumbs.

'It's okay. Have a nice day.'

'I'll phone from Northampton as soon as I'm finished,' he said, pulling on a glove.

'Bye,' she said, leaning forward and kissing him briefly for the last time.

Hilary opened the door for him, the blast of cold air making her shiver, and Bob waved from the gate, turned, and walked off to the station. Hilary was about to close the door when she noticed the vans outside. She peered out to see what all the activity was about, but, apart from the flashing lights, she could see nothing. She had thought of going back to bed for an hour, but if they were going to start digging up the road, there wasn't much point. She closed the door behind her and picked up the toast, popping it into her mouth. She swept the crumbs into her hand, straightened the photo of the girls on the hall table – two freckly, giggling 12-year olds – and went back to the kitchen. The house was on a corner and from where she stood by the sink she could see the road more clearly. For the first time she realised that it was gas men working outside. The thought suddenly occurred to her that if they were working on the main, they might have to turn the supply off. Damn, she thought, that's all I need, with half the cooking still to be done! She drew the curtains back and stared outside, wondering how long she'd have and whether it was worth tryingto get the mince pies into the oven.

'What the fuck's she doing?'

'Dunno. Just watching, far as I can tell.'

The men's voices echoed around the inside of the van. The first to speak joined the other and replaced him at a spy hole in the side of the van. He could see the middle-aged woman standing in her kitchen, the net curtain pulled to one side.

'What if she rings ...' began the other.

'I know!' he hissed. He turned from the spy hole, looking grim. His long black hair was pulled back from his face and tied in a pony-tail. A tiny shaft of light entered the dark interior of the van and fell across his face, picking out a scar that slanted down his forehead and cheek. His brow contracted in furious concentration and his cold dark eyes flashed. His companions watched him, waiting patiently for orders.

'Okay!' said the man with the scar. 'Dairy, come with me. And bring the shooter.'

Hilary had finished her now lukewarm cup of tea and had decided to get dressed. She was climbing the stairs when the back door of the house opened and two men wearing balaclavas crept into the kitchen. Hilary heard a noise, but thought that it was the cat-flap. She paused on the staircase and leaned over the balustrade.

'Billy?' she called.

The two men stormed into the hallway and ran at her. It was so fast and unexpected that although Hilary drew a breath to cry out she had no time before her dressing gown hem was pulled hard. She leaned back to prevent herself falling head-first, her slippers slid on the stair carpet, and she found herself being dragged on her back down the stairs. Her bottom hit the hall floor hard and then she let out a startled cry, cut short as a gloved hand was clapped roughly across her mouth. One man grabbed her feet and the other her shoulders, and they half-carried, half-dragged her into the dining room. They slung her on the floor with such force that the breath was knocked out of her. As she lay there gasping for air, one of them sat astride her waist, pinning her hands to the floor on either side of her head. Hilary felt a ball of material shoved hard into her mouth, so forcefully she almost gagged. She felt a draft of cold air around her buttocks and thighs, and realised that her dressing gown had been pulled open. I'm going to be raped! she thought, and she started writhing furiously.

'Grab her feet!' ordered the man on top of her. Hilary started kicking even harder. She felt a sudden blow across her face.

'Pack that in!' She looked up at the speaker. The hand he had used to strike her was now holding a revolver half an inch from her nose.

'You either lie there quietly while we tie you up, or I'll kill you here and now.'

Hilary went suddenly still and looked into the eyes of her attacker. He stared back at her, his chest heaving from the struggle, but his eyes calm and steady. She believed him.

'That's better. Now if you're sensible, this'll all be over in ten minutes, and you'll be fine. If not…' He waggled the gun in his hand, and shrugged.

Hilary felt the belt of her dressing gown being pulled from under her waist, and then her feet were being tied. The man astride her got off.

'Roll over onto your front,' he ordered. Hilary complied, her nightie rucked up and her bottom showing. The man tying her ankles pulled her nightie down for her and she felt a sudden wave of gratitude to him. He fastened her ankles and brought the belt up to her back. Hilary felt her wrists being pulled down. He was trying to tie them with the end of the same belt but it was not quite long enough.

'For God's sake, give it to me!' ordered the other.

He yanked her feet up behind her and Hilary was bent like a bow, her stomach on the ground and her shoulders and knees pulled into the air. Her body suddenly convulsed, her feet thrashing, striking her attacker in the face. She was thrown violently onto her back again, her feet still tied together but her arms free, and the gun was pointed at her head. She seemed not to notice it. Her hands clutched at her breast and her eyes stared wildly. Her two attackers gaped at her, uncomprehending.

'What's she doing, Kenny?' asked one, his voice taut with fear. Kenny brandished the gun again, putting it right to her forehead. He saw beads of perspiration starting from her brow and her face, only seconds ago red and flushed from the struggle, was now a dull grey colour. He pulled the gag from her mouth with his free hand but it made no difference. Hilary tried to sit up but only managed to raise her head a few inches above the carpet. Her torso shook once, twice, three times, and then with a gasp, her hands fell from her chest, and she sank back to the floor, completely still. The room was suddenly and completely quiet.

'Jesus Christ! Jesus, Kenny, look at her! Jesus Christ!'

'Shut the fuck up, Ray!' ordered Kenny, leaning across Hilary's body, trying to locate a heartbeat.

'Jesus Christ!' repeated Ray.

'I said shut up!' hissed Kenny savagely. He pressed his ear to her left breast. Nothing. He stood back and looked at her face again. The sheen of perspiration on her grey face made it look like wet concrete and her lips were tinged with blue.

'Is she dead? Kenny? Is she dead?' Ray's voice rose half an octave with each question.

'It fuckin' looks that way, don't it?'

'But how? How, Kenny? We barely touched her.'

'How the fuck do I know? I ain't no doctor. Heart attack, looked like.'

'Oh Jesus –'

'If you say that once more, I'll fuckin' do *you*, I swear it.'

'What're we gonna do?'

Kenny paused. 'Get her shoulders,' he ordered, untying her ankles and stuffing the belt in his pocket. Ray stood there, his eyes vacant, his mouth open. 'I said get her shoulders, you nonce!'

They carried her back to the hall.

'Stand her up a minute,' ordered Kenny. Ray slid his hands under Hilary's armpits and, with an effort, lifted her upright. He held her in a tight embrace, conscious of her breasts pressing into his chest. His face was buried in her tousled hair, and he suddenly recognised the smell of her shampoo – one his ex-wife used to use – and he felt a sudden confusing wave of arousal, sadness and sympathy for the dead woman in his arms.

Kenny rearranged her nightie and dressing gown, threading the belt back in its loops, and tied it again across her front.

'Keep her upright while I grab her feet,' he ordered.

They arranged her body at the foot of the stairs with her feet pointing to the front door, her bottom on the lowest stair and her head three or four above that.

'There,' said Kenny with some satisfaction. 'The lady fell down the stairs and had a heart attack. Or the other way round.' He examined her ankles. They'd been lucky. The belt was made of towelling and had barely left a mark on her.

'You can see something there,' pointed out Ray.

'Yeh, but you do get marks and so on if you fall down stairs, don't you? She's probably got a bruise on her bum too, where she fell, right?'

'Christ, Kenny, I never expected this…' whined Ray.

'For God's sake, Ray, what d'you expect me to do? It was an accident, but she's dead, right? There ain't nothing we can do about it.' He looked at his watch. 'Come on. The van'll be along any second.'

Kenny strode off down the hallway and into the kitchen at the back of the house. Ray didn't move. He was staring at Hilary's body, his face contorted.

'I bet she was a nice woman,' he said quietly. He crouched down and gently brushed the hair off Hilary's face, a gesture strangely reminiscent of Hilary's own, five minutes earlier, when she sat on the bed for the last time with her husband. 'I'm so sorry, missus,' whispered Ray.

Then Kenny was by his side, hauling him up by the sleeve and dragging him through the kitchen, back out into the cold dawn.

chapter 1

'Will the foreman of the jury please rise?'

'Where the bloody hell is West?' swore Bruce Withers Q.C. under his breath. The case had been running for two weeks, and it seemed as if Detective Sergeant West, who was supposed to co-ordinate the smooth running of the prosecution, had lost interest in it. Rather like he had lost the Crown's star witness, an out of work milkman, Ray "Dairy" Dunlop. Withers scanned the bench behind him where the officer should have been sitting, and looked in vain for the case file.

The clerk of the court addressed the foreman of the jury, a tired-looking middle-aged man in a crumpled cheap suit. 'Please answer the next question either "Yes" or "No": have you reached a verdict on any of the counts on the indictment, in respect of which all of you are agreed?'

A young police officer appeared at the back of the court and scurried to the bench behind the prosecution barristers.

'Sorry I'm late,' he whispered. 'I didn't hear the tannoy.'

'And who might you be?' asked Withers icily.

'PC Simpson. DS West asked me to stand in for him. He's busy somewhere else.'

'"*He's busy somewhere else*"?' repeated Withers. 'I see.

You weren't part of the investigation team were you? And you know nothing whatsoever about this case, do you?'

The young policeman flushed and shook his head.

'As I thought. Well,' hissed Withers with controlled irritation, 'this is the retrial of the Coulsdon diamond robbery; the jury are about to be discharged; and I am about to offer no evidence. I assume that would be in line with your instructions?'

The young man shrugged and was about to say something, but Withers cut him short. 'Yes, thank you.'

The police officer sat back in his seat, his face burning, and looked around him. At the far side of the court, hanging from a tall metal tripod and facing the jury, was a screen, and beside him on the solicitors' bench, emanating heat and apparently recently switched off, was an overhead projector. Spread across the solicitors' bench were piles of transparencies bearing artists' impressions of various defendants. Next to the screen, almost behind the judge's head, was a tall noticeboard on which were pinned location and portrait photographs, maps and sketch plans, joined by long stretches of multi-coloured tape. It formed an intricate web of connections between people and places. At the centre of the board was a large black and white photograph of a half burnt-out security van on its side.

The foreman of the jury spoke wearily, his voice betraying the two days of argument in the jury room. 'No, my Lord, we are still divided.'

Mr Justice Griffith drew a long breath. The cost of the

four-week trial was enormous. To discharge yet another jury...

'Is there no assistance I could give you?' he asked hopefully. He had asked the same question on numerous occasions since the jury retired two days before.

'I don't think so, no, thank you, my Lord.'

'Do you think,' asked the judge, 'that you might break your deadlock if given further time?'

The foreman spread his arms wide in eloquent answer. Several of the jury members shook their heads and Withers thought he detected one or two of them glancing at the back of a particular head or heads in the front row.

'As I have said before, if you think you might be able to bring in a verdict, whether it be guilty or not guilty, on any one or more of the charges faced by Lyall, I shall ask you to retire further.'

The foreman looked round at the two ranks of faces for guidance. There were a few resigned shrugs, but most shook their heads again.

At the mention of the accused's name, PC Simpson looked across at the dock for the first time. A large square-faced man sat looking at his feet. His lips were pursed together and it was unclear whether he was stifling a grin or a yawn. He wore a dark blue pin-striped suit, a light blue shirt and a red silk tie. He might have been a banker or a stockbroker had it not been for the very long black hair swept up from his forehead and falling lank onto his shoulders. That, and a scar that disfigured his temple, starting in his hairline and slanting in towards his nose. The knife – or, perhaps, bottle – that had caused it must have just missed the eyeball, as the scar continued faintly on his cheek until it was lost in the crease of his nose. The pallor of his complexion betrayed a long period on remand.

'Mr Withers?' asked the judge.

Withers rose slowly to his feet. Robert Bruce Withers QC, known to everyone at the criminal Bar simply as "Bruce", had been a barrister since the turn of the century. Matinée idol looks, a commanding, almost intimidating, magnetism and one of the best brains ever to take up practice in the Law, Withers had been the acknowledged star of his generation. He was in his early eighties now, but still a striking figure. Even with the slight hunch that the years had wrought on his spine, he stood over six feet tall. His face was creased and folded into angular planes like weathered granite, but penetrating light blue eyes still spied like a bird's from under bushy white eyebrows.

'With regret, Mr Withers, I feel that the time has come for me to discharge this jury. Has the Crown considered its position?'

'It has, my Lord.'

'So be it. Members of the jury,' said the judge, turning to address them, 'I now discharge you from giving a verdict in this case. I would like to thank you for the great amount of time and effort you've put into your public duty, at a cost, I know, of great inconvenience to many of you. You'll be pleased to know that your duty has now been discharged, and that you will not be required to sit on any other cases. I shall direct the jury bailiff to make a note that you should not be called again for jury service for a considerable period.' He smiled, and the relief among the eight men and four women jury members was obvious. 'You may stay and watch what happens now, or you may leave.'

The judge turned again to Withers. 'Mr Withers.'

'My Lord. The jury having been unable to agree on two separate occasions,' said the Queen's Counsel, 'and bearing in mind the enormous public cost committed to two inconclusive trials, the Crown takes the view that it would not be in the public interest for this defendant to be tried a third time. In all the circumstances, the Crown offers no further evidence against him.'

'Do you have any comment, Mr Blackburne?'

'No, my Lord,' replied the defence barrister, speaking for the first time that morning.

'Very well. Stand up Lyall.' The accused man stood in the dock. 'I formally record a verdict of Not Guilty against you in respect of all charges on the indictment. You may leave the dock. Are there any other matters gentlemen? No? I shall rise.'

'Court rise!' called an usher, and the judge swept out.

The court relaxed, a parade permitted to stand at ease. There was a sudden clamour from the public gallery and the reporters rushed out to file their stories.

Withers turned to the stand-in officer in the case. 'Simpson.'

'Sir?'

'Don't go anywhere. You'll be needed.'

Lyall was taken by the arm by the dock officer. His hand

rested on the rail on top of the dock for a moment and he was about to descend the steps into the cells, when a man approached him.

Simpson recognised him as a prominent defence solicitor. The solicitor didn't speak, but instead patted Lyall's hand. Lyall nodded briefly in response. The solicitor turned away and didn't see the look Lyall gave his departing back. It was not a look that Simpson would have liked directed at *his* back. Lyall then descended out of sight into the cells to collect his belongings.

Simpson turned to Withers and the junior who were busy stacking their papers. A man was weaving his way down the aisle towards them, pushing through the lawyers and journalists making their way out of the court. He was a stocky, heavy-jowled man in a grey suit. He looked uncomfortable, as if his shirt were a size too small, and he was sweating profusely. His hair was cropped extremely short and light reflected from his scalp. He resembled an unhappy bloodhound, which, in a sense, is exactly what he was. He marched up to Withers and, without a word, thrust out a hand containing a thin sheet of paper.

'Ah, Sergeant West. How good of you to pop by,' said Withers, dryly.

'Read it,' ordered West and then, remembering who he was talking to, added: 'sir. I've been waiting for the last hour. Just off the teleprinter,' he explained.

Withers's eyes narrowed. He took the document and read the contents. He sighed deeply, shook his head and returned the paper to the sergeant. 'Hanged.'

'That's definitely the cause of death. But I don't buy suicide. Ray Dunlop was a nice bloke, family bloke. He was in well over his depth and terrified; but suicide? No, I just don't buy it.'

Withers looked over to the now empty dock.

'There's nothing more we can do today. I've already offered no evidence, and even if we could prove that Lyall was involved, it'd have to be the subject of another indictment. Let's await the result of the inquest.'

'And this?' West lifted his right hand and revealed a briefcase handcuffed to his wrist.

'It's got to be returned. We've been through this already.'

'But it's the proceeds of crime!' protested the sergeant.

'That may very well be. But Lyall called evidence to the contrary which we were unable to damage.'

'But the handwriting evidence – ' interrupted the sergeant.

'– was inconclusive. There is no power in English law to confiscate property in these cases. Mr Smith,' replied Withers, indicating his junior, 'has written a very detailed Advice which deals with that, and I agree entirely with his conclusions. Come along,' he concluded, cutting short any further argument.

The two barristers led Simpson and the sergeant out of court. Lyall, now released from the cells, stood outside, a broad grin on his disfigured face, conferring with his solicitor. There was a young woman with them. She had a mass of blonde hair, large breasts only notionally covered by a diaphanous white blouse and long brown legs that disappeared into the shortest of leather mini-skirts at the last permissible moment. She clung resolutely to Lyall's arm. She had watched every day of the two trials from the public gallery. Now her man was free, and about to become eighty thousand pounds richer; she wasn't about to let go.

'Mr Robeson,' called Withers. Lyall's solicitor motioned for Lyall to stay where he was, and approached the Q.C. 'Sergeant West here has the cash found at your client's home.'

'Ah, yes,' said Robeson. 'Are you really going to waste everyone's time and money requiring us to make a formal application for it? Without, what was his name ... Pritchard? Pilchard? – whatever – without the teller, there's no way the Crown could even start to prove –'

'I can save you the trouble, Mr Robeson,' interrupted Withers. 'I am authorised to return the money to your client. This young man here,' he indicated Simpson, 'and Sergeant West, will deal with it immediately. We shall require a receipt.'

Robeson smiled. 'Of course. Shall we go into the interview room over there?'

Robeson led the way. Lyall untangled the blonde from his arm and followed him. Simpson and the disconsolate Sergeant West brought up the rear.

Simpson closed the door behind them. Without speaking West unlocked first the handcuffs and then the locks on the briefcase. All eyes in the room fixed on the briefcase as it opened.

'Eighty-four thousand, one hundred and fifty-five pounds,' announced the sergeant. Simpson looked at the old ten pound notes held together with rubber bands in bundles inside the briefcase. It was more money than he had ever seen before. Sergeant West tipped the cash onto the table in front of him. Robeson eyed at him quizzically.

'It's my briefcase,' explained West. He produced a small pad from his jacket pocket. The top sheet was a formal "Metropolitan Police" receipt. It was already completed and required only a signature. He handed it to Lyall with a pen. 'Sign there,' he said.

'What?' asked Lyall, his soft voice contrasting surprisingly with the scarred face and muscular build. 'How do I know it's all there?'

''Cos I say so.'

'Well, I'm sorry, mate, but that ain't good enough – ' began Lyall. He would have said more, but Robeson held up his hand to silence him.

'Sergeant, I'm sure that it's all there, every tenner of it – ' Sergeant West nodded and breathed a sigh of relief – which was cut short by the rest of Robeson's words: ' – but I do think it should still be counted, formally, so to speak. So there can never be any question about it in the future.'

The sergeant glared at the solicitor, but the latter simply smiled at him benignly. West looked to Withers for guidance. The Q.C. nodded. West's lips formed a thin horizontal line, and he glared at Lyall with such aggression that Simpson took a step forward, expecting his sergeant to throw a punch.

'Okay, if you've got all day…' replied West, simultaneously dragging a chair with his foot towards the table and pulling the rubber band off the first bundle. He sat down heavily and started counting. 'Ten…twenty…thirty…'

Lyall ignored the counting and watched the sergeant's face, smiling. This was scant revenge for the months spent on remand, but it still tasted sweet.

'Funny things, juries,' said Lyall, so quietly that it might have been to himself. 'All that evidence too – '

The sergeant dropped the bundle he was counting and stood, his face inches from that of Lyall.

'That's enough!' commanded Withers, stepping between the two men. He turned towards Lyall and drew himself up to his full height. Although only two or three inches taller than the scarred man, Withers's large craggy face and his black flowing robes suddenly made him look intimidating. Lyall's smirk faded slightly.

'Now you look here, Mr Lyall,' Withers said with soft menace. 'Let me tell you something: I *know* you robbed that convoy. Well, you got off; you played the system and you won. But don't push your luck. I'm warning you.'

Lyall continued to smile, but Simpson could see that it was bravado. The old barrister had rattled him.

'Now,' continued Withers, 'go and wait outside. Mr Robeson here will protect your interests, and your money. Simpson: stand outside and guard the door. We don't want your sergeant being interrupted.'

Simpson opened the door and held it open. Lyall nodded slowly, and after a moment backed away. He looked at the group, nodded again, and departed. Simpson followed him outside and stood with his back to the closed door. West resumed his seat and started counting again. A few minutes later the barristers left, sweeping past Lyall in their black robes without a word.

The sergeant was clearly unused to counting large sums of money. He made a number of mistakes and had to go back and recount several bundles, and it was over an hour later by the time he came to the final bundle. So tired were his fingers that he knocked that bundle and the one before it onto the floor. At last he was finished. Robeson knocked on the door and Simpson turned and opened it.

'We're done,' said Robeson.

Simpson called Lyall over. West was holding out a pen as Lyall stepped back into the room. 'Sign here.'

Lyall looked at his solicitor and Robeson nodded. Lyall took the proffered pen and made his mark on the receipt. Robeson began to gather the bundles from the table and put them in his briefcase.

'Here!' protested Lyall, placing Robeson's wrist in a vice-like grip. He leaned over and grabbed a couple of the bundles. 'Pocket money,' he said. 'And I'll have a receipt from you too, Mr Robeson,' he added, placing a strange emphasis on the "Mister". He turned back to Sergeant West. 'As for you: I'll be seeing you,' he said with an unpleasant smile.

'That you will, son, that you will,' replied the sergeant with feeling.

'Yeh, but not before I've got me'self a suntan,' said Lyall, with a broad smile, patting his pockets where the bundles of notes spoilt the line of his Hepworth suit.

The others watched him leave the room, collect the blonde, and walk off, his hand resting lightly on the woman's buttocks. The sergeant stood, hands in pockets, watching Lyall's departing back. Then he smiled to himself as his fingers closed around the crumpled banknote he had palmed from the bundle of spilled notes. The sleight of hand had been entirely opportunistic and, at that moment, Sergeant "Tricky" West of the infamous Robbery Squad had not considered quite what he was going to do with the marked note. But "Don't get mad; get even" was a philosophy that had always appealed to him, and the tenner now nestling in his pocket would, he was sure, come in handy sooner or later.

chapter 2

A pester of reporters swarmed up to Robeson as he emerged
onto the pavement. He ignored their pleas for a comment
and, squinting in the bright afternoon sun, peered about
for a taxi. One was just pulling up on the far side of the
street. Robeson brushed his way through the questions
without speaking and trotted across the road. He jumped
in as the previous occupants were still getting out, pulling
the window up tightly and resolutely turning his head away
from the newspapermen banging on the window. As soon
as the taxi's previous two passengers has finished paying
Robeson leaned forward and gave his directions to the
cabbie, who quickly pulled away from the kerb.

The two men just delivered to their destination walked
up the steps into the entrance hall of the Old Bailey. As
always when he crossed the polished marble floor, Charles
Holborne, Barrister-at-Law, looked up at the mural
depicting the scene following the bombing of the court
during theBlitz. His father had been one of the fire wardens
responsible for extinguishing the fires and carrying the dead
and wounded to the ambulances.

'Charming,' said the younger, referring to Robeson's
capture of their cab. Charles smiled and shrugged. They

climbed the stairs that would take them to the barristers' robing room. Charles was glad to be back in the Old Bailey, even on a relatively minor case such as this. It was a step in the right direction.

'Good to be back?' asked the younger barrister.

Charles smiled wryly. 'Yes, and I am grateful to you, Peter. But taking returns from one's ex-pupil is a little humbling.'

'I'm sure it's only a matter of time, Charles,' replied Peter with warmth.

He looked across at his friend with concern. Charles was in his late thirties, with a few stray grey hairs amid sleek black curls, his dark eyes framed by long lashes. But the shadows that had developed under his eyes in the last few months, and what was becoming an almost permanent worried frown, made him appear older.

'I thought Barbara was beginning to get some work in?' asked Peter.

'Oh yes. I spent a fascinating month in various Petty Sessions and Magistrates' Courts applying for adjournments, with the occasional careless driver thrown in for variety. So useful was the experience, I'm writing the definitive text entitled "Holborne on Remands", a two-volume book with a loose-leaf index.'

Peter laughed. 'That bad, huh?

'That bad. I finally persuaded our lovely clerk that despite being virtually unemployed for the last six months, even I don't need that sort of exposure. If a man of 14 years' call spends all his time prosecuting careless drivers, he can't be much good. So much for that nonsense about taking silk.'

'It wasn't nonsense. This time last year, you had more work – quality work too – than you could handle. You'd certainly have been appointed had you applied. And in chambers where you were the odd-man out, the only criminal practitioner.'

'Whereas now we're in a specialist criminal set, and I can't get anyone to instruct me.'

'What does she say about it?'

'Barbara? Depends on the day of the week, or the tides, or something. At first it was "Things always take a while to get going after a move, sir". Then there was "It takes a while for our solicitors to get to know your name, sir" – alternating with "Your old firms haven't got used to the new address, sir". She recently tried "It's often slack at this time of year, sir" – but even she wasn't enthusiastic about that one, especially after six months.' Peter laughed sympathetically. 'The truth is, Peter, that barristers aren't often charged with the murder of their wives, but when they are, it tends to cause an understandable reluctance on the part of the legal profession to instruct them.'

The two men arrived at the head of the stairs and together opened the polished swing doors of the robing room. They walked to the centre of the room where there stood an enormous inlaid table bearing a shoal of identical black, shiny, gold-stencilled wig tins. They pushed the oval tins to one side to make enough space for their own, and took out their wigs and wing collars. They replaced their normal collars and ties with wing collars and bands, pulled on their black barristers' robes, and donned their wigs.

'Ready?' asked Peter.

Charles checked the position of his wig one last time in the mirror, and nodded. 'Ready.'

'I'm sure this will be the first of many,' said Peter, patting his former pupil master gently on the shoulder. The gesture was meant kindly, but Charles bridled inwardly and forced a smile.

They descended the stairs again and went into Court 2. An usher approached Charles. 'Hello, Mr Holborne. How are you? Haven't seen you here in ages.'

'Hello. It's Brian isn't it? What're you doing here? Weren't you at Rochester Assizes?'

'I was. But we moved further in, so I applied for a transfer.'

'And the Lord Chancellor said yes?'

'I persuaded him in the end,' joked the usher. 'Are you in this plea?'

'Yes, with Mr Bateman here, who is also in Court 6 on another case.'

'That one's listed for two thirty,' explained Peter with a frown, 'and will take about ten minutes. Am I going to be alright?'

'You're in luck, sir,' replied the usher. 'We're going to be a bit late starting, three at the earliest. The jury in the case before has been discharged, and so all this stuff has to be moved.' The usher indicated the court behind him. A team of clerks from the chambers of the barristers who had just left court were busily boxing up documents, exhibits, projectors and screens.

'Oh, so this is where the Coulsdon retrial was?' asked Charles. 'I wondered why Harry was rushing off.'

'Harry?' asked Peter.

'Yes, the chap who pinched our cab. Harry Robeson. Don't you know Harry? I thought *everyone* knew Harry.' Charles looked at his watch. 'That means we have time for a cuppa. Come on. I'll fill you in.'

•

Harry Robeson stepped nimbly out of the taxi, handed the cabbie a pound note, and crossed the road, dodging the traffic. He walked briskly down a side street until he came to a silver-coloured Austin Princess. He looked behind him, but the quiet street was deserted. He slid into the leather seat, turned the key in the ignition and the strains of *Please, Please Me*, still at No. 1 weeks after its release, suddenly blared from the radio. He turned the volume down, but despite his preference for classical music, he left the Beatles playing. Their optimistic boisterousness suited his upbeat mood.

Robeson started the engine, executed a smart three-point turn, and waited for a gap in the traffic to enable him to turn out into the main road. A blue Ford Anglia pulled in almost immediately opposite the mouth of the junction. Robeson smiled grimly. The driver of the blue car was looking around frantically, up and down the thoroughfare. Robeson fought the impulse to sound his horn at the man.

This was a game they'd been playing for nearly a month now. So well had Robeson come to know the two men following him, this one and the one who drove the black MGA, that he'd given them nicknames. The one in the Anglia had a thin face and fairish hair.

Robeson had first seen him out of his car when at a funeral three weeks before. As he watched the interment by the graveside, Robeson had turned and there was the man, pretending to be a mourner. He was tall with skinny legs, and a way of walking that reminded Robeson of an anglepoise lamp, angular and slightly bent. He had thus been christened "Filament", "Fil" for short. The other man appeared to be shorter, but as Robeson hadn't been able to catch sight of him outside the MGA, he couldn't judge accurately; but he had ferociously bushy eyebrows, and so had been christened "Denis", after the MP, Denis Healey.

Robeson had initially been alarmed at the surveillance, fearing the Colonel's handiwork, but he learned within hours that Fil and Denis were not very expert at their task. The solicitor knew well that to mount an effective and undetectable surveillance operation on one man a minimum of four or five followers were required. Even allowing for that, these two were pretty hopeless. The ineptitude, the shortage of manpower and, most of all, their cheap suits meant that they were almost certainly policemen. The Colonel's boys were usually sharp dressers.

Robeson's deductions had been confirmed during the second week when attending a Magistrates' Court in north London. Fil had followed him into court and had been loudly greeted by the court inspector. Robeson, to protect the other's feelings as much as anything, had pretended not to hear and had gone about his business as if unaware that he was being followed. From then on he had waited for something to happen. Nothing had.

Fil had had difficulty keeping up with the cabbie, partly no doubt because Robeson had offered the latter double fare if he could lose the blue Ford Anglia behind, a challenge which the cabbie had accepted with glee.

Robeson pulled out into the traffic and passed directly in front of the other car. Even then, Fil, who was looking behind him, almost missed the large silver car, but he turned round just in time, and ducked down in his seat. Robeson waited a few seconds and then glanced into his rear-view mirror. The Anglia was directly behind him, and Robeson chuckled at the relief on Fil's face.

As he drove along The Strand towards Charing Cross Robeson noticed an unusually large number of policemen. He took his foot off the accelerator and paid more attention to the pavements. They were thronging with students carrying flags and banners.

'Bugger,' he muttered to himself. He'd forgotten the "Ban the Bomb" march which was due to finish with an enormous rally in Trafalgar Square later that day. Robeson executed a sharp right hand turn off The Strand and looked back in his mirror. Fil had been surprised by the manoeuvre and his progress had been halted by two buses travelling east towards the city. Robeson laughed; almost by accident, he'd shaken off Fil's attentions.

Robeson guided the Austin Princess smoothly northwards through the narrow streets, keeping further to the east rather than the route he would normally have taken through the West End. By the time he reached Camden Town he deemed it safe to return to his normal route and, within another ten minutes, he saw Fil's Ford Anglia one or two cars back.

'Well done,' he quietly congratulated the police officer.

As he arrived outside the gates to his drive, on impulse, Robeson decided to have some fun.

Rather than entering the drive and parking the car in the garage as he usually did, he left it parked on the road. He deliberately looked furtive as he closed the door, and then he ran into the house as fast as he could. That should be enough to attract Fil's attention, thought Robeson, just in case he'd thought of slipping off for a cup of tea. Once inside the house Robeson raced upstairs and closed the curtains in the front bedroom. He threw off his court suit, delved into his wardrobe, and came up with an old pair of trousers, a soft cotton shirt, a brown cardigan with patched sleeves, and a cloth cap. He threw them on, and stood momentarily before the full-length mirror.

'Perfect,' he declared.

He ran back downstairs and, pulling on a waterproof jacket, slipped out of the front door. He put his head down and plodded down the drive, emerging onto the pavement through the tradesmen's entrance, a small gate set into the hedge a few yards from the main gates. The Anglia was parked further up the road. Fil looked up at Robeson but appeared to dismiss the grubby chap in the hat, and transferred his gaze back to the gates of the house. Robeson could see the car radio in the policeman's hand, and Fil spoke into it like a ventriloquist, trying not to move his lips.

Robeson had not wanted his disguise to be that effective, so he crossed the road directly in front of Fil's car, studiously looking the other way. That was enough; Fil looked again at the gardener trudging up the hill away from him, spoke animatedly into his radio for a few seconds, and got out of the car.

Robeson led the policeman on a two-mile trek round the streets of Hampstead and Highgate, trying to look as suspicious and furtive as he could without actually getting himself arrested. After 40 minutes of fast walking, by which time he was getting bored, he brought the game to an end. He turned into a road that led towards Queen's Wood and almost immediately entered an alleyway between two houses. Once hidden from view he raced to the other end and opened a wooden gate set in a tall fence to his right. He was in a large garden. To the right was a substantial Georgian house and to the left the garden was divided by flimsy fencing into long strips, suggesting, as was the case, that the house was in multiple occupation. Robeson walked to the furthest section which was set out as a vegetable patch. To one side, leaning on a spade, was an elderly man, peering intently at something in the soil. He looked up as Robeson approached and reached behind his ear to turn on a hearing aid.

'Hello, there, Harry,' he called in a gravelly cockney

voice. 'I didn't expect yer today. Why dincha ring?'

Harry put his finger to his lips and went over to the man, stepping carefully over the neat lines of vegetables.

'Hello, Pop. I'm playing hide and seek. I'll explain in a sec.' He held up his hand for silence. He could hear movement in the tall weeds on the other side of the fence. The fence was however over six feet tall, and close-boarded; Fil would have trouble seeing into the garden unless he started climbing. Robeson smiled in satisfaction.

'What you up to, Harry?' asked Pop.

Robeson laughed. 'Nothing. I've got some idiot policeman following me, and I've been leading him a dance.'

'You ain't in trouble, are yer?'

Robeson laughed again. 'No more than usual.'

'You be careful, young man. Your dad'd turn in his grave if he thought –'

'I know, I know, I know,' interrupted Robeson. He cocked his head and strained to hear what was happening behind the fence. He heard footsteps receding down the alley. 'Come on, Pop, let's get back to your leeks. What've you done since I was here last?'

Robeson didn't hear the conversation that occurred once Fil got back to his car radio, but he would have been satisfied.

'Car 16? Car 16?'

'16 over,' replied Fil.

'Repeat that address will you?'

'2 Queens Wood Lane, N6, over.'

'Thought so. You've been had. It's his uncle's flat.

Popeye Robeson, d.o.b.: 2nd Feb 1890. Nothing known. Had a fish stall in the East End, now retired. West says Robeson's always there, helping the old bloke with his garden. So much for your "undercover liaison". Harry's taking the piss.'

Fil's reply, had it been transmitted, might have constituted an offence under the Obscene Publications Act 1959.

•

Charles had led the way back upstairs into the barristers' mess where he'd purchased the drinks. He couldn't shake off the tradition of the pupil-master paying for the pupil's snacks, notwithstanding the fact that Peter was no longer his pupil and had certainly earned twice as much as Charles in the last quarter. The two men sat at a table, wigs off and case papers tied in pink ribbon by their feet.

'Robeson, Harold. About fifty, and as canny as they come. He became a solicitor the hard way – by being a clerk for umpteen years, just learning the trade as he went. Been at it for over thirty years, I guess. He's a one-man firm and represents all the major villains. Remember the Camden rapist last year, and … what was his name … Billingsworth, Billingsgate …?'

'Billington, the "Brixton Butcher",' said Peter, the alliteration rolling off his tongue with relish.

'That's the one. He likes that high-profile stuff – well, who doesn't? But in fact his meat and drink is the London criminal fraternity, the top blaggers like Kenny Lyall. And, they say, the Kray Twins.'

'The Krays? He's bent, then?'

Charles shrugged. 'There are rumours, of course. That can't be helped when you defend major-league villains. I don't know any solicitor with that practice who hasn't been accused once or twice. But in his case there's no evidence, as far as I know.'

'How does a one-man band like that get such classy work?'

Charles regarded the younger man. He liked Peter, although their histories could not have been more different. Peter's background was privileged. His grandfather had been a senior member of the Great War government and his father had recently retired from the Court of Appeal bench. His upbringing had been comfortable, Eton and then Oxford, and on his call to the Bar his family had bought him a small flat in Mayfair to provide him with rent-free accommodation in London. Charles had been the first cockney – and the first Jew – he had ever met, but despite their differences, they'd both been surprised to find they shared the same attitudes and ambition and, the factor that cemented a genuine friendship, irreverence. During the course of Peter's pupillage, they'd often rendered each other incapable with giggling.

'He gets results,' answered Charles. 'His work's mostly privately paid too, no legal aid for the Kenny Lyalls of this world.'

'But isn't Blackburne representing him? He must charge the earth. And then there's the junior…'

'Sure. Professional criminals regard it as a necessary

business expense. Lyall'll be paying out of the proceeds of his last job but one.'

'Tax deductible,' said Peter with a grin.

'If he ever paid tax. They say Robeson's got a very good way with his clients. He speaks their language.'

'Like you.'

Charles looked up sharply at Peter to see if he was teasing, but the young man's face showed genuine admiration. Charles smiled. 'I suppose so,' he conceded. 'Like me, Robeson grew up in the East End, working class family. He understands how they think.'

'I met a copper the other day who'd just arrested two of his cousins. Caught them red-handed burgling an off-licence in Whitechapel.'

'I bet he was popular with his relatives.'

'He was pretty philosophical about it. He reckoned they'd all had the same choice of career: villain or copper. He jumped one way and his cousins jumped the other. Said the money was worse as a copper, but the hours were better.'

Charles laughed wryly, and shrugged. 'It's not uncommon where I come from. And think how many coppers we know who don't jump *at all* – just sit on the fence.'

'True. Remember last year's pornography trial?' said Peter.

Charles took a sip of now-cold tea. 'That was an extreme example. Bernie Silver has the entire Obscene Publications Squad on his payroll.' Charles sighed. 'I sometimes think the best we can hope for nowadays is a police force that catches more crooks than it employs.'

'Why do we bother?'

'Because someone has to.'

The two men sat in silence for a while.

'So what about that pillar of the establishment, Harry Robeson?' asked Peter.

'Ah, yes, Harry,' said Charles, brightening up. 'I think he'd love to be a pillar of the establishment, but he never went to university, working class roots and all that … But he does try hard. He's on the board of half a dozen charities – and they say he's very generous with his own money.'

'Trying too hard, perhaps?'

Charles studied the younger man's face intently. 'Maybe. But I understand that impulse, too.' Charles glanced at his watch. 'Come on,' he said, knocking back the last of his tea and putting on his wig, 'we can't keep his Lordship waiting.'

chapter 3

A gust of wind almost dislodged DS West's trilby from his head and he clamped his right hand down hard on the hat to hold it in place, his other hand holding tightly to the guard rail. His raincoat flapped and billowed in the wind and every now and then a particularly fierce wave showered his face with fine droplets of sea spray. He'd made the crossing from Portsmouth to Fishbourne on half a dozen occasions during his career but this was the roughest he could remember. DS West was no sailor, and every time the bow of the ferry dipped it left his stomach behind, but despite that he remained on deck. He found himself enjoying the sharp salt air on his face, the smell of the sea and the wider vistas offered by the crossing. It made a pleasant change from the claustrophobia of London, the cramped smoky offices at Bow Street, the smelly court buildings and the ever-present smog. That had been particularly pervasive this spring, and the smoke-stained London buildings seemed to crowd together and narrow the streets oppressively.

West heard, or rather felt through the deck, the frequency of the engine revolutions drop, and the ferry slowed as it entered Wootton Creek. The up and down movement of the deck subsided quickly and West felt able to take his hand from the rail. His fingers felt slick with salt and water and he took out a handkerchief to wipe them clean. The clouds suddenly parted and sunlight flooded the creek. The ferry chugged through blue-grey water between green fields and massed trees on both sides. Shrieking gulls swooped and dived above the ferry. The scene was so startlingly different from the sergeant's usual milieu that for a moment it felt like he was on holiday.

The tannoy announced that the ferry would be docking shortly and that passengers travelling by car should return to their vehicles. West took one long further look at the bucolic scene, and then made his way to the head of the stairs leading to the vehicle deck.

•

Almost exactly two hours later the enormous oak doors of Camp Hill Prison closed with a thud behind DS West. He wore a rare smile. Clutched in his hand was a manila folder inside which could be found the cause of his happiness: a signed statement from a jeweller named Avram Goldstein. He waved farewell to the officer from Hampshire police who had assisted him and, as he got back in his car, he looked at his watch. He had over an hour before his return ferry: just enough time for a celebratory pint and sandwich at the Castle Arms in Newport.

Back inside Camp Hill, a Category C training prison for low security and vulnerable prisoners, the prison officer who had escorted DS West to the gates returned to his shift overseeing the engineering shop. Goldstein had already been returned to his bench and was bent over making paint brushes. The officer looked down on the jeweller's skullcapped, bowed head and watched his deft hands as he worked. A trustee carrying a newly-manufactured rubbish bin climbed the steps towards the officer. As the trustee passed behind him, he slipped a small piece of paper into the other's hand.

'It's urgent,' he hissed between lips that barely moved, before walking on.

.

'CID Office.'

'Is Jack there?'

'Who's speaking, please?'

'I said is Jack there?'

'No, sir, I'm afraid not. Who's speaking?'

'When's he due back?'

'He's on leave today. He'll be in tomorrow. Can I help?'

'Are any of the Compass Team there?'

'No, I'm sorry. Can you give me your name sir?'

'No.' Pause. 'Look, just tell Jack that it's been arranged for a fortnight tomorrow, right? If he wants to know more, he'll have to get in touch with me before then.'

'And who's the message from?'

'Just tell him "Stinker".'

'Does he know how to get – ' But the line was cut.

chapter 4

Charles opened the door to his tiny flat in New Fetter Lane and tossed his jacket, his briefcase and the red cloth bag in which he carried his court robes onto the sofa. The red bag was now an embarrassment and an accusation, and Charles had considered throwing it away more than once. It was an uncomfortable relic of former glories: given to him years before by a leader to mark exceptional work on a murder case, when Charles had been the up-and-coming junior of the day.

He walked the five paces to the kitchen and examined the bottle of whisky on the counter: almost empty. He unscrewed the lid and lifted the bottle to his lips, about to swallow the last inch.

'Get a glass, Charles, for God's sake,' said Henrietta from her grave. With such clarity did Charles imagine he heard the voice, he almost looked round. Henrietta's vocal intrusions were becoming more frequent the longer he tried, and failed, to darn together the torn fabric of his life. What was worse, she seemed no more sympathetic now than during the last years of their marriage, which Charles thought rather unfair seeing as she had the benefit of the afterlife and, he supposed, a less parochial perspective.

Nonetheless, he obeyed, and poured the remnants of the bottle into the nearest receptacle, a coffee mug taken from the drainer. He took the mug and the day's newspaper, which he had left open on the counter that morning, and went to sit down. For a few minutes he flicked through the newspaper, reading how Dr Richard Beeching proposed to decimate the railway industry. Then he turned to the back pages to read the previews of the Spurs match against Atletico Madrid for the European Cup Winners' Cup in a few days' time.

Until the year before he'd rarely had time to read a newspaper. He'd pick up *The Times* every morning to read the Law Report but otherwise, except for scanning the headlines, he was too busy. He was in court almost every day and would spend the evenings doing paperwork or preparing for the next day's cross-examination or speech. How things had changed. Today, he'd endured another morning of pacing about Chambers waiting in vain for scraps from someone else's table, but by mid-afternoon he could see from the diary that there was no real prospect of work for the following Monday. Even if there had been a sudden influx around 4:30 pm, which did occasionally occur, there were several names above his in the diary with precedence, so he'd given up and returned early to the flat.

The last time Charles had been in a senior court was Peter's return, almost a month before, and he was reluctantly coming to the conclusion that unless things turned round soon, he'd have to find a job. A real job, one that paid a salary every month. The insurance company had eventually decided that Charles had not murdered his wife, and had paid out on Henrietta's life policy. That, the sale of their heavily-mortgaged home in Buckinghamshire and the backlog of unpaid fees had together given him a few months' grace. But next to the empty bottle of whisky was the second "*Please-note-that-your-current-balance-is*" letter from his bank manager, and that boded ill. He'd started to scan the legal appointments in the paper, merely out of idle curiosity, he told himself. So far he'd found a reason to reject as unsuitable every position he'd seen advertised, but the excuses were beginning to sound hollow even to himself.

He threw down the newspaper and wandered into the cupboard that posed as a bathroom, taking his drink with him. He peered at himself in the unforgiving glare of the light above the mirror. He was only slightly over average height but had an extremely broad barrel chest and heavily muscled arms, partly courtesy of his paternal genes and partly due to 20 years of boxing and weightlifting at the Rupert Browning Institute, a gym at Elephant and Castle used by professional boxers. He still trained regularly, but the last fight of his short career was now sixteen years behind him. Was it his imagination, or did his creased white shirt appear to hang rather more loosely on his shoulders than usual? His face certainly did look rather thin, and the dark circles under his eyes were apparently a new fixture.

He returned to the living room and opened his briefcase. He should be getting ready to go out, but he couldn't face doing anything for a while, so he again picked up the newspaper and looked at what he would be missing on television that evening. No television at his parents' house on Friday nights.

His telephone rang, and he reached for it in anticipation. Barbara with a late return for Monday? There was that distinctive click of connection that signified a long-distance call, and then a woman's voice.

'Charles?'

'Rachel?'

'Yes. God, I can hardly hear anything. Can you hear me?'

There was a pause. 'Just about. How are you? What time is it over there?' he asked, trying to remember the time difference.

There was another long pause. 'About nine in the morning?' she hazarded.

There was a lot of noise on the line, but much of it came from what sounded like a party in progress at the other end.

'Are you at a party? Isn't it a bit early?'

'No,' she shouted, 'It's very late! We haven't been to bed yet.'

'I'm pleased you are having such a good time,' said Charles dryly.

Rachel didn't detect the sarcasm. 'Wonderful!' she replied, a very slight, but detectable slur in her speech.

'And when do you suppose these dismal shores will once more be illuminated by your presence?'

'What? You'll have to shout, Charles, there's a lot of noise at this end.'

'I said, when're you coming home, darling?'

Rachel had had a promising ballet career until one of the London Festival Ballet's periodical financial crises, which saw her and several other members of the corps cut to save costs. The setback appeared to have brought her aspirations to an end; having failed to find a home in another company Rachel had given up and got a secretarial job. But then, two months later, she'd received an unexpected call from an old friend who was the director of a small dance company. He desperately needed a replacement for one of his girls who had fallen pregnant, and did Rachel know of anyone? They'd be required for a three-week engagement in the United States and had to be ready to start rehearsals immediately. When Rachel told him nervously that she was available, he instantly offered her the place. Charles had insisted that she go. He would be perfectly able to look after himself, and he could flat- and cat-sit for her. She had now been away for five weeks.

'Well, that's why I'm ringing. We've been asked to stay on. It's fantastic Charles, but we're sold out! They want to extend the run for another month. You don't mind, do you?'

'Of course not – ' he started to say, but was interrupted by her. 'I tried – sorry? What did you say, Charles?'

Charles realised that there was one of those infuriating delays on the line which made sensible conversation almost impossible. They would both speak at the same time, and then both wait for the other.

Rachel was trying again. 'I tried ringing the flat most of last week and I could never get you.'

'Yes, I'm sorry – '

'Sorry?'

'I said I'm sorry you've not been able to get me. I decided to move back into my place. I pop over to Dalston every day or two to keep an eye on things, but all my books are here and I can make as much mess as I like. It's also much nearer the Temple. I brought Moggie with me, so don't worry.'

'Her name's Philomena.'

'Whatever you say. When are you likely to be back, Rae?' he asked, suddenly conscious of how much he was missing her.

'I really don't know. Probably another six weeks. You really don't mind, do you? It's a wonderful opportunity – '

'No, I really don't mind,' said Charles, minding quite a lot but trying hard to sound as though he didn't.

'Look, I can't hear you, and I have to go anyway. Don't work too hard, will you? I'll call again at the end of the week. I love – ' she began, but the line was cut.

Charles replaced the handset more miserable than ever. He looked at his watch. The off-licence on Shoe Lane might still be open, and the prospect of replenishing his supply of whisky and spending the evening getting very drunk was infinitely more appealing than the prospect of Sabbath supper with his parents. Reluctantly he knocked back the last of his drink, and returned to the bathroom to wash.

•

By contrast, the sounds of a quite different Friday night celebration rang out over Greenwich. Kenny Lyall, late of Pentonville Prison, was back from the Costa de Sol with his new suntan, and was holding court at The Victory public house. Its name was apt, but it was also one of very few local pubs with a private room where a discreet party could be held. The event had started with Lyall drinking quietly with a few close associates, but as the afternoon wore on the landlord, a quiet Irishman known locally as "Paddy" but whose name was in fact Michael McGuinness, had noted with increasing anxiety the heavy-set men who entered his saloon bar, looked around cautiously, and then slipped up the stairs to join the party. Then, when he had to pass by the foot of the stairs to change a barrel, two men standing guard who he'd never seen before demanded to know his business. The Victory was still part of Lyall's manor and McGuinness paid well for Lyall's protection. But another publican only a mile distant had recently found himself in the middle of a turf war between Lyall's gang and that of the Richardsons, and for a short period was forced to pay protection to both. A division of the protection spoils had eventually been negotiated, but not before the publican's car had been burnt out by one side and he'd received a nasty knife wound to his chest from the other.

•

Approximately six miles away a battered Commer van pulled up outside a terraced house in Leyton. The van bore the legend "Terry Cooper, Plumbing Contractor". A young man in stained overalls climbed out of the van carrying a bag of tools, slammed the door closed behind him, and raced inside.

'Is that you, Terry?'

'Yes, mum.' He put the bag of tools down in the hall and met his mother on the threshold of the kitchen. He kissed her briefly on the cheek.

'Don't leave them there,' she remonstrated with him, pointing at the tools. He turned and picked them up and set off upstairs. His mother returned to the kitchen, from whence emanated the smell of Terry's favourite tea, lamb hotpot, made with stout. Mrs Cooper shouted up to her son. 'You're back late.'

'Yeh,' he called from upstairs. 'Had a problem on that job in Hainault.'

'You back there tomorrow then?'

'No; got it all sorted. Just took longer than I expected. Have you had a call from the overflow in Stratford?'

'No, dear, no one's called. Don't be long, Tel, your tea's ready.'

'I can't stay, Mum, I told you.'

Mrs Cooper came to the foot of the stairs. 'Oh, you're joking, Terry. I've made hotpot.'

He came to the top of the stairs. He was naked to the waist and was towelling himself down from his wash. 'I'm sorry, Mum, but I did tell you. It's the darts match over Greenwich-way.'

A sudden catarrhal cough from the front room revealed that there was a third person in the house. It was followed by a gurgling laugh. 'You remember, Enid, the boy's been challenged by that girls' team. Eh, boy? Ain't that right?'

'Yes dad,' called Terry, without enthusiasm.

His father had been ribbing him about it for weeks. Terry was the captain of the darts team of his local, The Rising Sun. Their last match had been at home against The Victory. The visiting team had arrived two hours late having gone to the wrong venue, by which time Terry and the rest of The Rising Sun team had assumed they'd won by default. By the time the match had started, the home team had had a couple of pints too many and they were thrashed. So heavy was the defeat, the visitors' girlfriends had suggested that they could give The Rising Sun first team a run for their money. His male ego rather bruised, Terry had issued a drunken challenge to the girls, which was instantly accepted. By the time he found out The Victory's women's team were the current Southern Region Ladies Champions it was too late to back out. Tonight was the night of the big match. Not only was Terry's male pride at stake, but probably his position as captain.

'I'd give a week's wages to watch this one,' said Terry's father, his laughter tailing off into coughing.

'Well that wouldn't come to much, would it?' retorted Mrs Cooper, 'seeing's you ain't worked in four years!'

Terry came downstairs, pulling on a clean shirt. 'What time you off?' asked Mrs Cooper.

'Right now.'

'Can't you even stop for a sandwich?' asked his mother, wondering if the last of the ham had gone the day before.

'No, sorry, Mum. I'm picking up Roy and Adam in ten minutes. Anyway, I'm feelin' a bit off,' he said, rubbing his stomach speculatively.

'Why? What d'you have for lunch?' interrogated Mrs Cooper, eying him carefully.

'A pork pie from the newsagent's next door to the job.'

Mrs Cooper shook her head. 'Serves you right then. Shall I keep the hotpot for you?'

'Yeh. I'll see how I feel when I get in. Ta-ra,' he said, and kissed her again. He put his head round the door to where his father sat, a rug over his knees, his head inclined towards the radio as he listened to a repeat of "Take It from Here" on the Light Programme. 'See you, Dad.'

'Cheers, boy. You better win,' he called out after his son, 'or they'll never let you in The Sun again,' but Terry had closed the front door and was striding to his van.

•

The upstairs party at The Victory was now in full swing. As afternoon had turned to evening more of the men arriving had women on their arms, and the atmosphere upstairs had changed. The clientele had moved upmarket too. The car park now contained some very expensive luxury motors, and the women were better dressed and better looking: high heeled shoes, beehive hairdos, fur stoles and jewellery teetered up the stairs, minutes later sending their escorts down for trays of cocktails and Babycham. On his last trip upstairs to collect glasses, the publican found the thick fug of cigarette smoke now laced with Marcel Rochas and Dior. Back downstairs, pulling pints in the saloon bar for his regulars, he began to relax slightly as the prospect of violence upstairs seemed to recede.

He thus paid little attention to a slim young man wearing a suit and bootlace tie and sporting heavily Brylcreemed black hair who entered the saloon bar alone. The young man, a real pretty boy, wore rings on every finger, an expensive overcoat and highly polished shoes. He stood just inside the door and scanned the bar carefully. He then re-opened the door and gave a signal. A giant of a man entered, followed closely by dark-haired twins. They too were expensively dressed, both wearing dark blue suits and matching silk ties, silver tie pins and cufflinks. One had an overcoat draped over his shoulders, so as to display to best effect the lush red silk lining. Everyone in the saloon bar knew their names. They stopped between the door and the foot of the stairs and the bar fell into silence. Michael McGuinness froze, halfway through pulling a pint. He put the glass down, wiped his hands hurriedly on a cloth and lifted the hatch to step out from behind the bar to greet the newcomers.

'Ronnie, Reggie,' he said to the twins. 'Good to see you again. I didn't know you were coming, or I'd've got some food in.'

'Don't you worry about that, Paddy,' replied Reggie. 'We'll only be here for a mo. Just here to congratulate Kenny upstairs.'

'Of course. Shall I bring up some drinks for you?'

Reggie Kray turned to his brother, eyebrows raised. Ronnie gave an almost imperceptible shake of his head and without making eye contact with McGuinness started up the stairs.

'I think we're fine, thanks,' replied Reggie.

The Krays' party disappeared up the staircase, which was temporarily unguarded, leaving McGuinness standing on his own in the centre of the bar. He listened for the effect of the new arrivals on the boisterous celebration above him, and was not disappointed.

Kenny Lyall was sitting in an armchair in the far corner of the room, his blonde girlfriend perched on the arm. One of her manicured hands stroked the back of his neck while the other twirled an empty cocktail glass. Some of the people closest to Lyall were also seated, but further out into the room almost everyone else was standing. Silence fell as the guests appreciated who was standing at the head of the stairs. Several of the men around Lyall stood nervously, but he remained in his armchair. The twins approached the table, the other guests parting like a diamanté sea.

'Ronnie, Reggie,' said Lyall, rising at last. 'I'm pleased you could make it.'

'It's our pleasure, Kenny,' replied Reggie. 'Good to see you looking so well.'

'Will you sit down?' invited Lyall.

Ronnie Kray stepped forward and took one of the recently vacated seats. Reggie smiled, and did the same. The room settled, and the buzz of conversation resumed. Lyall leaned forward and kept his voice low despite the noise building again in the low-ceilinged room.

'I'm glad you came. I wanted to thank you for keeping an eye on mum while I was away. She'd never have managed without the Away Society, especially since dad passed.'

'Our pleasure,' replied Reggie. 'You know we look after our own.'

'Yeah, well. Mum got a little gift for Vi.'

Lyall reached into his pocket and drew out a small velvet box. He opened the lid and showed the contents to the Krays. Ronnie reached over and took it, holding the open box at eye level. It contained a floral brooch pin featuring tiny milky glass florets on gold branches. He turned it round in the light, and then stared at Lyall, his head slightly tilted.

'Well I never,' said Ronnie, speaking for the first time since he had arrived. 'You never struck me as having class, Kenny, but that's a classy piece. Did you choose it or was it Gloria?' He looked up with a sneer at the nervous blonde sitting opposite him.

'In fact it belonged to me auntie Dolly,' said Lyall. 'Mum always loved it, but like I said, she's real grateful.'

Ronnie snapped the hinged lid of the box shut and put it in his jacket pocket. He leaned forward and stared again at Lyall, all traces of warmth gone.

'Are we good?' asked Lyall.

Ronnie continued staring at Lyall without speaking. Then Reggie put a hand on his brother's arm and Ronnie slowly sat back.

'Just listen to me in future, all right? We had it all sorted, and you very nearly fucked it all up.'

Lyall nodded. 'I know. It's just that – '

Ronnie cut him short with a warning finger. 'Don't start. Just listen to me!'

Lyall drew a deep breath and nodded again. 'Alright. You're the Colonel.'

Ronnie smiled slowly. 'That's right.'

•

Harry Robeson, also bound for The Victory, was as un-enthusiastic about his evening's prospective entertainment as was Charles, but he knew that to refuse Lyall's invitation would only ratchet up the tension between them a further notch. He intended to put in an early appearance and leave after an hour or so. He peered through the foggy windscreen of his Austin Princess and at the same time reached for the switch to extinguish Beethoven. He couldn't concentrate with the music at full volume, and he wasn't sure of his way. He turned left slowly and saw the public house ahead of him on his right. As he indicated to turn into the car park a large saloon with four passengers cruised out slowly. He recognised the young driver and the twins in the rear seat, and breathed a sigh of relief. That was one additional complication he was happy to have avoided. He drove into the car park and stopped in the space just vacated, next to the toilet block, the pungent presence of which he was unable to avoid as he got out of his car.

•

Terry's two team-mates were waiting for him as he came round the Green, and they both squeezed into the front seat.

'Sorry I'm late,' he said. Then he noticed their clothes.

'A bit posh for a darts match, aren't we?'

'Well, Tel,' replied Adam, 'the evening has interesting possibilities, don't you think?'

'Yeh,' agreed the third member of the party, Roy. 'It was you what said you only accepted the challenge so's to get your leg over that Sandra.'

Terry groaned. 'Did I?' He was feeling worse by the minute.

As the darts team negotiated the Friday night traffic towards Greenwich two other cars travelling in convoy approached the car park of The Victory. One pulled up by the pavement and extinguished its lights. The second, a white Ford Zephyr with sharp fins, entered the car park. It crawled up the aisles of parked cars, and the three men inside the dark interior peered intently at they passed vehicles on each side, looking for something or someone. As the Ford was about to turn to go round again, one of the occupants, the rear-seat passenger, pointed to the silver Austin Princess in the corner, by the toilets. The driver stopped, reversed out onto the road, and parked next to the first car. Men got out of both cars. The driver of the Ford Zephyr, DS "Tricky" West, pointed swiftly to the two entrances to the pub and two men jogged across the road, each taking up a position close to the entrance. West and two of the other men walked through the lines of cars in the car park and stopped by the Austin Princess. There was a short whispered conversation and after a moment DS West and one of the others walked towards the saloon door of The Victory and went inside. The other, a very tall man with a peculiar bent-over gait, waited outside in sight of the Austin Princess, but hidden from view in the shadows.

•

Charles walked across Fleet Street to the Temple where he parked his car. He still drove the battered old MG Sprite, despite the fact that what had been the family's principal car, the Jaguar, was still locked in a garage in Buckinghamshire. He didn't really know why. Perhaps because it reminded him too sharply of Henrietta, who used to drive it most; perhaps because with his present practice he couldn't afford to run it; but at the same time he avoided confronting the logic of selling it – that would involve the admission that his practice really had failed. So the Jaguar gathered dust at a cost of seven shillings and sixpence per week, and Charles drove a draughty, damp, unreliable car, suitable for a man half his age.

He moved out into the heavy rush hour traffic and headed north towards Hendon, where his parents had moved two years before. His mother, Millie Horowitz, considered the move to have been a betrayal of their East End roots; she had been born, schooled, married, and had given birth to her sons, all within a mile of her parent's home in Stepney, and the wider roads and gardens of suburban Hendon were alien to her. To what it was she was being disloyal was not clear even to her husband, Harry; most of their friends had moved out years before, replaced by the new generation of immigrants, the Asians; minicab offices, pungent restaurants, shops open on Saturdays – the place of Harry's birth had altered beyond recognition. But still Millie pined for a way of life that no longer existed, and couldn't settle in suburbia.

Charles stopped briefly to buy his mother some flowers outside Hendon Central tube station, and drove the last mile to his parents' home. He sat outside the row of neat semi-detached homes with their privet hedges and closed curtains for a few minutes, steeling himself. Then, with a sigh, he got out of the car and walked up the path that divided the garden in two, to the front door. He rang the bell. He heard footsteps approaching, and Harry Horowitz opened the door.

'Hello, Charles,' said Harry softly. He hugged his son and kissed him on the cheek. There had been little demonstration of affection between them before Charles had married; a gruff handshake or a pat on the back were the only clues to the almost unbearable love and pride Harry had for his firstborn son, the lawyer. Harry more than anyone else had been devastated by Charles's decision to change his name and then, to commit the ultimate sin, to "marry out". He had sat *shiva* for Charles – torn his clothes, and mourned for five days, as if bereaved. Thereafter for Harry Charles had ceased to exist, but part of Harry had died too. But when, against all expectation, Charles had returned, hounded and bereaved himself, Harry's emotional floodgates had opened. Even now, almost a year later, Charles sometimes caught his father looking at him from across the room, a smile on his lips and tears glistening in his eyes.

'How are you, Dad?' asked Charles.

'Not bad,' replied Harry. 'Go in. Your mother's waiting.'

Charles resolutely fixed a smile to his face and went into the dining room. The table was laid for Sabbath dinner, laden with the foods Charles associated with his youth, chopped liver, pickled and salted herring and an enormous plaited loaf of crusty bread. In the middle of the table were the cup of wine and the unlit candles. Charles's brother David sat at the far side of the table in whispered conversation with his recent bride, Sonia. Their heads were bent together, and Charles could see David's hand in Sonia's lap, gently caressing her arm as he spoke. David looked up as Charles entered.

'Charles,' he said, standing and holding out his hand across the table. Charles took his hand and shook it warmly.

'Hello, Davie. How are you, Sonia?'

She was young, twenty-three perhaps, and ten years David's junior. She was not so much pretty as handsome, with a full figure and long lustrous hair. Charles liked her open, frank, face and her serious eyes which missed nothing. She too stood and leaned over the table, kissing Charles on the cheek.

'I'm very well, thanks, Charles.'

Millie Horowitz entered the room from the kitchen, a large box of matches in her hand.

Charles firmed up his smile.

'Good Shabbos, Mum,' he said, approaching her, holding out the flowers.

'Why is it always *you* who has to be late?' she said, brushing past him. 'I was about to light the candles without you.'

•

Terry and the team from The Rising Sun had arrived to find The Victory's car park full. They too parked on the street and went inside the public bar. The ladies team was already there with a large number of good-natured but partisan supporters. The lads from Leyton received a boisterous, though not unfriendly, welcome. Terry and Roy began practising while Adam bought some drinks. Adam watched with apprehension from the bar as the ladies also took some extremely accurate practice shots. Unnoticed among the noisy young people sat DS West and his colleague. They wore casual clothes but they didn't appear to be relaxed. They sat at a table from which they could see through the archway into the saloon bar, and the staircase that led to the private room upstairs. They spoke little, looked frequently at their watches, and appeared to survey the room periodically. A careful observer might have seen that their jacket pockets bulged. After a few minutes, the very tall man who had been waiting outside, DC North, came in and sat beside them. He whispered something in West's ear. West put down his pint and went outside with North.

The match was about to start. Terry, as captain, was to play first against the ladies' captain, Sandra, over whom he had rashly promised to get his leg. He was, however, feeling very ill indeed. He usually had a stomach like cast iron, but he was certain he was going to be sick. He took a swig from his pint in an effort to calm his queasy stomach but it had just the opposite effect. There was nothing for it: he was going to have to excuse himself. To hearty catcalls ('Lost your bottle, mate?' 'He's scared shitless!') and stinging laughter, he asked where the gents was located, and rushed out, impervious to the embarrassed protests of Adam and Roy.

Terry reached the toilet block but, once there, he found the only cubicle occupied. The smell of the place was dreadful. He returned as far as the door, made it into the shadow of a large silver car, and parted company with his lunch.

•

'Don't you agree, Sonia?' asked Millie.

Sonia stood at the table ladling chicken soup intently. It was a tricky job, as the soup contained *kreplach*, triangular dumplings filled with cooked meat, and they tended to fall into the soup bowls with a splash, causing marks on the white lace tablecloth. Sonia looked guiltily towards the kitchen where Millie Horowitz was slicing bread, but her transgression hadn't been noticed.

She caught the eye of her father-in-law sitting patiently at the head of the table, and he winked at her. David entered the room from the hall, having removed his jacket now that the candles were alight, and the blessings over bread and wine completed. As he passed behind his wife he pinched her lightly on the buttock. Sonia responded with a gentle smile and continued to serve the soup.

Millie Horowitz entered from the kitchen, in her hand a breadboard piled high with the bread she had just sliced.

'Don't you agree?' she repeated. 'It's like a criminal, hiding behind a false name.' This was a favourite subject. Charles had been foolish enough to tell the family an anecdote about an incident in court which included a reference to his name. The ritual of the Sabbath meal seemed to goad Millie, and, like a terrier with an old rag, every week she would worry at the frayed edges of Charles's relationship with his religion.

'I don't know, Mum,' Sonia replied uncomfortably, without looking up. 'I can see it from Charles's point of view too.'

'Well I can't. It's nothing to be ashamed about, having a Jewish name.'

'I never said it was,' protested Charles. 'Plenty of people anglicise their names. What about those friends of yours … Betty and Robert …' Charles groped in vain for their surname.

'Green,' assisted David, regretting it the instant his mother's glare landed on him.

'Yes, thank you,' said Charles. 'They were Greenbaum for forty years, and then all of a sudden they lost the "Baum".'

'They should be ashamed too,' replied Millie, putting the breadboard down too hard on the table.

'Mum,' said Charles gently, 'it's just assimilation. Look at any period in Jewish history, when there's been no persecution – '

'I don't need a history lesson from you.'

'Look where you live, and who your friends are now. Compared with a generation ago …' Charles's voice faltered as he saw, too late, his father's expression of warning. 'Let's change the subject eh? Please let's not argue this time.'

Millie hesitated, about to speak, but thought better of it.

For a while here was silence except for the clink of soup spoons against the bowls. Charles watched his father's bowed head as he ate. The ever-thinning silver hair, and the almost imperceptible tremble in his hand as it lifted the spoon to his lips, reminded Charles suddenly that his father was grown old, and he wondered if it wasn't partly his fault. Ever since Charles had returned to the family, Harry had had to endure weekly internecine warfare between the two people he loved most. Whereas the two combatants recovered each week so as to be able to rejoin battle the succeeding Friday, Harry was left exhausted and despairing. Charles vowed again, as he did every week, that he wouldn't allow himself to be drawn into more rows.

'Aren't these lovely dishes,' said Sonia, replacing her spoon in her empty soup bowl.

'Thank you darling,' said Harry. 'They came from my grandmother.'

'By the way,' said Millie. Everyone else round the table held their breath. 'That reminds me.' It was said in a conversational tone that allayed suspicion. 'I've got something for you two,' and she nodded to David and Sonia.

'What, more?' asked David. 'Every time we come here

you give us something – '

'It's just some fish knives, that's all. They were your grandmother's, and I never use them. You might as well have them now as when I die. I'm just delighted I have someone to give them to,' she concluded.

The implication that the widowed Charles could not, in the circumstances, be the recipient of fish knives was not missed by anyone in the room.

'I've got an announcement,' interjected David, trying again to divert the attack from his brother.

'I've been waiting for one of you – '

'Mum!' protested David, demanding his mother's attention.

'Yes? Harry, would you put this on the sideboard?' she said, handing to him a plate, now empty, that had contained pickled herring.

David shook his head in exasperation. 'If anyone's interested – '

'I'm interested,' replied Charles.

'So am I,' said his father. 'So give us your announcement already.'

'Well,' said David, looking at his wife, who returned his glance with a smile, 'I've been promoted. I am now a managing consultant.'

'Mazeltov!' cried Harry and Millie together. 'And what's a managing consultant?' asked Harry.

'It's a consultant who manages the team which services the client; it's one step above senior consultant, and, most importantly, it's one step below associate, which means,' and

David paused dramatically so that even his mother stopped fussing with the cruet and watched him, 'which means, that there's a real prospect of partnership in the next few years.'

'Even with a Jewish name,' said Millie.

David threw his hands up in mock horror and shrugged to Charles.

'For heaven's sake, Mum, it's hardly the same thing. Half the partners in David's consultancy are Jewish!'

'Sure, and they've done even better than Davie. *They're* partners already,' she concluded with impeccable logic.

The cutlery jangled as Charles's fist thumped the table top. His mother ignored him and swallowed a mouthful of soup. Charles took a deep breath, and tried to remain calm.

'Look,' he said softly, attempting conciliation. He took his mother's hand in his own, and squeezed it gently. 'Maybe you're right. Maybe I shouldn't have changed my name. And maybe if I had my time again, I wouldn't do it. There's a lot of things I wouldn't do. But it's done now. My entire career is based on that name. It's the one that I'm known by. It's too late to change back now – I've been Charles Holborne for fifteen years.'

Millie should not have answered. She should have accepted the proffered olive branch. She should have bitten her tongue and offered her new daughter-in-law some more bread. Instead she answered with venom: 'And a fat lot of good the name's doing you now, eh? Now you're the Jewish barrister with the English name, the one who was charged with murdering his *shiksa* wife. And a great help *that* must be to your career.'

Charles shook his head. 'Nothing I can possibly say will make this right, will it? Whatever I say, whatever I do, you're going to punish me! Well, Mum, I've had a depressing day to end a depressing week, and, if you don't mind, I can do without this tonight!' Charles rose, threw his napkin to the table. 'I'm sorry, Dad,' he said, and stormed out.

•

Terry Cooper wanted to die. He had emptied the contents of his stomach over the rear wheel of the silver car but he was still retching, and bringing nothing up. His eyes watered, his legs felt like jelly, and his insides hurt like hell. He heard, but paid no attention to, footsteps tentatively approaching the corner of the car park where he crouched. He was however quite startled to hear someone fiddling with something at the back of the very car behind which he was hiding. Oh, Jesus, he thought, that's all I need! The boot swung open. Terry kept his head down. The owner was not likely to be pleased at the mess Terry's pork pie had made of the wheel and paintwork and Terry, never a coward when in control of his insides, didn't feel able to deal at that moment with an irate, and probably wealthy, driver. Terry succeeded in suppressing the spasms while the owner closed the boot again, and the footsteps receded in the direction of the pub.

Inside the pub DS West and DC North returned to their colleague at the table, who knocked back the last of his pint, and stood. The three of them navigated their way through the crowd around the darts board, where, to the evident delight of the home supporters, it appeared that a ladies' team were giving their male opponents quite a thrashing. They sidled through the drinkers in the saloon bar towards the foot of the stairs. One of the two bouncers who had earlier challenged McGuinness was on guard. The three police officers surrounded him and two flashed warrant cards. The bouncer made to go up the stairs and was restrained gently. DS West and DC North started up the staircase, leaving their colleague at the foot of the stairs with one hand on the bouncer's arm.

At the head of the stairs they were confronted by the second bouncer. He studied their faces for a moment and stood back, allowing them entrance.

Kenny Lyall was still sitting at the table in the far corner of the room. A short man with a cigarette clamped in the corner of his mouth was bending down from behind Lyall's chair, whispering in Lyall's ear, his cigarette bobbing up and down as he spoke through lips that barely moved. Despite the throng of drinkers Lyall spotted the two new arrivals almost immediately, and put up a hand to halt the short man's flow. The conversation around his table stopped and, like ripples spreading outwards from a stone dropped in a pond, silence gradually worked its way to the margins of the party. All eyes in the room fixed on the two newcomers.

Lyall rose, the noise of his chair scraping on the floorboards sharp and loud. 'Well, well,' he said. 'Tricky West. You've got some nerve. What the fuck do you want?'

The policeman raised his voice so as to be heard at the

back of the room. 'Well, we don't want any trouble, Mr Lyall. I want a word with one of your guests. Is Mr Harry Robeson here?'

There was movement, and the guests parted to allow Robeson to the front.

'Yes, Sergeant?' he said as he arrived before the two men. He was a good-looking man, and although in his mid-fifties, still in good shape. He had clear grey eyes surrounded by tiny wrinkles, suggesting, as was the case, that their owner smiled a lot. He was smiling now, an open, curious smile.

'We've had a report that a silver Austin Princess in the car park has been tampered with,' said Sergeant West.

Robeson's eyes narrowed slightly. The sergeant's head glistened through his cropped hair. He must get through buckets of anti-perspirant, thought Robeson. 'And you just happened to be in the vicinity, did you? Two Met detectives off their patch having a quiet drink?'

'Would you like to come down, sir?'

Robeson paused to consider his position before answering and then took a deep breath. 'I guess I'll play this one out. Lead on.'

West led the way with Robeson between him and the other officer. Several of the other partygoers followed to watch the excitement, while others gathered at the windows overlooking the carpark. Lyall remained standing at his table. The short man caught his eye, and winked almost imperceptibly.

At the foot of the stairs the third policeman held the

door of the saloon bar open and the party filed outside into the cold night air. The earlier clouds had gone and the sky was bright and starlit.

West led the way to the corner of the car park where the group of onlookers created a semicircle at a slight distance, their breath creating vapour trails. Some of the women in unsuitably thin clothing hugged themselves and hopped from foot to foot. Robeson had the bizarre sensation that he was in a drama with all the actors having hit their marks perfectly. The stage was set.

'This is your vehicle, sir?' asked West.

'It is. As you well know.'

'Can you confirm if it has been tampered with?'

All eyes followed Robeson as he walked slowly around the car, looking at each of the doors and peering through the windows. Robeson was careful not to touch any of the door handles.

'Looks fine,' he replied. He caught a worried glance passing between the two other policemen. 'Except,' he added, pointing to the rear nearside wheel, 'that someone's thrown up all over this wheel.'

'Did you have anything of value in the boot?' asked West.

'No.'

'Would you mind checking please, sir?'

Robeson smiled at the police sergeant. 'There's no point. The boot's usually empty.'

'We have specific information that someone was tampering with the boot. Would you mind checking, please?'

Robeson knew he was being set up. The question was,

with what and by whom? He could refuse and just walk back to The Victory – or even get in the car and drive off – but he didn't think Tricky West would permit that. The policeman was a long way off his patch and this meeting was obviously planned. The corrupt sergeant had earned his nickname over many years and he was not to be underestimated. He would have other cards up his sleeve if Robeson refused, and the canny solicitor made the decision to play the hand out here and now, where at least there were witnesses.

He reached into his jacket pocket and took out his keys. He opened the boot and it slowly lifted up. West looked over Robeson's shoulder and then pushed past him. He leaned into the boot, and stood up. There was a shotgun in his hand.

'Is this yours, sir?'

'No, it is not,' said Robeson very calmly. 'As you know very well, *officer*, I have never seen it before.'

West turned to the others with a triumphant smile and turned back to Robeson. 'Harry Robeson: you are under arrest on suspicion of unlawful possession of a firearm. You need not say anything unless you wish to do so, but anything you say will be taken down and given in evidence. Handcuff him, Walker.'

chapter 5

The last week had seen Charles's position progress from bad to worse. The day before he had received the politest of summonses to the room of his head of Chambers. Huw Evans Q.C. was a friendly man, with a soft Welsh accent and a gentle sense of humour, but the request to be in his room at six o'clock that evening still made Charles feel like a schoolboy sent to the head for a caning.

The interview had been amiable and inconsequential. They had chatted over Chambers business, what was now being called "the Profumo Affair" which was all over the newspapers, and the case on which Evans was engaged. Only as the silk was rising at the end of twenty minutes did the real purpose of the meeting become evident. He reminded Charles, in the most charming way, that his rent was almost a quarter in arrears and that the previous quarter had eventually been paid seven weeks late. There was no threat and the discussion remained friendly, but he made the position quite clear. It was not really fair for other members of Chambers to support one member – we all have our overdrafts to manage, don't we Charles? joked Evans. He was sure that Charles wouldn't want to embarrass any of his colleagues. He was also sure that Charles would make certain that the rent was paid within the next fourteen days. If that were not possible, although Chambers would obviously try to be as flexible as it could – we all have bad patches, don't we? – some other arrangement would have to be made. He was sure Charles understood.

Charles understood. Red bills from the GPO and the City of London had sat unopened on his desk at the flat for the last two weeks. He had exceeded his overdraft by over two hundred pounds, and had been invited for yet another meeting.

Today he had appeared at Westminster Sessions to act on behalf of a client summonsed under the Metropolitan Streets Act 1867 for obstruction of the footway by unnecessary deposit of goods. The brief, originally destined for one of the Chambers pupils, had been marked with the princely sum of two guineas. It was now six o'clock, Barbara was turning off the lights before locking up for the night, and Charles was, again, unemployed on the morrow. He dug into his pockets, and came up with 12/6. He had some whisky left at the flat, but he didn't want to be alone, so he turned right out of Chambers and walked across the Temple towards the "Witness Box". It was not a pub he used often, but it was right outside the eastern gate of the Inner Temple and there was generally a friendly atmosphere in both bars. There was a private party in progress upstairs, and so he went down to the basement, bought himself a pint, and sat at a small table.

'Hello, Mr Holborne,' said a woman's voice from the table behind him. Charles turned in his seat. Two young women were just finishing their drinks.

'Well, hello Sally.'

Sally had been the junior clerk at Chancery Court, Charles's old chambers. She'd started there as an office girl cum typist but had soon been promoted. Last Christmas however, Stanley, the senior clerk for twenty years, had suffered a severe heart attack, and although still technically in charge, he only came in three days a week, and even then would often leave early. So Sally found herself in charge of the set on a daily basis, and, from what Charles had heard, was making quite a success of it.

She was in her early twenties, but at only just over five-foot tall and with almost a child-like openness to her face, she looked much younger. She was the one person from his old set who Charles really missed.

'How're you doing, sir?' she asked.

'I'm alright,' he said, pleased to see her. He rose slightly and turned his chair so he was sitting at her table. 'Can I get you and your friend a drink?' he asked, forgetting the fact that he had only loose change in his pocket and nothing in his wallet.

Sally's companion answered. 'No, thanks. I've got to go, Sal. See you tomorrow, eh?' she said, getting up and putting on a raincoat. She collected her bags, and departed with a wave.

'Will you join me?' asked Charles.

'Alright,' said Sally, 'just for a quick one. I've got to get my train. But I'll get them: I haven't seen you for ages. Brown ale?' she asked, pointing at his glass and moving off to the bar before he could object. Charles watched her departing rear, and wondered, not for the first time, what it would look like naked. She returned with a pint of stout and what looked like a lemonade for herself, and sat opposite Charles.

'Well then, Mr Holborne, how's the new set?'

Charles grimaced. 'Look, I'm not sure of the protocol here, Sally, but I really would prefer you to call me Charles, not Mr Holborne. You're not my clerk anymore. And for heaven's sake, not "sir"! Particularly outside office hours.'

'We never meet outside office hours,' she replied with a coy smile.

'That can be remedied,' he said with a grin.

'Ooh, sir, now you're being naughty,' she said, in a passable imitation of Barbara Windsor. 'Anyway, if you don't mind, I'll call you "Charlie".'

'Good.'

He'd half-expected her to decline the familiarity, and was pleased she had not. He was also strangely pleased that she preferred "Charlie" to "Charles". No one else called him Charlie.

'I've always thought of you as "Charlie" ever since that … incident, you know?'

Charles remembered. He'd been in Chambers late one night when he had discovered Sally, dishevelled and distraught, having been molested by another member of chambers the worse for drink. Charles had been her "knight in shining armour" – he had even saved her job by somehow getting the barrister responsible to resign. She'd never known how he'd accomplished that, and she'd never asked, but ever since Charles had held a special place in her affections. She called him "Charlie" that night and, briefly, had held his hand. When she thought of the events of that night, which she still did every now and then, she was always surprised to find that her principal feeling was not one of fear at the thought of how close she had come to being raped, but of that moment of intimacy with Charles.

'Charlie will be fine,' he said softly, savouring the echoes of that evening. He paused. 'Please don't be offended by this,' he hazarded tentatively. 'But … but what happened to the accent? And the hair? It's like you're a new person.'

Sally smiled and even in the pub's poor lighting Charles saw her cheeks colour. 'Wotcha mean, the cheeky cockney sparrer bit?' she asked, with a self-conscious grin.

'Yes, exactly.'

'Well, that's all very well for a junior clerk and tea-girl,' Sally replied, 'but I reckoned I needed to smarten up a bit if I was going to make it as senior clerk.'

'Really?' asked Charles. 'There's a long and honourable tradition of cockney clerks in the Temple.'

'Well, we all want to get on. And we all use our masks, don't we, Mr *Holborne*?' she replied, pointedly.

'Touché,' replied Charles, softly. 'Well, whatever it is, it's working.'

'So, you like it?' she asked, pointing at her sleek black hair, and suddenly aware that his answer was important to her.

Charles smiled. 'You look fantastic,' he replied with enthusiasm. 'And everyone I speak to says you're flying as a senior clerk. The youngest in the Temple.'

'They'll find me out soon enough. And you? Busy?'

That was always the first greeting in the Temple, or so it now seemed to Charles, since he had been unable breezily to respond with his customary: 'Submerged!' He took a deep breath. He didn't know quite how to answer. The Temple was a hothouse of intrigue and gossip, particularly among a particular group of the criminal lawyers who appeared to have nothing to do after five o'clock except drink and chat. He couldn't allow his failed practice to become common knowledge; that would certainly have been the kiss of death. At the same time, he didn't want to lie to Sally.

She saved him the problem of further deliberation.

'I hear things aren't too good,' she said simply. Charles had been a favourite topic of conversation round the Temple ever since Henrietta's murder. Everyone knew that his career had taken a nose-dive.

He nodded grimly. 'Not great,' he confirmed.

'What're you going to do?' she asked.

He shrugged. 'To be honest, I haven't a clue. It's not the chambers themselves; they've so much work they don't know what to do with it. Anyway, I wouldn't exactly be attractive to another set. At least when I left Chancery Court, I was the young flier who'd murdered his wife. Now I'm the one with no practice who was cleared of murdering his wife.'

'Are things really a dead loss there, then?'

'As dead a loss as you could imagine.'

Sally pulled a face, her big brown eyes – surrounded by heavily mascaraed lashes – full of sympathy. It's not fair, she thought. Unlike most clerks she actually took the trouble to see her guv'nors in action now and then, so she could talk of their abilities with authority when asked by instructing solicitors. She'd slipped into court on three or four occasions when Charles was in her chambers to watch him from the back of the public gallery. Charles was one of the best barristers she'd ever seen. He had real charisma and commanded the court the minute he walked in, he was very sharp, and he had a down to earth directness that juries loved. What's more, she thought, he's a decent bloke.

'I think it's rotten, what's happened to you, Charlie,' she said softly.

'I agree, Sally. It's perfectly rotten. But there's no point moping about it. I won't be the first barrister to give up because of bad breaks.'

'Give up?' exclaimed Sally.

Charles shrugged. 'I'm going to have to get a job. In fact, right this very second I've decided to start looking tomorrow.'

'You can't do that, Charlie.'

Charles spread his arms wide in a gesture of helplessness. Sally frowned and thought to herself. She desperately wanted to help him in some way but there was little she could do personally. Most clerks had an excess of work at times, and usually returned briefs first to the chambers where their friends were clerks, but Sally's set did civil work, and so even when there was an excess of work at Chancery Court, it would be of no use to Charles. But she was popular in the Temple and she knew most of the clerks. She determined to have a word with a couple in criminal sets and see if something could be put Charlie's way. There might be another route she could try, too.

Charles broke into her reverie. 'Where are you off to now?' he asked.

'Crikey!' she exclaimed, looking at her watch. 'I've got to go.'

'Boyfriend?'

Sally regarded Charles for a moment, her head tilted slightly to one side and her dark eyes bright. She looked like an inquisitive robin, thought Charles. Her lips curved in a faint smile as she tried to guess what, if anything, lay behind his question.

'No, my mother,' she answered eventually. 'Since my younger sister got married I'm the only one left at home, and my mother's one of those people who, they say, enjoys ill health.'

'What's wrong with her?'

'You name it, she's got it – plus quite a few with no names. And there'll be hell to pay if she doesn't get her tea on time,' she laughed, resignedly.

She stood, grabbed her bag and bent down to plant a kiss on Charles's cheek. At the same moment Charles half-rose and, as he turned his head, Sally's lips landed on his. Her eyes registered surprise but she didn't pull away. Her mouth softened, and her hand touched the back of his head lightly. She straightened up and looked at Charles in silence for a second.

'Keep smiling,' she said softly. 'Something'll turn up.'

She rushed off, turning to give him a wave as she ran up the stairs. Charles sat down with the dregs of his pint, noting that his heartbeat had quickened.

Charles arrived at Chambers the next morning only to be sent off to court where he spent the entire day waiting for his case to be called on, and so his decision to find a "real" job was deferred for a further day. Nonetheless, the next day he was again unemployed, and he went into the Temple bright and early to start his search in earnest. As usual, he was the first to arrive. On the mat inside the door was a manila envelope marked "To the Clerk to Mr Charles Holborne". Charles tore open the envelope. Inside was a brief. It was headed "In the Central Criminal Court". Charles gave a little whoop of pleasure, and took the papers into his room to read them.

•

THE QUEEN
– and –
HAROLD JOSEPH ROBESON

BRIEF FOR THE DEFENDANT

Enclosures:
1. *Certificate on committal*
2. *Full bundle of prosecution depositions*

3. *Copy charge sheet*
4. *Copy custody record*

Counsel is instructed on behalf of Harold Joseph Robeson, who is charged with conspiracy to rob. An indictment has yet to be received from the Central Criminal Court, but Instructing Solicitors enclose as Item 3 herewith a copy of the charge before the committing Magistrates' Court. It is not expected that the count on the Indictment will differ significantly from the original charge.

Instructing Solicitors do not propose to set out in detail the facts alleged by the Crown as they will be apparent from the prosecution depositions, but Counsel will see that it is alleged that Mr Robeson conspired with Kenneth Lyall, Peter Simons, Raymond Dunlop and persons unknown to rob the South African Gem Corporation of a quantity of diamonds worth almost £1 million. Counsel may be aware that while Dunlop has since died, Simons and various others have been convicted of their respective parts in the robbery, Goldstein has been convicted of handling the diamonds, and Lyall has been acquitted, following two trials at which the juries could not agree.

Mr Robeson is, as Counsel will be aware, a solicitor of the Supreme Court of thirty years' standing, and acted for a number of the Defendants in these trials.

Instructing Solicitors apologise for the lack of a Proof of Evidence from the Defendant. Mr Robeson is presently in custody, but arrangements have been made for a Proof to be prepared and for comments on the depositions to be obtained as soon as possible. The Defendant will however be pleading not guilty to the charge (and indeed any charge that may appear on the indictment). Instructing Solicitors appreciate that the evidence against the Defendant is very substantial, but the Defendant strenuously denies any criminality, and asserts that he has been "framed" by certain police officers in response to Lyall's acquittal. In particular, he asserts that the gun found in his car (see Bundle 1) was "planted" there.

Instructing Solicitors anticipate instructing Counsel shortly to make an application for bail on Mr Robeson's behalf, and details of sureties and other relevant matters will be forwarded to Counsel in due course. For the present Counsel is instructed to represent the Defendant at the Old Bailey at his trial.

Robeson & Co.

'Well I'll be damned,' said Charles to himself. Why Robeson should have chosen to instruct him was a mystery. The wily old solicitor had his own select coterie of barristers with whom he worked regularly, some of them among the very best in the profession. Why he should choose to be represented on the most important trial of his life – his own – by a junior who was not only unknown to him, but also on the way out, was completely inexplicable. Charles turned the brief over again to the backsheet to make sure that it was indeed intended for him, but there were his name and address in the clearest of capitals.

He pushed his chair back and, backsheet in hand, walked into the clerks' room. Barbara had just arrived. She was a tall, elegant redhead with sharp features and a refined Edinburgh accent.

She had been one of the first women in the Temple to be appointed senior clerk, and she had a formidable reputation. Most of Charles's junior colleagues in Chambers were afraid of her.

'Look at this,' said Charles, putting it on the desk before her.

Barbara finished hanging her coat on the hook behind her desk and picked up the backsheet. She frowned, and turned it over once or twice in her hands. Then she handed it back. 'I'll need it back so I can start a new case file,' she said simply.

'But why have I got it?'

'I don't know sir,' replied Barbara, sitting at her desk and not making eye contact with him.

'But I've never worked for him in my life! It doesn't make sense.'

'I agree.'

'Why hasn't it gone to Fifer, or Blackburne, or one of his other regulars?'

'I really don't know, Mr Holborne. You tell me.' She looked up at him from opening the post and regarded him carefully.

'What do you mean?'

She swivelled round in her chair and reached up to the filing cabinet behind her. 'These came in late last night, just before I left,' she said, throwing onto her desk half a dozen briefs tied with pink ribbon, all held together with a fat rubber band. 'I haven't had time to book them in yet. Have a look.'

Charles bent over her desk. There were seven new sets of Instructions, all marked with his name. The names of the defendants and the courts were all different, but the name of the instructing solicitor was the same in each case: Robeson & Co. Charles dragged a chair from the adjoining desk and sat down heavily.

'What the hell's going on?' he asked.

'You really don't know?'

Charles shook his head. 'Of course I don't. I've never worked for Robeson in my professional life. What do you think? Should I take them?'

'Can you afford *not* to? Mr Evans has kept me informed about your … situation. And it's all good work, sir. A couple of trials at the Sessions but mostly at the Assizes and, you will note, not one of them legal aid. The first one's a plea this afternoon at Inner London. It's for possession of a dangerous drug and … it's marked at twenty guineas.'

'Jesus Christ!'

'Quite. The next one's in a week's time. It appears to be a theft by a company director listed as a fixture for three days. There's seventy-five guineas on the brief, and twenty-five on the refreshers. That just over £131 for three days' work. Not bad.'

'Not bad? It's incredible.'

'But …' started Barbara.

'But what?'

'Well, sir, there's bound to be … gossip.'

'There's been gossip for the last year.'

'This'll be worse. Barristers instructed by him tend to acquire a certain reputation by association. And with your unfortunate history …' She left the sentence unfinished.

'Yes, I know. But what about the cab-rank rule? They're in a field in which I purport to practise, I'm available – I assume I'm available?' The clerk nodded with wry grin. 'And if I'm available, I *have* to take them. Isn't that one of our important constitutional safeguards on which the Bar Council places so much reliance when justifying our exclusive rights of audience?'

'Mr Holborne,' she said gently, holding up her hand to stop him. 'I can see nothing wrong with any of these briefs, and no good reason why you shouldn't act in them, particularly in view of the trouble we've had getting you re-started since your move. And it may be the very fact that you *haven't* acquired the reputation some of his regulars have, is why he wants *you*. You're untainted – everyone knows you've never worked with him before. The small stuff – ' she pointed at the briefs on her desk '– is to see if you know what you're doing. His own case – ' and she pointed at the back sheet in Charles's hand '– is the big fish.'

Charles considered the point and nodded. 'That makes sense.'

'Unless perhaps he heard that you were very quiet, and decided to help out.'

'Very funny. Charity's one thing; risking your own liberty on a junior who's on the way out, is something else altogether.'

'I agree, although I wouldn't have said you were on your way out,' said Barbara.

'You have to say that – you're my clerk. My bank manager has a different perspective.'

Barbara laughed. 'Then take the cases, pay some of the red bills, and ignore the inevitable whispering.'

Charles rose. 'I'll start on Robeson's own trial first. When you've booked the others in, give me a call. Please can you prioritise the one for this afternoon?'

Charles returned to his room via the kitchen, and sat down with a cup of coffee to read the case of *The Queen versus Harold Joseph Robeson*.

chapter 6

Michael O'Connor took one last look around the tiny room that had been his home for the last eight months. He'd never liked the place: it was too small and frequently too noisy, especially in the mornings when they wanted him up and all he wanted to do was sleep and not allow himself to remember where he was and why he was there. Still, he would miss it. It was safe, and it was familiar. And when he had bad days, when the pain came surging back or when he fell a lot, there was always someone there to cheer him up or tell him off for being self-absorbed.

That was what Patty called him when he was down: self-absorbed. He didn't think he was "self-absorbed" – he guessed she probably meant self-pitying – but he understood what she was getting at. Big, blonde, Geordie Patty, with her crisp manner and crisp uniform. A girl he would once have fancied. A girl he would once have "pulled" with no difficulty with his dark locks, blue eyes and ready smile. Now it was all different. Now all he could do was imagine. On his better days he'd still have a laugh, flirt with her, just as he'd have done before, but it wasn't any good. It always stopped short of the point where he would ask "D'ya fancy a drink tonight when you're off?" or "Have you seen the new film at the ABC?"

So he'd lay in bed in the dark, following the loom of the ambulance headlights as they swept across his dark ceiling, his insensate erection making a tent of the sheets.

He spun the wheelchair around. 'Let's go,' he commanded the porter standing patiently behind him with his suitcase. 'I can't wait to get outta this place!'

The ambulance transport took him to his new council flat where the social worker and the district nurse met him. He said nothing as they showed him round and checked to see if he could negotiate the wheelchair through the widened doorways without skinning his knuckles. He nodded without comment at the newly-installed stairlift, the bath board and the raised lavatory seat. They asked him when his sister would arrive and he lied, saying that she'd be there within the hour. So they left him for a while to find his way round, with promises to return later. Only then, once alone, did he slacken the firm grip he had maintained all day, and weep bitter, angry tears for his useless legs.

•

Deposition of Michael James O'Connor
Occupation: Security Guard
Address: Care of Stoke Mandeville Hospital.
Magistrates Court Rules 1952: This deposition of
Michael James O'Connor, Security Guard, care of
Stoke Mandeville Hospital, Aylesbury, was sworn before
me, Michael Harrison Cartwright, MBE, Justice of

the Peace, on 18 January 1963 in the presence of the accused, Harold Robeson, at the Croydon Magistrates' Court.
Signed: MH Cartwright, MBE
Signature of deponent: MJ O'Connor

Michael O'Connor WILL SAY AS FOLLOWS:

I am a security guard employed by Securicor. On 20th. December 1962 I was employed as part of a team to escort a consignment of uncut jewels from Gatwick Airport where they had arrived on a special flight from South Africa, to a bank in London. I was the driver of the transport, and occupied the front cab with one other guard, Paul Curtis. Two other members of the team, Roger and Steven Woodleigh travelled in the van with the consignment.

At approximately 5.20 am we left the airport and proceeded towards London on the A23. We reached Coulsdon without incident at about 6.10 am. At the junction of the Brighton Road and The Avenue there were what appeared to be roadworks. There were two gas board lorries parked on the west side of Brighton Road, and the road was narrowed so it only permitted alternating traffic. I noticed at the time that there was a Wolsey motor car parked by the side of the road between the two lorries, as I felt sorry for the owner who would have trouble getting out in the morning.

We were waved through as we approached. Before we reached the end of the narrowed area a gas van pulled out from the pavement directly into our path. I braked hard but had not quite come to a halt when there was a sudden series of bangs, perhaps five or six, and the van seemed to jolt on each one. I realised that we were under fire. I put the van into reverse, but from the steering I knew that all of its tyres had been shot. Another vehicle appeared behind us, preventing us from moving further.

Five or six men surrounded our van. They were wearing balaclava helmets and identical boilersuits. One man, who appeared taller than the rest, positioned himself in front of the van, slightly to the passenger side, and demanded that we get out. He was carrying a gun. From the width of the barrel and the stock it appeared to be a double-barrelled shotgun with the front part of the barrels sawn off. Another of the men, who was shorter and broader than the first man, also had a gun. It was a pistol, black in colour, with a barrel about five inches long. He held it with both hands, his arms outstretched, and pointed it directly at my head from his position just outside my door. The leader again shouted at us to get out, and pointed his shotgun at the front windscreen. At the same time, I felt the van jerk upwards at the side. I could also hear a "ratchet" sound beneath us, and I realised that the van was being jacked up at the side. I was forced to my left, on top of my co-driver. There was then the sound of a drill cutting into the metal of the underside of the van. That lasted for about two minutes. The van was jacked up so far on that side that I feared that it would topple onto its side. The man at the front then told us that there was a grenade placed through the armour on the underside of the van, and that he was giving us twenty seconds to get out. *I did not believe him, but we were in any event preparing to get out. The angle of the van made it difficult to open the door and we were both still in the cab when there was a huge explosion. I remember being forced back onto Paul, and the sensation of flying, rather like when you drive over a hump-backed bridge at speed.*

I remember nothing more of the events. I awoke in hospital. I suffered a broken back in the explosion and I am paralysed from the lower chest downwards. I have been in hospital from the date of the robbery until now, and I am told that I shall remain here or in a different hospital for several months longer so that I may receive training. It was my impression at the time that the leader did not really care whether we got out of the van or not. He certainly did not wait for us to try to get out, despite the fact that it must have been obvious that that was what we were doing.

Signed: Michael O'Connor

•

'And, of course, with that model you get a radio.'

'How much did you say it was?' asked the woman.

'To buy outright, six hundred and ninety-nine and, as I say, it's well underpriced only because of the left-hand drive. But, of course, if as you say you're going round Europe in it, well, you're getting the benefit aren't you? But, let me repeat: we offer very competitive finance deals. Basically, we can tailor one exactly to your needs, based on what you can afford monthly.'

The young couple looked at each other. He was already

sold. He'd fallen in love with the first Vauxhall Victor model when it came out in 1957 and had been waiting for the second-hand price to fall ever since. She was much less sure. The VW Camper they'd seen the day before was half the price and much more sensible: they could sleep in it and save on hotel bills. As far as she was concerned, she would as soon as go to Canvey Island again with her parents as go on this long and expensive drive around Normandy, but if they really had to go, a campervan was so much more practical. *Her* friends didn't drive about flashy cars like Vauxhall Victors, whatever Stewart's new colleagues did. A caravan had been good enough for her parents for all those years at Canvey, and it would be good enough for her.

'Erm, Mr...?' she said tentatively.

'Rattle. But like I said, call me Rodney, everyone does.'

'Yes, well, how many miles does it do to the gallon? See, we have a long journey to do ...' she tailed off.

'I'd say twenty-eight to thirty, on a run,' said Rodney confidently.

'Really? My dad thought nearer to eighteen or twenty ...' said the woman.

Rodney gritted his teeth and smiled. 'Well, it's true that they used to be very poor on fuel consumption, but over the last few years they solved that problem. No. I can't guarantee it mind, but I'd be very surprised if you got less than thirty.' He turned back to the man. Rodney Rattle had been in the used car business for almost twenty years, since he was sixteen, and he could smell a sale at a hundred paces. Mister was almost hooked; whatever Missus might say. If I can just get him talking figures, he thought.

'How were you thinking of paying? Let's assume the vehicle's all right for a minute, how were you going to pay? Cash? Finance? Have you got a vehicle in part-exchange?'

'Well, we've got enough for quite a bit of it …' Mister started, but felt his wife's hand on his arm.

'Look, come inside and I'll show you the tables,' said Rodney quickly. 'You'd be amazed at how reasonable the monthly repayments are. And frankly,' and here he dropped his voice conspiratorially, 'we might even be able to do something about the interest rates, eh? I know the chap at the finance company and, well, with a bit of arm-twisting, I might even be able to get him down a point or two.'

Rodney was cut short by a hand on his arm. He turned to see a tall young man dressed in a dark suit. He was holding up a card. A Metropolitan Police warrant card. Rodney contained his anger and smiled. The last thing he wanted was a copper nosing around just when he had punters in the yard.

'Mr Rattle?'

'Yes?'

'I'm Detective Constable McMillan. Mr Beeman, your boss, said you could help me. We need the records relating to a car you sold a while back.'

'There was no problem with it, was there?' said Rodney, glancing at his punters, who were listening intently.

'Oh, no, sir. It wasn't stolen or anything.'

Rodney smiled nervously at Mr and Mrs Punter. 'Look,' he said to the policeman, 'I'm a bit tied up at the present.

Could you come back later; tomorrow maybe?'

'No, I'm sorry sir, but this is an important inquiry.'

Rodney looked around. He could see Beeman talking to his secretary in the office, but everyone else was out on road tests or at lunch.

'What records are you after, officer?'

'The bill of sale, an H.P. form, any document that might bear the handwriting of the purchaser.'

'Oh, I don't think we keep anything of that sort – '

'Look, Mr Rattle, I've already been through this with your boss. Your company keeps all the records. I've even seen the filing cabinet. What neither Mr Beeman nor I know, is where the hell you filed them! Now stop messing me about, and dig them out for me. It'll only take ten seconds.'

Rodney doubted that; filing was not his strong suit. He looked anxiously at Mr and Mrs Punter. 'Would you excuse me for just a second? I'll be right back.' He turned to go, and then turned back. 'Perhaps you'd like a cup of tea while you're waiting? I can ask Joanne to bring you some out.'

Mister was about to accept the offer but again Missus intervened. 'No, thanks,' she said, smiling, but looking at her watch.

Rodney fretted for another second, knowing that if he left now he might well lose the sale.

Then, seeing the officer's face, he trotted off to the office, the policeman at his heels explaining what it was he required. Inside the office Rodney dived into the filing cabinet, throwing out files onto the desk, keeping one eye on the Punters outside. They were deep in conversation, with

Missus making the running. Hold on, son, he willed Mr Punter. I'll be right out, just hang on in there! If he could only find the blasted file and get back there, he'd close the sale – he was sure of it. The pile of files on the desk grew and one or two fell to the floor, to be joined by others as Rodney took his eyes off what he was doing to look through the window. As he watched, he saw Mister's resistance grow ever weaker. He was barely answering back now, just feebly gesticulating with his hands, trying to stem his wife's flow of words.

Finally, with a triumphant 'Here!' Rodney found the relevant file and thrust it into the policeman's hand. He raced back out to the yard, but in the seconds it took to run down the corridor, Mister had finally surrendered unconditionally. The yard was bare.

'Shit!' swore Rodney.

•

Deposition of Rodney Baxter Rattle
Occupation: Car Dealer
Address: Performance Motors, 88 Kingsland St.,
London, E8.
Magistrates Court Rules 1952: This deposition of
Rodney Baxter Rattle, Car Dealer, of Performance
Motors of Kingsland Street. London, E8, was sworn
before me, Michael Harrison Cartwright, MBE, Justice
of the Peace, on 18 January 1963 in the presence of the
accused, Harold Robeson, at the Croydon Magistrates'
Court.

Signed: MH Cartwright, MBE
Signature of deponent: RB Rattle
Rodney Baxter Rattle WILL SAY AS FOLLOWS:

I am a car salesman employed by Performance Motors of Kingsland Street. E8. On 12th. December 1962 a man came in and asked about a Wolsey 16/60 automatic, licence number 273 RYU we had for sale on the forecourt at £720. It was a top of the range model with leather upholstery and pile carpets. He asked about the car and gave it a very thorough mechanical check. He was so expert that I took him to be a dealer or a mechanic, but I could not understand why he was prepared to pay retail prices if that were so. He took the car on a road test. When he came back, he paid the full asking price, mainly in £50 notes, without haggling. He paid in cash and therefore filled in no forms at all. The invoice is now produced and shown to me marked RBR 1.

I would describe the man as white, in his thirties, with short fair hair and a moustache. He was about five foot eight in height, and of slender build.

Signed: Rodney Baxter Rattle.

Charles put the bundle down and made some notes. Then he picked it up again and flicked through it, looking for something. Yes: three statements further on, another car dealer, only two days later, this time a Ford Zephyr. Cost: £800. That made over £1,520 on transport alone. Whoever set up this job, two things were clear. Firstly, they took no chances. Many would have simply stolen two cars and put on false plates. By buying legitimately, for cash, there was absolutely no risk of being traced through the vehicles or of being caught while trying to steal them. Secondly, money clearly was not a problem. They were playing for high stakes, and someone had a lot of money to play with. Charles took a sip of now-cold tea, grimaced, and started to read again.

•

May Charlotte Barlow pulled back her net curtains for the thirtieth time that morning and peered out of the front window of her Surrey cottage at the village green. It had been a quiet morning. The Jacksons opposite had had their milk and post delivered as normal, and then, at teatime (around quarter to eleven if May didn't go to the shops, and half past if she did) someone had arrived to deliver a parcel. Mrs Jackson was out at the time and May was about to go over and offer to take it in when Mrs Titherleigh from next door had appeared, and she had signed for it. Mrs Titherleigh had been in her garden cutting her privet hedge, and May had heard the click-click of her shears all morning. It was reassuring, that sound. May didn't like to be alone. The village was so isolated, and anything could happen. The nice lady from the council had helped get a telephone put in the winter before, just in case May needed to be in touch in an emergency.

May heard the sound of a vehicle approaching, and she craned her old neck round to see who it was. It was the plumber for number 21. He'd been there the night before.

May understood from Mrs Smith that their toilet had blocked once more. I expect it's the baby putting things down it again, thought May. Last time it had blocked, Mrs Smith had told her, the plumber had pulled a plastic Mickey Mouse toy out of the U-bend.

May watched as the plumber got out of his van and walked up the garden path. Steve, his name was. He lived in the next village, and she'd first met his aunt in the Wrens during the war. They'd been friends ever since, at least until she'd stopped going to the WI. She really wasn't up to it anymore, not since her last fall. Steve knocked on the door of number 21 and was allowed in by the eldest girl, Julia. My goodness, she's almost undressed! thought May, looking with horror at the 17-year-old's tiny miniskirt and almost see-through blouse. She watched Steve all the way in until the door closed. You can't be too careful, she often said to her daughter. Her daughter, Ellen, lived near Guildford, but she still popped in at least twice a week. She was a good girl, and May counted herself lucky. Mrs Bolley up the road at number 1 had no one, not even on Christmas Day.

Ellen always teased her mother about her nosiness, but it wasn't nosiness really. Even the police approved of people keeping an eye open, didn't they? And where would they have been without her being nosey, eh? That's what she asked Ellen when she poked fun. If she'd not kept her eyes open, they would never have caught those awful criminals. And, for once, May was quite right.

•

Deposition of May Charlotte Brown
Occupation: Housewife
Address: "Lime Tree Cottage", Orchard Lane, Lower
Barnsthorne, Surrey.
Magistrates Court Rules 1952: This deposition of May
Charlotte Brown, housewife, of Lime Tree Cottage,
Orchard Lane, Lower Barnsthorne, Surrey, was sworn
before me, Michael Harrison Cartwright, MBE, Justice
of the Peace, on 18 January 1963 in the presence of the
accused, Harold Robeson, at the Croydon Magistrates'
Court.
Signed: MH Cartwright, MBE
Signature of deponent: MC Brown

May Charlotte Brown WILL SAY AS FOLLOWS:

I live at the above address and have done so for the last thirty
years. The house next door to mine, called "Staplecroft",
is owned by a Professor Wilson who is presently away in
America. Since he has been away the house has been let out to
various people, mainly teachers from the college. On Friday
14th. December 1962 a new set of tenants moved in. I know
it was that day because the previous tenants had been students
and they made a lot of noise the night before with a party. The
first new tenant to arrive was a man in his thirties, tall, dark,
and with very long hair down to his shoulders. He had it tied
back in a ponytail, a style which I had never seen before on a
man. I spoke to him, and he said that he and some friends were
moving in for a week or so on a business course at the college.

I was surprised, as it was so near Christmas, but he said that that was why the course was held then, when the college was otherwise empty. A day later two other men arrived. One was shortish, with fair hair. I only saw him briefly, and so I could not estimate his age. The third man was very dark-skinned, not like an Indian, but more like someone with a very good tan. He appeared younger than the others, in his twenties, and very fit and muscular. I think there were one or two others, as I heard their voices, but I did not see them.

The men had two cars. I do not know much about cars, but I am sure one of them was just like the car used by Stratford Johns on Z Cars, which I have been told is a Ford Zephyr. I remember the second car very clearly as it was the same as my son-in-law's company car, a Wolsey 16/60. Its registration number was 273 DBB. The reason I can be sure of the number is because it had the initials of my late sister-in-law, Dilly Beatrice Barlow.

About a week after the men arrived next door, I saw a report in the local newspaper of a robbery, and of a car being found abandoned. I saw then that the registration number of that car was the same as the number of the Wolsey driven by the men next door. I reported the fact to the police.

Signed: May Charlotte Barlow.

Before Charles could pick up the next statement, his telephone rang.

'Mrs Horowitz, sir,' said Philip, the junior clerk, and he put the call through.

'Hello, Mum?' asked Charles, quite surprised. He

had not spoken to her since the last row, weeks before. 'Everything alright?'

'Does there have to be something wrong before I can ring my son at work?'

'No, of course not,' he replied with a sigh. Less than ten words spoken, and already he was smoothing ruffled feelings. 'How are you?'

'I'm fine.' She paused. Charles sensed that something was indeed wrong. 'And Dad?' he asked.

'He's okay. You know your father; he won't take things easy.'

'Why? What's happened?'

'Nothing's *happened*…' she said, implying the contrary.

'But?' prompted Charles.

'He's been having one of his morbid patches. Talking about his will, how he couldn't bear to die with his family fighting, that sort of thing. He wants you to come to supper.' She paused again, struggling with what she had to say. 'And he wants me to apologise.'

Now Charles was certain something was wrong. He couldn't remember the last time his mother had apologised for anything.

'Mum, will you please tell me if he's alright?'

'He's okay. He's had another of his "turns".'

Harry Horowitz had suffered from "turns" for some years. It was not unusual after such an attack for mortality to weigh heavily on him. He refused to see a doctor for fear of confirmation.

'A bad one?' asked Charles.

'As bad as I can remember,' replied his mother, at last her voice betraying how worried she really was.

'Do you want me to come over?' he asked, looking at his watch. He was due at Inner London at 2 pm, and realised that he would probably not be able to make it to Hendon and back in time.

'No, it's not that bad. The doctor's been, and your father's got to stay in bed for the next while, that's all.'

'Are David and Sonia coming on Friday?'

'I expect so.'

'Shall I come too?

'Yes, please. He wants to see you.'

'Fine. I'll phone tonight and see how he is.'

After he had finished speaking to his mother, Charles read for a further hour and then tied up the Robeson papers to finish reading them that night. Having tidied his desk, he picked up the telephone again and dialled a London number.

'News Desk, please,' he said when the call was answered.

'Farrow,' announced the person to whom he had been put through.

'Percy,' said Charles.

'Charles?'

'Yes. How are you?'

'I'm fine, old chum,' replied the journalist in his wheezy voice. 'How are you, and that lovely dancer of yours?'

'I'm very well. As for Rachel, at the last report she was having a wonderful, if rather inebriated, time of it.'

Percy laughed. 'Is she still away? I thought she was due back some time ago. If you're still on your own, why don't you come to the club for dinner? Can't have you starving while she's away. Is this a social call, or can I do something for you?'

'Well, you could lend me a hand actually. You know Harry Robeson?'

'I know *of* him, of course,' replied the journalist. 'Solicitor, does dirty crime, and salves his conscience by sitting on a couple of charitable boards. Theatres too. Isn't it the Old Vic?'

'Haven't a clue. That snippet of information's new to me. But that's why I called. I guess you've got a file on him somewhere.'

'Not me personally, but – '

'But the paper will, right? Any chance that I could see what there is?'

'Can I ask why?'

'You know he's been committed to stand trial on conspiracy charges?

'Yes. I covered it.'

'Thought so. Well, I'm representing him. I just want to know a bit about the man I'm dealing with.'

There was a pause on the line while Farrow framed his next comment carefully. 'Are you sure this is a good idea, Charles?'

'I am aware how it'll be perceived,' replied Charles, 'but frankly, Percy, I've run out of choices. It's this or bankruptcy. Your colleagues' attentions over the last year have done for me.'

'I know, Charles, and believe me I'm really sorry. It is our job you know. But surely this is only going to make things worse?'

'Like I said Percy, no choice.'

'Well, in that case, congratulations. And, yes, I expect I can help out an ex-employee.'

'That was 15 years ago,' laughed Charles. Like many young barristers just starting out, he made ends meet by overnight reading of several of the Fleet Street dailies, checking for libel.

'Do you want to come and browse?' asked Percy.

'I'm afraid I can't; it's a bit too urgent.'

'Okay. I'll see what I can dig up. We've just acquired one of those xerographic machines, so I may even be able to make you some copies.'

'Xerographic?'

'Yes, it makes copies of paper documents. Absolutely bloody brilliant. Actually, come to think of it, you're only in New Fetter Lane, aren't you? I'll drop them in tonight after work. I'm going to the Aldwych Theatre this evening.'

'That's terrific, Percy. Thanks a lot. I owe you one.'

'In that case you can treat me to dinner.'

'Agreed. Look, I've got to run. I'll give you a call. Bye.'

'Bye.'

Charles collected the brief from Barbara and rushed off to court.

chapter 7

The woman tied her scarf more tightly round her head, seized the hand of a child in each of hers, and joined the back of the queue. It was a damp and miserable day, and the wind swirled around her, seeking out the gaps in her thin clothing and chilling her bones. There were more visitors today than she had seen before and she despaired of keeping the boys occupied for what would be a long wait before they were allowed in. Two men in suits carrying briefcases walked to the door, ignoring the queue. They knocked, spoke a few words to the man who opened the door, and were allowed in. Legal visits, I suppose, thought the woman; they don't have to wait. Look what you get to know about, she thought to herself. I never expected to become an expert in prison procedure.

Her youngest son, Raphael, began struggling, trying to twist his hand out of hers. She gripped tighter.

'Keep still Rafi, please,' she said without looking down. The boy quietened for a few seconds and then aimed a kick at his older brother who was standing on the other side of her.

'Stop that!' she hissed.

'He kicked me first,' complained the child.

The woman looked at the boy on her right. He was studiously examining his shoes and avoiding her gaze – corroborative evidence that he had provoked the kick.

'Please, Hershel, be a good boy,' she begged. He didn't respond, but looked at her out of the corner of his eye. He had become so sullen, so sly. He would goad the others, particularly Rafi, until he prompted retaliation, and then he would run and tell tales or, worse, hurt them out of all proportion to the retaliation. That formed another entry in the account of bitterness she kept awaiting the day of her husband's release. My husband the criminal, she said to herself for the thousandth time. They'd never had a moment's trouble with the children until the day Avram threw away his sanity and his good name, and landed himself in prison. Now they were all wild, even the two girls whom she had persuaded her mother to take for the day. She simply could not manage the trip to the Isle of Wight with four children – even assuming she could have afforded it – so she took them two at a time, alternating boys and girls. This month was the turn of the boys to see their father, the criminal.

'Can we go and sit down over there, Mama?' asked Hershel, pointing to a tiny patch of muddy grass.

'Will you be good, and play with Rafi?'

'Yes,' he replied.

'Go on then.'

She watched the two boys run over and begin chasing each other. It was likely to end with one or both of them crying, but for the moment she hadn't enough energy to

111

stop them. A number of heads among the waiting families turned and watched them. The boys' skullcaps, strange clothes, and the long curled locks at the side of their heads always attracted attention at the prison. Then the woman would feel herself the object of scrutiny, and her face would burn. A Jew – one of the "pious ones", a *hasid* no less – a common criminal. At those moments she would hate Avram with an intensity that, even after months, still surprised her, for having brought such shame upon them.

As always when, finally, she faced her husband over the table in that disgusting room filled with the smell of institutional non-kosher cooking, she did her best to put on a brave face. She knew that he lived only for her monthly visits and tried to blot out the days in between. Last month, the eldest girl, Naomi, had developed mumps and had forced the visit to be cancelled at the last minute, and Avram had sent a letter so piteous that Ruth had cried for days. She knew too that however bad it was for her and the children – the ostracism of her friends and relatives, the endless self-vindication of his parents – for him, the last year had been hell; sheer, living hell. And she knew finally that thoughts of suicide were his constant companion. The knowledge that he had available that means of escape (and he claimed, to her distress, that he had contrived at least two certain methods of accomplishing it) was his only refuge from total despair.

They talked for a while about the flat, her mother's health and Hershel's school work, but in the silence that followed, the false cheer slipped from her grasp as it did every month, and tears again welled in her eyes and ran down her plain cheeks to land in two puddles on the table. Rafi clung to her skirts and began to cry. Avram picked up her hand, bent his bearded head towards it, and kissed it repeatedly.

'Razel, Razel,' he whispered her pet name softly, 'please do not do this!'

'I can't help it, Avram. You don't understand ...' she sobbed, shaking her head.

He stared at the table between them, stroking her hand. 'Listen my love, I have good news.' She didn't hear him through her sobs until he repeated himself. 'Ruth, I have good news.'

'What news?'

He bent forward and lowered his voice. 'There's a possibility of parole soon,' he said.

'How?' she replied incredulously. 'You told me another year.'

He looked down at the scratched table. 'Things have changed.'

'What things?' She eyed him carefully but although he continued to hold her hand tightly, he avoided her gaze. 'Look at me Avram. What things?'

He lifted his head. She knew his face so well, but it was a moment or two before she recognised his expression, so unexpected was it: he looked guilty. 'What have you done, Avram? What have you done now?'

'I would have told you last month, but you didn't come. Razel you must understand: I can't bear it in here. I cannot tell you what it is like. For *them*, the goyim, I suppose it isn't so bad, but for me … it's unspeakable.'

'What have you *done*?' she repeated.

•

Deposition of Avram Shimon Goldstein
Occupation: Jeweller
Address: Camp Hill Prison, Newport, Isle of Wight
Magistrates Court Rules 1952: This deposition of
Avram Shimon Goldstein, Prisoner number 1249862 HM
Prison Camp Hill, Newport, Isle of Wight, was sworn
before me, Michael Harrison Cartwright, MBE, Justice
of the Peace, on 18 January 1963 in the presence of the
accused, Harold Robeson, at the Croydon Magistrates'
Court.
Signed: MH Cartwright, MBE
Signature of deponent: AS Goldstein

Avram Shimon Goldstein WILL SAY AS FOLLOWS:

I am a jeweller with premises in Hatton Garden, London, and I am expert in the valuation of diamonds. Through the course of my business I met a man I knew as Kenneth Lyall. He started coming into my shop to buy jewellery some years ago, probably in the late 1950s. At that time, I thought that he was a successful businessman. He came in infrequently, but when he did, he would spend up to £1,000 at a time.

One day, in the middle of 1962, he came in and bought a

small pendant. He also mentioned that he was owed a large sum of money by a business associate, who was unable to pay. He had been offered payment by way of certain jewellery, but he didn't know if it was real, or, if so, whether or not it was worth the amount of the debt. He asked me if I would be prepared to value the jewellery. At that stage I did not realise that anything might be illegal about the transaction, and I agreed. I am often asked, by people in the trade and by others, to give valuations.

I heard nothing more for some months, and had entirely forgotten about it until one night just after Christmas 1962 he arrived at my shop with another man just as I was about to close for the night. He asked me to go with them to value the jewellery. I said that I had to go home, and invited them to return the next day. Lyall became very upset and said that I had made a deal, and that he stood to lose the chance to take this jewellery unless it was valued that night. He offered me £200 to do the valuation, which is much more than a valuation is worth, but I was expected at home and I still refused. He then became angry, and said that he would hold me personally responsible if he lost his chance to recover his debt. I began to realise that the story of the debt was not true, and I suspected that he was doing something dishonest. However, he was very insistent, and I was quite frightened. He and the other man were young and looked tough, and I was alone in the shop. He then offered me £300 for what he said was only a couple of hours' work, £100 in advance in cash. I agreed, and he gave me the £100 which I put immediately in the safe.

an honest man

I was taken to a car parked outside my shop and I got in the rear with Lyall. The other man, who did not speak at all throughout the evening, drove. After we got out of the centre of London, Lyall asked to blindfold me. He said that the location of the meeting was a secret, and that it would be better for me if I did not know where it was being held. I thought it was a strange request, but I did not feel as if I could protest. After that we travelled for nearly an hour. Much of the middle part of the journey was on a fast road like a dual carriageway, as I could feel that we were travelling at speed and there were no stops at all for some miles. We arrived at a house that I think was in the country, as I could hear very little traffic and there was the sound of wind blowing in a lot of trees.

I was taken to a room upstairs and the blindfold was taken off me. I was shown to a desk on which there was a lamp, and asked to look at a total of 35 cut and polished diamonds. The diamonds were among the largest and most beautiful I had ever seen. Together, I valued them at just under £1 million. While I was at the house I only saw one other person. He was a middle-aged man, wearing expensive clothes. He stayed at the back of the room out of the light, and watched me while I worked. He did not speak while I was there. I saw him quite clearly as I stood up to leave. I believe I would recognise him again.

I was then returned, blindfolded, to my shop in Hatton Garden, and had to make my own way home. Kenny Lyall had also watched me working, and, as I was getting out of the car, he gave me a diamond that I had valued at £500. He told me to keep the change. I have since been convicted of handling

*stolen goods, namely, that diamond, and I have received a
sentence of imprisonment of 20 months.*

*On 7th. June 1963 a police officer came to H.M. Prison
Camp Hill with an album of photographs. One of the
photographs was of the man who was in the bedroom of the
house where I did the valuation, and I pointed this person out
to the officer.*

Signed: Avram Shimon Goldstein.

Charles picked up his pen and made some further notes.
The cross-examination of Goldstein would be a crucial part
of the case. There were a number of ways in which he could
be impugned, not least the fact that by giving evidence for
the Crown he obviously hoped to improve his chances of
parole. Charles was also curious about the diamond: had
Goldstein returned it? The statement made no mention of
it. Charles made a further note to ask the solicitors to check
whether Goldstein had ever been in trouble with the police
before this incident. In a case like this, where his client was
a man of "good character" – without previous convictions
– any dirt Charles could throw at the prosecution witnesses
would be invaluable.

He returned to the bundle of prosecution statements
and leafed ahead. It appeared at a glance that the rest of
the witnesses were policemen or Home Office experts.
The next statement was by an Inspector Bathington of the
Hampshire Constabulary, and he confirmed that he had
shown an album of unnamed photographs to Goldstein,
and that Goldstein had, as Charles expected, picked

out the photograph of Robeson as the man at the house. Charles grimaced as he read on to discover that Inspector Bathington had had nothing whatsoever to do with the primary investigation itself; he had simply been asked to show the album to a witness and record his reaction. There was therefore very little prospect of suggesting that he had done anything improper. If Goldstein had been "primed" to pick out the right man, it had happened in advance of the identification. Charles went back to Goldstein's statement. It was dated the same day as the identification, 7th. June, only two days after Lyall's acquittal. Charles scribbled a few further comments, and returned to the papers. He got no further than finding his page, when the telephone rang.

'Yes?' he asked.

'Mr Holborne? It's Barbara. I have Robeson & Co. on the telephone. They want you to go on a conference at Brixton *this afternoon.*'

'Oh, come on! I'm working on something. Why can't they make an appointment like anyone else?'

'I've told them all that. But the client they want you to meet is Robeson himself.'

'Oh. I see. I wonder what all the rush is? I haven't finished the papers yet.'

'I told them that too, but they don't mind. They realise you've only had them for a couple of days, but the client is very anxious to meet you before you come to any conclusions. They've set the conference up for 2 o'clock. You'd have to leave almost immediately. If you really can't make it, they'll cancel, but – '

'No. Don't cancel. I'll do it. Do they want to speak to me?'

'No, I'll just tell them you're on your way. Oh, by the way, a cheque for the case at Inner London Sessions arrived yesterday.'

'What?' asked Charles, utterly astonished. The average time barristers wait for payment from solicitors is measured in years, not days, and because barristers can't sue for their fees, there's nothing they can do about it. He had scores of cases on his records that had been unpaid for ten years and more, and his position was no different to that of any other criminal barrister. To be paid by the next day was almost unheard of.

'I know. But they just *happened* to receive funds from the client yesterday, and they just *happened* to have a clerk from their office near Chambers, and so they thought they'd drop it in by hand.'

'My God.'

'So you can have the cheque on the way out –' for which Charles silently thanked Barbara, as it usually took three days to go through the accounting system before it reached the barrister concerned, '– and you'd better be very nice to them this afternoon.'

Charles hung up, a broad smile on his face. If this was seduction, he could grow to like it. He returned to the papers. He only had a few minutes, so he skimmed the last few statements. The first two, almost identical, were from the police officers who found the gun in the boot of Robeson's car. The third was in standard form and was the statement of a ballistics expert, confirming that the gun was one that had been fired at the robbery. The last was from the police officer who had interviewed Robeson under caution, although the solicitor had wisely declined to answer any of the questions. Altogether, a strong, but not impossible case, thought Charles. Goldstein was clearly a flawed witness. Given the two acquittals of Lyall, it wouldn't be wholly incredible to suggest to a jury that a frustrated policeman had overstepped the bounds of propriety and "assisted" the evidence by planting the gun. Not wholly incredible; but enough for reasonable doubt? wondered Charles. He re-tied the brief in its pink ribbon, grabbed a new notebook, and set off for Brixton Prison.

chapter 8

Charles parked his car in a side road off Brixton Hill in the certain belief that it would not be there, or at least intact, when he returned. His certainty was not in the least based on experience – he'd parked his car there on each of the dozen or so occasions that he'd had to visit clients at Brixton Prison and it had never apparently been touched – but on the fact that the area itself seemed so villainous. To what extent that feeling was prompted by the knowledge that at any time a quarter of London's less successful male criminals were housed in the rambling brick buildings across the road, he had not considered.

He walked down the long access road to the prison entrance and identified himself to the officer on guard at the entrance. He walked through the security procedures – the frisking, the emptying of pockets – with only half his mind on what was happening. He was thinking of Harry Robeson, solicitor of the Supreme Court. What must he be going through now, thought Charles, whether guilty or not? This was no old lag, for whom prison was no more than a business risk, inconvenient, but, with experience and patience, endurable. According to the newspaper clippings that Percy Farrow had posted through Charles's door, this was a civilised man, a bon vivant; a man reputed to be expert in wine, architecture, and the history of Italian opera; a man whose knowledge of the classics – self-taught, too – was said would rival that of an academic don. Charles was curious to see what incarceration would do to such a man, incarceration with men that must have been as foreign to Robeson as if they had been Tibetan. A few hours in police custody were the worst hours Charles had ever endured; imprisonment had always held a particular terror for him.

He was shown to a tiny interview room and awaited Robeson's arrival. Footsteps sounded along the corridor and Robeson entered. As a prisoner on remand he was entitled to wear his own clothes, and possibly because he had never seen him in anything else, Charles, foolishly, had expected him to be wearing a suit. In fact, Robeson was wearing comfortable slacks and a lambswool jumper. His greying hair was combed neatly and he smelled slightly of aftershave – aftershave which, curiously enough, Charles recognised, as he used the same one himself. Robeson greeted Charles warmly.

'Charles,' he said, extending a hand. 'Delighted to meet you. I hope you don't mind the use of your first name?'

Charles did mind. It always irritated him when strangers used his first name without prior permission but he nonetheless smiled, shrugged, and shook the other's hand. Robeson had a firm grip, and he looked Charles straight in the eye for a few seconds, as if evaluating him. Charles returned the look with equal steadiness. Although he'd never actually met the solicitor before Charles had the odd sensation of recognising something in the other man. It was a sort of openness, a frankness in the wide grey eyes and the bluff, square face that made Charles feel comfortable. Robeson reminded him, for some inexplicable reason, of a Yorkshire cricketer.

'Charles will do,' replied Charles, offering the solicitor a seat.

'Good,' said Robeson with approval as he sat down, 'I don't know why, but I would rather call you Charles. I thought about it, and decided that if I were not the client, I would call you "Mister Holborne", and be quite miffed if the client didn't do likewise. Strange, eh? Anyway, I don't think I could bear it if you kept calling me "Mister Robeson", so let's start as we mean to go on, okay?'

'Fair enough,' said Charles, smiling. 'I must warn you, Harry, that I haven't been through the papers in detail. I've read them once, but –'

'Forget it, forget it,' replied Robeson quickly with a wave of his hand. 'You've only had them a minute. I gather you had a result yesterday?'

Charles raised his eyebrows in surprise. The man was facing a life sentence if convicted, in prison for the first time in his life, and he looked for all the world as if he were relaxing after a round of golf. Now he was asking Charles about yesterday's case, a relatively trivial prosecution under the Dangerous Drugs Regulations. Charles looked hard at Robeson, trying to judge whether this was just bravado, but the solicitor regarded him steadily and with what appeared to be genuine interest.

'We did alright,' replied Charles carefully. 'We were able to undermine their identification evidence.'

'That's very modest of you, Charles, but when you say "we", what you mean is "you". You got the charges dismissed, I understand?'

'Yes.'

'And you were expecting a plea, which speaks of quick thinking, so well done. Bernice was very impressed with you,' said Robeson, referring to the clerk who had attended at court on the firm's behalf. 'But then, the opinion of a 20-year-old typist with a couple of O levels and two years' experience of the law might not be much of a testimonial.'

He said it with a completely straight face and a twinkle in his eye, and Charles couldn't help but grin. One of the particular applications of Sod's Law to practice at the Bar was that one's greatest forensic triumphs were always achieved before an audience consisting of a legally aided client, a part-time judge, the instructing solicitors' temporary secretary, and a drunk in the public gallery sheltering from the rain, none of whom could affect one's future career in the slightest, however impressed they might have been with the brilliant advocacy. On the other hand, when things went wrong, the cock-up was always witnessed by a High Court Judge, a substantial litigious client who could have guaranteed the barrister's income for life, and the senior partner of a prestigious firm of city solicitors. It was an insight into practice that had occurred to many a barrister, but was one which Charles would not have attributed to a solicitor.

Charles undid the ribbon on his brief, and opened his new notebook.

'Don't worry about that,' said Robeson. 'Have you got a light?' He produced a cigar and held it up. 'Do you?' he asked, offering another to Charles.

'I don't, thank you,' declined Charles, 'but I do have a light. Standard equipment on prison visits.'

Charles lit Robeson's cigar, and the solicitor leaned forward on the table.

'We both know there's no point in a con if you haven't read the papers properly. I didn't ask to see you to discuss the case, anyway. At least, not the evidence.'

'What, then?' asked Charles with some irritation.

'Don't fret, Charles,' chided Robeson gently, 'you'll be paid for the con, whether we talk about the case or the weather. And paid handsomely too. I want to get to know you,' he explained.

Charles stared at the older man, his fountain pen poised above his notebook, for a moment.

Then he shrugged, screwed the top back on his pen, and closed the notebook. 'As you wish.'

There was a knock on the door and a man in blue prison uniform put his head round the door. 'Tea or coffee, gents?' he asked.

Robeson raised his eyebrows at Charles. 'Coffee, please,' said Charles. 'Milk, no sugar.'

'Twice, please, Spike,' said Robeson. The trustee disappeared for a few seconds and then returned with the drinks, for which Charles paid.

'An ex-client,' commented Robeson after he had departed.

'Presumably a dissatisfied one then.'

'No. We represented him throughout his career until his last job. Then he was recommended to a firm in Islington with potted ferns and smoked glass windows. Got two years.'

'How are you finding it?' asked Charles.

'What, in here?' Robeson paused, wreathed in cigar smoke. Charles watched him ponder the question. 'It's funny what you miss. Not what you'd have thought at all. I miss my car.' Robeson glanced at Charles, slightly embarrassed at the confession. 'It's got this lovely smell of leather and polished wood. I look forward to getting into it every morning. Had it two years now, and I still feel exactly the same about it as on the day I took delivery. I had a background like yours, you know? East End. No money. Worked my way up the hard way. I've wanted an Austin Princess since they came out. The poor man's Rolls-Royce.'

'What do you know of my background?' asked Charles, surprised.

Robeson just smiled. 'I didn't just stick a pin in the Bar List, you know.'

'Alright. If this is a getting-to-know-you session, I'd like to ask you a question. What's more, it's one I've never asked a solicitor before, just in case I prompted him to ask it of himself: why did you choose me? You've never instructed me before. I'm not a silk. You could have chosen a dozen barristers more experienced than me. So why?'

'Are you a good barrister?'

'Yes, I think so.'

'So do others to whom I've spoken. Are you available to do the case?'

'Yes.'

'Do you think it's winnable?'

'How often do you give guarantees to your clients, Harry?' asked Charles with a smile.

Robeson didn't smile in reply. His voice was low and very serious. 'Agreed. But I'm not asking for any guarantees. I asked if it's "winnable", not whether we'll win.'

'In that case, yes, it is winnable. As you know, anything can, and often does, happen, but the Crown's case is far from water-tight. But that still doesn't answer my question. There are many very competent barristers who would be available.'

'Well,' replied Robeson slowly. 'I'm afraid I can't give you any better answer than that for the present. If you like, you can ask me again at the end of the trial. I don't promise to give any further answer then, though.'

Charles shrugged. This was certainly an unusual conference, but he was rather enjoying it. The usual format was that the barrister would ask questions about the evidence, the client would ask if he was likely to be convicted and, if so, how long he would get, and the barrister would leave.

Charles realised that he was waiting for Robeson to speak and that he had surrendered the initiative. He wondered if this had been Robeson's policy, to see how he would react.

Robeson regarded Charles for a long moment, and then nodded slowly as if satisfied. 'Now I have a more difficult question for you. Do you believe I did it?'

'That's not my job, Harry. It's irrelevant what I believe. I'm not the jury. All that matters is that I convince them to believe you – or at least, have enough doubt about the Crown's case that they can't convict. You know all this better than I.'

'Yes, Charles, I know all that. The number of times I have said exactly the same thing to my clients, and thought them dense for not understanding. But they're not being dense. I realise that now. What they're doing when they ask the question – what I suppose I'm doing – is making sure there's someone, *anyone*, who will believe in them. This is incredibly lonely, you know. Not just for me, but for any accused, and particularly on remand. We stand alone against the combined might of the Metropolitan Police, an able team of barristers and, very likely, an unsympathetic, prosecution-minded judge. All of them are striving for our conviction – and before you protest, yes I know that barristers instructed by the Crown aren't supposed to strive for convictions, but we both live in the real world. And when you sit in that cell, hour after hour, it comes home to you how alone you are, and how the odds are stacked against you, no matter how flawed the Crown's case may seem.' Robeson stood and began to pace up and down the interview room, trailing cigar smoke behind him.

'I understand.'

'No, you don't!' Robeson almost shouted, wheeling on

Charles as he did so. 'You don't,' he repeated more softly. Charles began to wonder whether under the urbane exterior Robeson was frightened. 'My whole life has been governed by this system. I believe in it. Sure, we all gripe from time to time. I'm not pretending it's perfect – we all know it isn't. But I've always believed it's the best there is.'

He paused for a while and sat down again, a frown creasing his brow. 'And?' prompted Charles.

'And now I'm on the receiving end, I'm not so sure. You try telling an innocent man who's just been convicted that, statistically, this happens less here than in other jurisdictions! What if I'm convicted? I'm innocent, you understand; I didn't do it. And yet I know that I may still be convicted. To you it's just another job – alright, maybe a good one, an important one, but a job all the same. For me,' and as he spoke, Robeson thumped himself on the chest for emphasis, 'this is my life! I can't just hand the case over to someone who may or may not believe in me, to whom it is just a job. Can you understand?'

'I can.'

Charles understood perfectly. He too had always believed in the system, but when he'd been accused wrongly of murdering Henrietta, and as the evidence piled up against him and no one believed him, it had been a profound shock. His faith in the system had never fully recovered.

'Well? I repeat: do you believe I'm innocent?' He leaned forward again, his face only inches from Charles's, staring directly into the barrister's eyes.

Charles wondered if this question were an even more

direct test. How could the man expect him to answer?

'Harry,' he answered slowly, 'if you were any old client, I could bullshit you, and say "Yes, of course I believe you". But the truth is, firstly, I haven't heard the evidence, and secondly, even if I had, I still wouldn't know whether you did it. I wasn't there, and I'm not God. All I can say is, I'll fight as hard as I can to have you acquitted. So far as my *opinion* is concerned, it's irrelevant.'

'What if I *demand* your opinion?'

'I can't and won't give it to you. If you like, you can ask me again at the end of the trial. But, like you, I don't promise to give any further answer then.'

Robeson threw back his head and laughed. 'Touché! Alright, Charles Holborne you'll do! I think you're straight, and I'll accept that for now.'

Robeson took another lungful of cigar smoke and sat back in his chair. The tension in the room had gone, and Robeson was as relaxed as when he first entered.

'Is that what all this was for, Harry? For you to decide if I'm "straight"?'

'Now, now, don't be offended, Charles. I am genuinely up against it here. And I wouldn't put much past Sergeant Tricky West. I had to know whether or not he could get to you.'

He saw Charles frown and realised he didn't know who Jack West was. 'Sergeant Jack West. Has the well-earned nickname of "Tricky" and is the principal investigating officer in my case. Unlike you and I, he doesn't believe in our system of justice – or at least, if he does, he believes it needs a leg up every now and then. He's been fighting his own little crusade for some years now. I started to keep a file on that man in 1952. Since then I have accumulated over thirty statements, various clients and witnesses, unrelated cases. Many involving people who, in truth, had never done anything worse than park on a yellow line.'

Robeson paused and spoke slowly, emphasising each word. 'Every one of them alleged that he's planted evidence, fabricated confessions, and bullied suspects. You know the sort of thing: threatening to charge their wives or have their children taken into care. On two occasions he's even bribed witnesses – presumably with his own money, so I guess he believes in what he's doing. I won't bore you with the details, you're welcome to see the file if you like. The point is, if West thought he could get round you, he'd do it.'

'I see. And you reckon he planted the gun?'

Robeson shrugged and raised his arms. 'How do I know? All I know is that *I* didn't put it there. I know too that West's been after me for years. He's lost too many cases against me. The Lyall re-trial was probably just the last straw. You know the score: if you defend important cases, and if you're any good, the time will come, sooner or later, when certain police officers start being sore losers. From then on, you're fair game.'

'You realise that it's not going to be possible to prove it?' warned Charles. 'Your dossier on Sergeant West isn't admissible in this case: it's only relevant so far as his creditworthiness is concerned and I couldn't go behind the answers he gives me in cross-examination. Most judges wouldn't even allow the questions.'

'I know that. I just want you to appreciate the situation. Thirty witnesses. They can't *all* be lying.' Robeson leaned forward once more, his face suddenly serious again. 'I was set up, Charles. And whether you believe me or not, I wanted to tell you, face-to-face, not just in some statement that my staff have prepared, but man-to-man. Maybe that's part of the reason I chose you. You were charged with murder, right? You were entirely innocent, but all the evidence seemed to point at you. You know as well as I do, the system didn't save you. The system would have had you hanged by the neck until dead. You had your back to the wall – just as mine is now – and you had to get yourself out of it. So, of all the barristers I know, you probably understand better than any, how I feel at this moment.'

Robeson rose. 'Anyway, Charles, I shan't take up any more of your time. You've got some work to do,' he said, indicating the brief with his cigar. He put the cigar back between his lips and offered his hand. 'I'll get the office to arrange a proper con in a few weeks. I'm going to ask you to make a bail application before then, for what good it'll do, so I'll see you at Court.'

Charles watched the solicitor walk off down the corridor. Then he packed his papers back into his briefcase, smiled to himself, and left.

chapter 9

Charles arrived back in Chambers just after six o'clock. Barbara had already left, but there, in his pigeon-hole, was another brief. It was from a firm of solicitors who had instructed him regularly at Chancery Court. He had long since given up hope of further work from them. Maybe my luck's really changed, he thought. There was a note under the ribbon from Barbara: *"Better late than never I suppose. Warned for next week. Con arranged for Friday 4.30 pm. Clear tomorrow."* Even the last sentence couldn't deflate him. On impulse, he picked up the telephone in the clerks' room and dialled a number he knew well.

'Chancery Court,' announced Sally.

'Hello Sally, it's Charles.'

'Hi,' she replied, the official tone leaving her voice.

'I'm glad I caught you.'

'Yes. Me too.'

Charles thought of the kiss, knowing that she was thinking of it too. It was as if they both knew that a line was about to be crossed, and both held their breath, savouring the moment.

'Have you time for a drink? I've something to celebrate.'

'Yes, I think so,' she answered. 'I'll have to make a phone call first. Charlie?'

'Yes?'

'Will I be quite late?'

'Yes.'

They met in the same pub. Charles arrived a minute or two before Sally. They kissed as soon as she walked in, this time with no hesitation. Thereafter they didn't touch again except by accident. They talked for the duration of a drink, and Charles told her briefly about Robeson and the sudden influx of work, but neither of them paid much attention. A mutual decision had already been made, and both were impatient. They left after fifteen minutes. Sally faced Charles as they emerged onto the pavement.

'Charlie, I missed lunch, and I'm really hungry. I'm sorry, but can we grab a quick bite first?'

'Sure,' he said, laughing. 'We've waited years; another couple of hours won't matter.'

'It will to me,' she said, squeezing his hand. 'But I reckon I could wait half an hour!'

They turned eastward on Fleet Street and went into the first restaurant they found, Il Ristorante, on the Strand. It was almost empty, and their single course arrived quickly. They spoke little, and neither paid much attention to what they were eating. Within 45 minutes Charles had left two £1 notes on the table and they were walking swiftly back towards Fetter Lane, hand-in-hand.

Charles entered the flat and put on the light. He took Sally's coat and hung it up while she disappeared into the bathroom. Charles took two glasses and what was left of his whisky into the bedroom, checking briefly that it wasn't too untidy. He threw some socks into the washing basket and Rachel's cat into the lounge. He smiled wryly at the irony, and wondered briefly why he didn't feel guilty. He slipped out of his shoes and socks. There was a light tap on the door, and Sally appeared in the doorway. She was wearing Charles's bathrobe which she'd found hanging in the bathroom. It was enormous on her and made her look even more like a child. Then she stepped towards Charles, and let the front of the bathrobe fall open, and she was no longer child-like. Charles's eyes travelled down her body. She was slim, but with much larger breasts than he had imagined, and small, dark brown nipples. His eyes continued down to the tidy triangle of hair between her legs and her slim perfectly shaped legs.

'Sally,' he whispered, 'I had no idea.'

Sally looked at him with her head slightly tilted and an amused smile on her rosebud lips. 'No idea?'

'That you were so … gorgeous!'

She took a step towards him and, without speaking, slid his jacket off his shoulders, hanging it over the back of a chair by the bed. He reached to unknot his tie but she gently pushed his hands down. 'I want to do it. I've thought about this a lot.'

Sally undid his tie and placed it neatly over the jacket. Then, with slow, deliberate precision, she undid each of the buttons on his white shirt from his neck to his waist and slipped her hands inside, following the contours of his pectoral muscles. She looked up at his face in surprise.

'Blimey, Charlie, where'd you get these muscles? You look like one of those wrestlers on TV.'

'Boxing.'

Sally's hands travelled round to his back and she pressed her face to his chest, inhaling his smell. Her tongue circled one of his nipples, and she felt it harden in response. After a second she stepped back again and continued undressing him, starting with his belt buckle and then his trouser buttons. She eased his flies open.

'I never knew you cared, Charlie,' she said, looking up at him.

'Oh,' he said, his throat constricted, 'oh, yes you did.'

'Hmmm,' she purred, looking coy. 'P'raps I did.'

Charles's pinstriped trousers dropped to the floor and he stepped out of them. He was going to kick them aside but Sally bent down and picked them up, folding them neatly with the rest of his clothes across on the back of the chair. She reached behind him and slipped her hands into the waistband of his pants, for a few moments caressing his buttocks with her small soft hands. Charles rested his chin on the top of Sally's head, inhaling the smell of her hair. Then, finally, she eased her hands, still inside his pants, round to the front and pulled the elastic away from him to free his erection. She pulled the pants down to Charles's ankles where she finally let him kick them free.

She snaked her arms back round his torso and snuggled into him, wriggling to open the bathrobe more widely so their bodies were in contact at chest, groin and thigh. Charles uttered a noise - part groan, part laugh - but mainly pure joy. He slipped the bathrobe off her shoulders and held her warm curvy body hard against his. He luxuriated in the warm softness of her and drank in her perfume.

'Oh, Charlie,' she breathed in his ear, 'I've imagined this for so long.'

'Me too.'

He wanted to take things slowly but his body was screaming to let go. His hands travelled down the silky depression of her spine to reach her bottom. He cupped her buttocks, and they fitted neatly in his huge palms. She tipped her head back and rose on tiptoe, her lips seeking out his. He lowered his head to hers and they kissed, mouths slightly open, tongues flirting. Charles moved his hands down so they were under her thighs, and he lifted her clear off the ground. Charles carried her, lips still joined, until his knees struck the side of the bed and then he lowered her to the mattress, the robe falling off her to the floor en route.

•

They lay in Charles's bed, still locked together, as their breathing subsided, the sounds of the late evening traffic coming faintly through the windows. Sally craned her neck to look at the clock on the bedside table.

'How long have you got?' asked Charles.

'I told Mum ten thirty at the latest.'

'Plenty of time, then. Do you want a drink? I've only got whisky, I'm afraid.'

'Go on then,' she said.

Charles disengaged from her and reached over to the whisky tumblers. He handed them to Sally, who sat up and held one glass steady on each of her thighs. Charles opened the bottle and was about to pour the remnants into the glasses. He paused, momentarily distracted by her swaying breasts. 'Come on; we haven't got all night!' she urged.

•

Sally went to the bathroom to clean up and Charles threw on some slacks and a sweater. He would shower when he returned and, in any case, he wanted Sally's scent on him for a while longer. He offered to drive her home, but she declined.

'It'll only set Mum off, asking questions, you know.'

'But I can't let you just get on a train.'

'Yes you can. You can walk me to the station if you like.'

Sally gathered her things, and stood by the door waiting for Charles. He opened the door and turned the light off, and the telephone rang.

'Damn,' he said, hesitating.

'Well, go on, answer it,' said Sally.

Charles put the light back on, and picked up the receiver. 'Charles?' It was Rachel.

'Hello.'

'How are you?'

'I'm fine. Where are you?'

'I'm in America. Remember?'

'No, I meant where exactly.'

'At a friend's house, just outside Los Angeles.' She sounded puzzled.

'Right.'

There was a pause. 'Charles, is there anything wrong?'

'No, why?'

'Well you sound very strange.' There was another pause. 'Have I called at an inconvenient time?'

'No, it's perfectly alright. I'm sorry.' He looked across at Sally. She smiled, and slipped out into the hall. He could hear her footsteps as she walked to the lift.

'Charles, look, I've got something to say. I'm sorry it has to be over the telephone. I meant to write, but never got round to it, and now I have to make a quick decision.' She stopped, clearly finding the conversation difficult. 'Look, I've been offered permanent work.'

'Oh. I thought you didn't want to dance full-time again.'

'I don't. They want me as a choreographer cum dancer. The work's really interesting, and the others in the company are fantastic.'

'I see. What are you going to do?'

'Well, that's what I wanted to discuss with you.'

'It sounds to me as if you've made up your mind already.'

'I suppose I have. But there's something else.'

'And that is?'

'Kieran, the theatre director, has been trying to get me a work permit. It's taken a month so far, and still no sign, and now my visa's about to expire. So… he's offered to marry me.'

'You applied a month ago?' asked Charles. 'So you've

known for a month you were going to stay?'

Rachel didn't answer.

'And don't they check up on that sort of thing?' asked Charles. 'Marriages of convenience?'

There was another long pause. 'It wouldn't be entirely a marriage of convenience.'

'What are you saying? Are you having an affair with this chap?'

'Sort of.' She paused for so long this time that Charles thought that the connection had been broken. 'Charles, I'm in love with him. That doesn't mean,' she added quickly, 'that I don't love you too, it's just that … well … I'm very happy over here, and, much as I care about you, I'm not sure I really want to come back, at least for the moment. I'm so sorry, Charles.'

'It's okay, Rachel. You don't owe me an apology. The last couple of months have shown our lives are moving in different directions.' Charles glanced to where Sally had been standing in the doorway.

'I do, I do. I've known for a while you see, but I sort of just hoped the problem would go away. For a while I thought it was just a holiday romance, you know? And that I'd get bored with it. But it hasn't happened like that.'

'Rachel, you really don't have to say any of this. We made no commitment. You know I wanted you to get your career back on track, and if you're happy there, and … attached to this bloke, you should certainly stay there.'

'Oh, Charles, please don't be so reasonable! Why don't you shout at me or something?'

Charles hesitated before speaking. 'I'm not sure how I feel, to be honest. But ... Well ... perhaps that's ... because something has happened to me, too.'

'Really? You're not just saying that to make me feel better, are you?'

'No, really.'

'Who ... and when? Sorry, sorry! None of my business.'

'Actually, Rachel, it was tonight.'

'Wow. And do you think ...?'

'I haven't a clue. But it feels right.'

'Wow,' repeated Rachel.

'So, go and marry Kieran if you have to, take the job, and be happy.'

'Okay. I'll do just that. I'll write and let you know what's happening. Do look after yourself, Charles. You're a lovely man, and she's very lucky, whoever she is. Oh, and can you deal with Philomena for while? I'll have to come back and sort out the flat and so on, but not for a couple of months I should think. I guess she's more attached to you by now anyway.'

'Sure. Take care, Rae.'

'And you, Charles.'

She broke the connection. Charles listened to the dialling tone for a moment, then hung up, turned off the light, and closed the front door behind him. He joined Sally at the end of the corridor. She was in the lift, with her finger hovering over the button. She raised her eyebrows in interrogation.

'Everything okay?' she asked.

Charles shook his head in disbelief, and shrugged. 'I

think so, yes.' He looked down at the oval face framed by her boyish bob, and felt a wave of warmth for her.

Charles closed the lift gates and, using her hand, pressed the button to descend. He turned and put his arms round her as the ancient lift clanked into life. He bent his head and kissed her softly, his eyes closed.

'Actually I don't think things could be more okay than they are, right now,' he said.

chapter 10

The sound of the telephone gradually percolated into Charles's deep sleep. He groaned and reached out blindly to lift the receiver and still the noise.

'Charles?'

'Yes? Hang on a sec, I can't find the light.' Charles fumbled with the switch to the bedside lamp, trying to turn the thing on. He eventually managed it.

'David? Is that you? Am I late?' For a moment he thought that he'd overslept for court and wondered why it was David who was telling him. He looked across to the bedside table to see the clock.

'Charles, wake up and listen to me. It's Dad. He's been taken ill.'

'What? What's wrong? Is he okay?' Fear filled Charles's veins like freezing water.

'He was in the ambulance when I arrived, but Mum says that he was paralysed down one side and he couldn't speak.'

'Oh, no.' For a split second, a vision so powerful that it blotted out what David was saying, swam before Charles's eyes. He saw himself and David standing before a coffin, reciting in unison the *Kaddish*, the prayer for the dead. It was a scene he had always known would come one day. He took control of himself, and attended to his brother.

'I'm at Hendon. Mum called us over while waiting for the ambulance. Dad's on his way to the Royal Free in Hampstead, and we're leaving now.'

'Okay. I'll meet you there. It's off Haverstock Hill, isn't it?'

'Yes. See you soon.'

'Twenty minutes.'

Charles leapt out of bed and ran to the wardrobe, catching his little toe painfully on the corner of the bed as he went. Yelping with pain, but not stopping, he struggled into his trousers. He tore the wardrobe apart looking for a clean shirt, shouting with frustration, and then gave up, and instead rummaged through the washing basket to come up with the one he had worn the night before. As he raced around the tiny apartment he urged himself on under his breath: 'Come on … come on … come on …' like a punter willing a horse to the finishing line.

'Shoe … shoes … shoes …' he repeated, as he turned the bedroom upside down in the search for them, not realising that they were next to the bed and covered by the edge of the blankets.

Eventually dressed, he grabbed the car keys from the kitchen table and raced into the cold night.

Once on the road the vision of his dead father returned to him. He offered a silent prayer to the God he didn't believe in not to let his father die.

Charles arrived at the hospital thirty minutes later. The

roads had been clear but he'd been caught by every red light between Gray's Inn Road and Haverstock Hill. Sonia was just inside the door to Casualty, an overcoat covering her nightclothes. She immediately took Charles to where David was being spoken to by a doctor and then went to find Millie who was waiting in the canteen.

'Doctor, this is my brother Charles,' said David, with an apparent calmness Charles envied. 'Can you start again please so that he can hear it too?' asked David.

'Yes, certainly. I'm Doctor Harris, the medical registrar on call.' Charles shook his hand. 'Your father has all the signs of having suffered a stroke, but he's already recovering.'

'Is that normal?' asked Charles.

'It can be with a particular type of stroke caused when there is a blockage in the internal carotid artery. A transient attack like this can see signs of recovery in a couple of hours.'

'Is there any treatment for it?' asked David.

'Well, your father's going to need bedrest once he's discharged, certainly for several days and possibly a couple of weeks. As for substantive treatment, he may be advised to have an endarterectomy, in which we remove part of the inside of the artery and any deposits that have formed there.'

'Will he have that tomorrow?' asked Charles.

'Oh no. He needs some tests first. If they confirm the diagnosis there's usually a waiting list for the operation. Perhaps in the next 12 weeks, but that would be a decision for the consultant, not me.'

'But what's to stop this happening again in the meantime?'

'Well, there are no guarantees, but he'll receive some dietary advice and he may have some drugs to thin his blood. Now I'm very sorry gentlemen, I have to go. I have other patients waiting for treatment.' The doctor began to move away.

'May we see him?' called Charles.

'He was asleep when I left him. I suggest you leave it 'til the morning.' He walked off, leaving the two brothers in the corridor.

'What now?' asked David.

'Let's find Mum and Sonia. I suggest we take Mum home.'

They found Millie and Sonia in the canteen. Millie's eyes were red and puffy. She sat nursing a mug of tea. Charles and David went over to her, and Charles crouched beside her and put his arm round her shoulder. She turned to him and began crying again.

'Oh, Charles!'

'It's alright, Mum, he's going to be fine.' She sobbed into his chest, her tea still in her hands, and Charles folded his arms round her. She felt unfamiliar, and he realised that he couldn't remember the last time he had hugged her.

'Shhhh, it's okay …' he soothed. 'Dad's comfortable, and he's asleep.'

'Mum,' said David, 'I think we should go home.' Millie began to protest, but he cut her short. 'We can't do any good here. Dad's asleep. You can't stay here all night, and he'll want to see you when he wakes up in the morning.'

'He's right, Mum,' confirmed Charles. 'You should try

and get some sleep. Dad's going to have to take it very easy when they discharge him, so you might want to think about making up a bed downstairs in the back room.'

Millie brightened up a little at the prospect of being able to do something. David winked at Charles over her head. Millie looked at Sonia for confirmation, and she nodded her agreement.

'Yes, Mum. I'll stay with you tonight, and help you get things ready tomorrow. We can come straight back to the hospital tomorrow morning,' she said.

'Okay,' said Millie. 'Take me home.'

•

By 10 am on the following morning Charles stood outside the door to the cells in the basement of the Old Bailey. He pressed the bell. One of the court's original centuries-old iron-studded oak doors had been preserved, and was retained opposite the new door to the cell area. While he waited for the officer to admit him, Charles regarded the old weathered oak, wondering how many men had passed by it on their way to the gallows or a life sentence. Eventually he heard the jangle of heavy keys, an interior door clanged open and closed, and the wicket in the outer door opened.

'Good morning,' said Charles, 'counsel for Mr Harry Robeson.'

The wicket swung shut, another key was selected, and the door opened to admit him. The familiar smell of frying bacon greeted Charles. It was always breakfast time in court kitchens, whatever the time of day. The prison officer closed the outer door and then opened the inner door, this one made of steel bars. Charles gave his name to another officer who, between reading "The Sketch" and drinking a cup of tea, noted the arrival and departure of legal visitors, and Charles was directed to a cell.

He rose as Robeson entered. 'Good morning, Harry.'

Robeson held out his hand and Charles took it. 'Are you okay, Charles? You look like you've had no sleep.'

Charles smiled ruefully as the two men took seats on opposite sides of the tiny table. 'That's because I spent most of the night at the Royal Free.'

Charles explained briefly.

'When's he being discharged?' asked Robeson.

'In the next couple of days I would guess. Then he has to have some investigations carried out and probably an operation, when the NHS can get round to it,' Charles replied with some bitterness.

'There's a waiting list?'

'Isn't there always?'

'Can't you do it on your health insurance?' asked Robeson.

'I'm afraid that that was one of the first casualties of last year's doldrums. I had cover for both my parents and myself, but I cancelled my subscription.'

'Oh. Bad luck.'

'Yes. Anyway, let's concentrate on your problems.'

'Are you going to be okay for today?'

'Of course. Working through the night is one of the unavoidable exigencies of the Criminal Bar. We've all done it, and you do get used to it as long as it's not too frequent. In fact, I got about three hours last night, and I feel fine. It tends to hit me late afternoon. So, let's get to work. I received the extra Instructions, thank you. Overall I think you've a reasonable chance of bail, albeit on strict conditions. The real problem will be persuading the court that you won't skip the country. You're not in the same position as most villains, who wouldn't have anywhere to go. The documents I've seen mention connections in Italy and in France. And I think you speak French …?'

'Afraid so. And some Italian.'

'Impressive but unhelpful in these circumstances. I suggest, Harry, that in addition to offering conditions such as reporting to a police station, surrender of passport and sureties, you offer a very substantial security.'

'What do you call "very substantial"?'

'Substantial enough to make it inconceivable that you'd risk forfeiting it. I like to offer even more than the client is alleged to have made from the job, but here the Crown aren't suggesting any particular figure. What about a hundred thousand pounds? Can you get that sort of cash to deposit?'

'The value of the jewels was a bit under a million, right?'

'Correct.'

'Let's offer two hundred and fifty grand.'

Charles whistled. 'You can get hold of that much in cash?'

'Not personally. But I know people who can.'

'Well, let's go for it.'

•

An hour later Charles again waited for Robeson to appear in the cell beneath the courts.

'Well done Charles!' he said as he entered. 'I thought you were being over-optimistic when you said we had a chance.'

'Thank you. How long will it take to get the money?'

'Somebody'll be along shortly. I should be out in an hour or so.'

'Do I want to know where the money's coming from?'

Robeson shook his head. 'No, you don't.'

'Fair enough. Look, Harry, would you mind terribly if I left you to it? I'd like to pop over to Mile End to see my father.'

'Sure. Mile End? I thought your parents lived in Hendon.'

'Good God, you're right. For a moment I completely forgot they'd moved.'

'You're tired. Whereabouts in Mile End did they live?'

'British Street.'

'What d'you know? I grew up on Eric Street; it's only a couple of streets away. Anyway, you get off. I'll give you a call in Chambers in the next few days. Sergeant West came down to see me just before you arrived. He was looking too happy by far.'

Charles's brow furrowed. 'I'd rather you didn't have any dealings with him at all without a witness present.'

'Don't worry, I shan't. He'll hand over my belongings, I'll sign for them, and that's it. I promise Mr Holborne, sir, I shan't open my mouth.'

chapter 11

It was early the next week that Charles discovered the nature of Sergeant West's good humour.

<u>IN THE CENTRAL CRIMINAL COURT</u>
<u>63/1021</u>

<u>THE QUEEN vs. HAROLD ROBESON</u>
<u>NOTICE OF ADDITIONAL EVIDENCE</u>

TAKE NOTICE that in addition to the evidence of the deponents whose names appear on the back of the Indictment, the Crown intends to rely on the statements of the witnesses attached hereto.

Statement of Peter Millard
Occupation: Estate Agent
Address: 13 High Street, Windlesham, Surrey.

I am an estate agent trading from the above address. My firm's principal business relates to the sale and purchase of residential properties, but we do have a letting service also. One of the properties on our books is called "Staplecroft",

Orchard Lane, Lower Barnsthorne, Surrey. It used to be owned by a Professor Wilson, but it was recently acquired for a company called Overbrooke (G.B.) Limited. We were asked to continue managing the house for the new owner. I was told that Overbrooke (G.B.) Limited owned a number of similar properties.

Just before Christmas 1962 I received an enquiry relating to the property from a Mr Smith. I think that this was after the company purchased the house, but I am not certain of that as we did not act on the purchase. I showed Mr Smith round the property, which he said he required for himself and a few colleagues while they attended a course at the polytechnic at Guildford. He decided to rent the house, and paid in full on that day in cash and took the keys. I did not see him again. I deal with so many people that I am afraid that I could not describe Mr Smith, except to say that he had long dark hair and a scar across his forehead and cheek. I might recognise him again.

I have spoken on the telephone to a Mr Carlysle who is, I understand, a director of Overbrooke (G.B.) Limited, but I have never met him nor any other officer of that company.

Signed Peter Millard.

Statement of Declan Mahoney
Occupation: Clerk
Address: c/o Companies House, 55 – 71 City Road, London EC1.
I am a clerk employed at Companies House by the Registrar of Companies. The Registrar is required by law to keep records

relating to all companies incorporated under the Companies Act 1948. I have been asked to make a search in relation to a company called "Overbrooke (G.B.) Limited". I can say that this company was incorporated on the 1st. June 1962. According to its Memorandum of Association, its principal object was to buy and sell residential and commercial properties. The identity of its directors has changed a number of times, but in December 1962 they were Robert Milton Carlysle, Jennifer Angela Carlysle and Frederick Costen. The company has an issued share capital of £100 divided into £1 shares. The three directors are each registered with one share, and the remaining 97 are registered to a company called Prince Estates (1960) Limited.

I have further caused a search to be made in relation to Prince Estates (1960) Limited. It is also a company set up to buy and sell residential properties. Its directors in December 1962 were Frederick Costen and Edward Albert Findlay. It has an issued share capital of £100 divided into £1 shares. The two directors each are registered with one share, and the remaining 98 shares are registered to a Harold Robeson.

Signed: Declan Mahoney.

Statement of Roger William Duncan
Age: Over 21
Occupation: Banker
Address: c/o Midland Bank, Fleet Street, London EC4

I am employed by the above bank, and I am authorised to make this statement pursuant to the Bankers Book Evidence Act 1879. A company named Prince Estates (1960) Limited holds an account at the above branch (number 41081004). On 8th. December 1962 the sum of £900 was withdrawn from the account. On 9th. December 1962 a further sum of £650 was withdrawn. The mandate held by the bank only requires one signature of the two authorised signatories on any cheque. The signatory in respect of each of the above withdrawals was Harold Robeson. I produce herewith the original cheques, and copies of the statement of the account for the relevant period marked "RWD 1".

Signed: Roger William Duncan.

Charles frowned and put the Notice of Additional Evidence to one side. Sergeant West had certainly been busy. The three statements forged a definite link between Robeson and the property used by the robbers, and showed that immediately before the two getaway cars were purchased he had withdrawn in cash almost exactly the sum required to buy them. For the first time, Charles was faced with evidence connecting Robeson to the crime that did not rely on the word of a police officer or a "grass". He would have to obtain instructions on the new statements, and he was curious to know how Robeson would explain them. Not for the first time, he pondered the strange conference he'd had with his client at Brixton, and its purpose.

Charles then turned to the last statement attached to the Notice. It was a statement from DS West himself.

Statement of Jonathan Peter West
Occupation: Detective Sergeant

Address: COO8, West End Central Police Station

On 1 August 1963 I was present at the Central Criminal Court when the accused re-applied for bail. As a result of his successful bail application I was required to return to him the personal belongings which were taken into custody following his arrest. The custody sheet prepared by the custody sergeant at Greenwich Police Station following the accused's arrest listed the property taken from him, which included a wallet containing £4. In addition, the accused had 6/9 in change in his pockets. The serial numbers of the 4 x £1 notes contained in the accused's wallet are listed in Appendix 1 hereto.

As I was going through the accused's wallet in preparation for returning it to him at the Central Criminal Court, found an additional £10 note folded into a book of stamps which was not immediately visible. I checked the serial number of the £10 note against the numbers listed in Appendix 1 hereto and realised that it had not been listed.

On a hunch I decided to compare the serial number of the £10 note against the numbers of the notes returned to Mr Kenneth Lyall following his acquittal of the Coulsdon Diamond Robbery. In excess of £84,000 was discovered at the home of Mr Lyall on his arrest but it could not be established that that cash was linked to the robbery and it was returned to him. The serial numbers of the notes returned to Mr Lyall are set out in Appendix 2 to this statement. It will be seen from page 31 of Appendix 2 that the £10 note found hidden in the wallet of the accused was one of those returned to Mr Lyall.

Signed Detective Sergeant West.

Before Charles could formulate his thoughts or make any notes on DS West's further evidence, the telephone rang. That was one of the penalties of working in Chambers; whatever work he started, he was interrupted every ten minutes.

'Yes?'

'Mrs Horowitz, sir,' said Barbara.

'Yes, Mum?' said Charles when she was put through. 'Is Dad alright?'

'Alright? He's fantastic. This hospital's wonderful! So much nicer than the Royal Free.'

'What hospital? Have they moved Dad?'

'What hospital, he asks me!' Millie thought he was joking.

'Mum, I'm serious. I haven't a clue what you're talking about.'

'Charles, stop kidding. We know it was you who arranged it. Harry told us.'

'Harry who?'

'Harry Robeson. He's been fantastic, Charles, a real *mensch*. Is he Jewish?'

Despite his confusion, Charles couldn't resist laughing. A Jew somehow could never quite understand why anyone but another Jew would do them a favour. Why should anyone *else* do them favours?

'Look, Mum, start at the beginning please.'

His mother sighed, tired of playing what she thought was a game. 'Alright. Harry came round, told us you'd arranged a room at a private hospital at Marble Arch, and said you'd asked him to give us a lift down. So now we're here. You should see the size of this room! And the menu! It's like a hotel!'

'Is Harry still there?'

'Sure.'

'Would you put him on, please?'

Charles heard his mother's voice as she held out the handset. 'It's Charles. The *meshuggener* wants to talk to you.'

'Charles?' asked Harry.

'Yes. What the hell's going on?'

Robeson's voice dropped. Charles could hear his mother and father chattering away in the background. 'I mentioned your situation to a consultant friend of mine – no names mentioned, I promise! – and he thought it unwise to delay your father's treatment. He made some enquiries, and called me back. There was space on the lists here, and I thought, well, we'd better grab it while we could. They're going to do the further tests today, if you're happy to proceed.'

'You had no right to do any of this, Harry,' replied Charles angrily. 'It's none of your business. I'm sure you meant it kindly, but this is my family. You've no right to interfere. How the hell are they going to pay for it?'

'Don't worry about that.'

'What do you mean "Don't worry"? You've created an expectation in them which I can't possibly meet! I haven't got the money for private hospitals!'

'I know that. Look at it as a favour from one East End boy made good to another.'

'I'm sorry, Harry, this won't do. I'll have to come and get Dad out of there.'

'Don't be ridiculous! He needs the tests, right? He could wait months on the NHS, and might die in the meantime. And even if he doesn't, you'll be worrying yourself sick and you won't be concentrating on my case. I'm entitled to your full attention. So, put your pride to one side and accept with good grace. If it makes you feel better, consider it a loan – part of your brief fee up front.'

Charles paused. Robeson was right about one thing: the minute he'd said that treatment could be available within days, Charles had felt a surge of relief. He *had* found it difficult to concentrate over the last 48 hours, and Robeson was entitled to his undivided attention. Robeson sensed his indecision.

'Charles? Listen my boy. Your father needs the treatment, and soon; you've got no money. Like I say, if you must, you can pay me back when things are better, but don't turn me down. *Gey gezinter heit.*'

chapter 12

Harry Robeson sat in his beloved Austin Princess on the drive of his Hampstead house, eyes closed, luxuriating in the smell of the leather seats, the sheen on the walnut dashboard, and the strains of Mendelssohn. He wondered how many weeks he had left to enjoy the car. Perhaps only a handful, he concluded. Then what?

'Walk away,' he whispered softly to himself. Start again somewhere else, far away. He opened his eyes, looked at the clock on the dash and shook himself out of his reverie. He started the engine and drove down the paved drive, through the ornate iron gates and onto the street.

He headed south towards the city. Traffic was light and he slowed down, realising that he'd arrive too early. The blue Ford two cars behind him was forced to drop further back as the cars in between overtook Robeson. DC North (or Fil, as Robeson knew him), driving the Ford, picked up his radio and reported the fact that he and his quarry had left the Hampstead house and were travelling south, destination unknown. North considered this entire operation to be a waste of time. DS West hoped that the pressure would cause Robeson to do something foolish, something they could use to augment their case.

North doubted it. Robeson was far too experienced to act rashly.

Robeson suddenly swerved towards the kerb and pulled over close to a corner, and watched with a smile as Fil had no choice but to continue past him for fear of being spotted. Robeson accelerated round the corner and sped to the end of the side turning where he turned immediately to his left again and brought the Austin to a halt next to a telephone box. He turned off the ignition and got out. The telephone box was in better condition than most, no stench of urine and only a little litter on the floor. Robeson picked up the handset, inserted some coins, and dialled.

When he heard a voice on the other end he pressed button A and the coins dropped. 'Hi. You're in early,' he said.

'Hello there. Busy day ahead. I wondered if you'd call.'

'How're things going?'

'Fine.'

'Are you enjoying yourself?'

'If you're referring to what I think you're referring, mind your own bloody business.'

Robeson grinned. 'Just thought I'd ask, that's all.'

'Is there anything I can do for you *Mister* Robeson? I have a job to do you know.'

'No, nothing. Just wanted a chat. I'm just … a bit worried, you know?'

Her voice softened. 'I know. I'm sorry. Shall I come over tonight before going home? Or do you want to come down for lunch?'

'Now, that *would* be silly, wouldn't it?'

'Yes, I suppose so. What about tonight then?'

'We'll see. I don't know what time I'm going to get in, and you've got to get back. I'll give you a call later.'

'Okay. Keep your chin up. I'm sure it'll be alright.'

'I wish I was.'

'I love you.'

'I love you too. Bye.'

'Bye.'

Robeson hung up and retraced his steps to the Austin. He scanned the road but it didn't appear that Fil had caught up with him. He completed the block and drove back to the main road to continue with his journey. Within quarter of a mile he spotted the MGA driven by Denis, Fil's partner, three cars behind his.

Follower and followed were by now in Camden Town. Robeson moved off quickly from a set of traffic lights, almost losing Denis who got caught behind a bus turning right. Denis followed the Austin down to Kingsway where it turned left into Lincoln's Inn Fields. Robeson circled the square looking for a parking space and was lucky to see a car backing out of one on his second lap. He parked the Austin and walked quickly into Lincoln's Inn, past the manicured lawn and barristers' chambers, and ducked under the old wooden door into Chancery Lane where he turned right.

It was a bright but very cold day, and Denis had jumped out of his car so quickly in an attempt to keep Robeson in sight that he'd left his jacket behind. His breath came in steamy clouds as he hurried to keep pace with Robeson who was walking at a remarkable pace for a man of his age. He watched Robeson cross Carey Street and then run lightly up the steps into the Law Society. Denis stood on the pavement by the black railings with the gold lions on top debating what to do next. Robeson might be hours in there. If Denis were to wait, he'd freeze and his double-parked car was certain to be towed. There was nowhere to watch the entrance that wasn't in plain sight, so he just stood at the foot of the stairs, pretending to wait for someone. He waited for ten minutes, becoming increasingly cold, solicitors entering and leaving the building regarding him with curiosity. Finally, he turned on his heel and retraced his steps back up Chancery Lane.

Robeson poked his head out of the door to the Law Society entrance, and watched the policemen's departing back with a smile. Making sure that Denis had disappeared into Lincoln's Inn, Robeson stepped back onto Chancery Lane and walked north. Near to the junction with High Holborn he entered a small door to his right next to the silver vaults. He walked down a wood-panelled empty corridor, his shoes ringing on stone flags. At the end of the corridor, next to a large leather-topped desk, stood a man in black morning suit and top hat. He stood ramrod straight, almost to attention. Robeson presented a card bearing his photograph to the guard. The man examined it and looked at Robeson.

'Good morning Mr Black,' he said.

He turned to a large card index bureau behind him and found the drawer marked "A" to "E". He opened it and flicked through the cards until he came to the one he sought. He brought it back to the desk, sat, and pushed a form towards Robeson.

'Please write the fifth and seventh keywords from your security phrase in the first two boxes, and then sign in the signature box,' he instructed.

Robeson took a pen from his pocket and completed the form as directed. The man checked Robeson's answers with those written on his card index and examined the two signatures closely.

'Thank you Mr Black,' he said, folding the completed form and placing it in a wire tray on his desk. He stood and pressed a discreet button on the wall to his right. 'My colleague Mr Smith will escort you to the vaults. Please present him with your card.'

Robeson waited as he heard footsteps approaching the steel door set in the wall behind the security desk. Keys jangled and the door swung inward.

'Thank you,' said Robeson stepping through. The door closed behind him.

'Good morning, sir. My name's Smith,' said the man, also in morning suit but wearing no hat. 'You haven't been to see us for a while.'

Robeson was in a discreetly lit oak-panelled room. It was luxuriously carpeted and the walls were hung with expensive-looking paintings. To one side of the room was a large polished table bearing glossy magazines, and comfortable chairs lined the walls. There were two or three other doors set into the panelling, but no windows. The room resembled a basement Harley Street waiting room. It smelt of leather, furniture polish and new carpet. Smith sat down behind a beautiful Queen Anne desk with graceful bowed legs. Robeson handed his card over for it to be examined again. Smith made some notes and returned the card.

'Thank you. If you would care to take a seat for a minute, I'll go and get your key. I understand there's to be another gentleman?'

'That's right.'

Smith disappeared through one of the doors set into the panelling and closed it soundlessly. As Robeson sat, the door through which he had entered the waiting room opened again. A young fair-haired man stepped into the room. Robeson rose to greet him.

'Mr Black,' said the other, extending a hand, 'how nice to meet you again. I hope I haven't kept you waiting?'

'Mr Connor,' said Robeson, shaking the proffered hand. 'Not at all. I trust you have them?'

'Of course, sir.'

Smith returned. 'If you would care to follow me Mr Black?'

Robeson left Connor in the waiting room and followed Smith through another panelled door and down a short corridor. At the end were the open steel gates of a large vault. He stepped inside. Before him was a wall composed of the fronts of safety deposit boxes.

'Sir?' said Smith, indicating a box at the bottom right of the bank with two slots for keys.

Robeson and Smith each inserted a key into the lock.

The lock turned. Smith removed his key. 'If you'd care to remove your key, please…?' he requested.

Robeson did as he was bid and Smith pulled out a long thin box. Robeson followed him back to the waiting room. Smith opened the final door in the panelled wall to reveal a small carpeted room with a table, chairs and a tray bearing a pot of coffee and cups. Smith placed the box on the table, and indicated to Robeson and Connor that they should enter.

'Please take as long as you like gentlemen. The room has been booked until noon.'

He turned to depart. As he did so he saw Connor out of the corner of his eye tipping something, or somethings, out of a small black velvet bag tied with a drawstring. Whatever it was, it glittered and sparkled. Gems, probably, thought the man. Perhaps krugerrands. One never knew. He was, after all, paid not to know. Smith closed the soundproofed door behind him and left the two men to their business.

•

The well-dressed young man with Brylcreemed black hair and fingers covered in gold rings climbed the stairs to the first floor flat on Selby Street, Bethnal Green, a shopping bag in one hand. The staircase, although worn and bare, was spotlessly clean, and the smell of cooking emanating from the flat at the head of the stairs made his mouth water. He paused at the head of the staircase and looked at the blue painted door ahead of him. There was no number on it, and no name of the occupants of the flat. He took a scrap of paper from his blue suit pocket and looked again at the address scribbled on it. Then he noticed the mezuzah on the door frame. The young man was not Jewish, but he had lived in the East End all his life amongst Jews, and he knew what the mezuzah signified. Satisfied, he replaced the scrap of paper in his pocket, looked for a doorbell and, finding none, knocked politely on the door with his knuckles. At first he thought he heard a child laugh, or perhaps cry, from behind the door, but now there was silence. He knocked again. Again silence. There was something about the stillness behind the door and the smell of cooking which convinced the young man that, despite the lack of response, there was indeed someone at home. He bent down and opened the letter box. That gave him a view of a small section of a narrow lobby covered in light blue linoleum, the corner of a patterned rug, and the legs of a small piece of furniture to the right. On the left, almost entirely out of sight but nonetheless still visible, was a pair of feet in women's shoes. The shoes were leather, but old, and the toes were saturated, as if they had recently been walking through the rain.

The young man lifted his head so his mouth was opposite the open letter box. 'I can see you're in,' he said. 'There's nothing to be frightened of, Mrs Goldstein. I'm a friend of Violet Kray's from round the corner in Vallance Street. She's asked me to look in on you. I've got something for you from her.'

The young man bent further and peered once again through the open letter box. The feet hadn't moved.

'Honest, Mrs Goldstein, I mean you no harm. Violet knows your situation, and wants to help.'

He watched as the feet moved hesitantly towards the door and he stood, allowing the letterbox to close with a snap. He sensed the woman standing on the other side of the door, hesitating. He could easily have kicked it open – his employers had required him to kick open many similar doors in the past – but he was under strict instructions. At least for this first visit. Then he heard the sound of a security chain being put into place and a shoot bolt being opened. The door opened inwardsa few inches, the security chain stretched taut at the same height as the young woman occupant's cheekbones.

'Do you recognise me, Mrs Goldstein?' asked the young man through the gap. 'I'm often around. I'm sure we seen one another up the 'igh street or at the Lane.'

Ruth Goldstein nodded fractionally. She looked as if she had just returned, as she still wore a raincoat and a wet umbrella rested just inside the threshold, a small puddle forming around its pointed end on the linoleum.

''ere,' said the young man offering her the shopping bag in his hand. 'Vi knows you'll be kosher, so rather than making a meal for you and the kids she asked me to get you some bagels and herring from Moishe's stall up Petticoat Lane. It's all fresh.'

Three small children, two boys and a girl, shyly approached the door and crowded round Mrs Goldstein's legs. They could smell the warm bagels.

'I can't pay for them,' said Mrs Goldstein.

'We know that. They're a gift. Look, can I come in for a sec? We've a message for your husband.'

The little trust the young man had built was suddenly gone and fear filled Ruth Goldstein's eyes. She made a move to close the front door but the young man's foot was now between the door and the doorpost.

'I give you my solemn word, Mrs Goldstein, you're perfectly safe. Vi and the twins want to help, and that involves getting a message to your husband when you next visit. Please let me in. I'll be gone within two minutes.'

Mrs Goldstein looked down at the boys. She reached out, took the offered shopping bag through the gap and handed it to the older of the two boys. 'Go into the living room, close the door and stay there. You can have one bagel each.' The children scampered off and a door to the left closed behind them. Their suppressed excited voices could be heard behind the door as they squabbled over the bagels.

'If you move your foot, I'll take off the chain,' said Ruth Goldstein to the young man.

He removed his foot, the door closed briefly, Mrs Goldstein removed the chain and the door opened wide.

'The kitchen,' she said, pointing at the only other door opening off the lobby.

The young man followed her direction and, skirting around a pram with a sleeping infant in it, he entered a small kitchen, no more than eight feet long and four feet wide. It contained a small table, a baby seat and three fold-up wooden chairs stacked under the window. Washing was drying on a pulley clothes airer just below the ceiling. The single sash window was covered in condensation and the walls were damp. The room smelled strongly of cooking – a pot simmered on the small stove – but also of mould.

Mrs Goldstein followed him in and shut the door. She gestured to the wooden chairs. 'Take a seat,' she said.

The young man politely opened two chairs and placed them on either side of the table, waiting for Mrs Goldstein to sit before he did so. He came straight to the point.

'Ronnie and Reggie are aware of your situation. You probably know that when one of their Firm is away they do what they can to make life a bit easier for those on the outside. May I ask, has Mr Lyall been sorting you out?' Mrs Goldstein shook her head. 'That's what we thought.' He reached into his inside jacket pocket and placed an envelope on the table. 'There's £100 in the envelope. It's a gift. You don't have to do nuffin'.'

Mrs Goldstein stared at the envelope on her kitchen table for a moment, and then shook her head. Very delicately, as if she didn't want to touch it at all, she pushed the envelope back across the table towards the young man with her index finger tip.

'We can't take your money.' Her voice was tired, resigned, but not frightened.

'Wouldn't you like to move back home? This flat's much too small for you all. And it don't smell right.'

'The landlord relet it.'

'That ain't a problem,' said the young man with a smile.

Mrs Goldstein shook her head again, this time more vigorously. 'No,' she said simply.

'Then what about food? And some winter clothes for you and the kids? It ain't charity; it's what we *do*. We look after one another, don't we?'

Mrs Goldstein stared at her hands folded on the table top, the envelope still in her peripheral vision. 'What would the message be?' she asked.

'OK. Well, we've heard from Camp Hill that your husband, Mr Goldstein, has given a statement to a certain police officer.'

Mrs Goldstein took a sharp intake of breath and for the first time since he had entered the tiny flat her eyes locked on to those of the man sitting opposite.

'You knew already?' he asked.

'Yes,' she whispered. 'He told me.'

'Did he tell you the statement he's given is false? Did he tell you the damage it might do?'

'The policeman wanted him to say he recognised someone, so he said it. I don't think it was true. He just pointed to the man he was supposed to point to. He wouldn't mean to do any harm, but he'd do anything to get out.'

'The thing is, Mrs Goldstein, life on the inside is bad enough for someone like your Avram. But as a grass…' he shrugged and left the sentence unfinished. 'And he's in a low security wing. Anyone can get at him, on the landing, in the workshop, in the showers. There's nothing we could do to protect him.' Mrs Goldstein's hands covered her mouth, her eyes wide with shock.

'But what can I do?'

'Talk to him. Make 'im understand this is a mistake.

He'd be sending an innocent man to take his place, and he'd be puttin' 'imself in danger. If he withdraws his statement, we can put the word out. No one'll touch 'im.'

Mrs Goldstein suddenly reached under the table and pulled out a handbag. She rummaged around in it and in her turn produced an envelope which she placed before the young man.

'Read it,' she offered. 'I was going to post it this morning when I went shopping, but I forgot. Go on, read it.'

The young man turned over the unsealed envelope. It was addressed in a firm angular hand in blue ink to Mr Avram Goldstein, c/o Camp Hill Prison, Newport, Isle of Wight. He took out the letter, unfolded it, and read:

My dearest Avram,

I am so sorry that I cannot come to see you this month. We are all well, but I feel that I cannot come again until you have thought some more about your decision. You cannot take back what you've already done, but you can decide to tell the truth later, when it matters.

How would you feel if an innocent man was behind those bars? Maybe an innocent man with a family like yours? Despite everything, I know you're a good man. I beg you, be a mensch. You'll never forgive yourself otherwise.

The children are well, and look forward to seeing you again. Maybe it will be better anyway if they don't see you until next year, as we originally thought. They have been so unsettled, not knowing when you're likely to be released. So, until I hear from you, I send all my love. Your Razel.

Mrs Goldstein watched him read, and then continued:

'He'll have to swear on the Torah – the Five Books of Moses, won't he?'

'In court?' The young man nodded. 'Yes.'

She shook her head. 'He doesn't realise. He's just desperate. But I know him. Avram's a weak man, but a devout Jew. To perjure himself like that – on the book of his fathers! – it'd destroy him.'

The young man regarded the Jewish woman carefully.

'You were really going to send this?'

She shrugged. 'I didn't know what else to do. If you don't believe me, you can take it and post it yourself.'

'My instructions were to get you to speak to him in person.'

She shook her head. 'If I see him, we'll both just start crying again. Having it in writing will give him time to think.'

'You don't mention the consequences of grassing.'

'Grassing?' She spoke the word as if spitting out a sour taste. 'What do I know about that? If you've got people inside that prison get *them* to explain "grassing" to him.'

The young man studied the tired, worn out woman carefully, nodded, and stood. He picked up the letter and envelope addressed to the prison and left the envelope containing the cash.

'Thank you, Mrs Goldstein. I'll tell Reggie and Ronnie what you said, but I'm sure it'll all be okay. If you need anything, pop round to Vallance Road, won't you? The Krays always pay their debts.'

chapter 13

THE QUEEN

– and –

HAROLD JOSEPH ROBESON

FURTHER INSTRUCTIONS TO COUNSEL

Enclosures:

1. *Proof of Evidence of Terence John Cooper*
2. *Proof of Evidence of William McCready*
3. *Defendant's comments on Notice of Further Evidence*
4. *Contract re: land at Holmbury St. Mary, Surrey.*
5. *Copy Bank Statements, company searches, and accounts of Prince Estates (1960) Limited.*

Counsel will be familiar with this case having advised throughout and having made a successful bail application on behalf of the Defendant.

Counsel will note from Enclosure 1 that Mr Cooper, who is an entirely independent witness, confirms that someone was at the boot of the Defendant's car during the course of the party at The Victory. Efforts have been made to trace Mr McGuinness, the publican of The Victory public house, but without success. Enquiries suggest that Mr McGuinness is taking an extended holiday somewhere abroad. It is unclear if the holiday is genuine or he is being kept out of sight, but enquiries have reached a dead end. However, a short statement has been obtained from a Mr McCready, a temporary member of bar staff at the time, and he appears to confirm that the person at the car cannot have been the accused. There is also a suggestion that the person was a policeman, but Instructing Solicitors are aware that that evidence is tenuous and may not survive cross-examination.

Counsel requested that we obtain details of any previous convictions recorded against Avram Goldstein, and we have been informed by the Crown that, save for the matter for which he is presently serving a sentence of imprisonment, he is of good character.

If counsel requires any further information, a further conference may be arranged.

Robeson & Co.

•

The scrawny unshaven man sat in his car and lit another cigarette. The ashtray in front of him was full and outside the driver's door there was a pyramid of cigarette butts where he had tipped the last full ashtray an hour or so before. He reached into his pocket again and took out the dog-eared list of names. His nicotine-stained index finger ran down the thirty-two names on the list, each followed by an address. Most of the addresses were in south London and half of those had postal districts that indicated that they were in Greenwich. All but three had been crossed through in a smudgy pencil, the same pencil that nestled on top of the man's left ear beneath his rather greasy black hair. He had cultivated the affectation when, as a youth, he had worked for a week in the classified ads department of a newspaper. The habit had stuck, though it was incongruous in his present profession.

The three names still to be struck through had something in common: their owners all lived in Leyton. The tall man had therefore left them until last, deciding to do them all in one afternoon.

An old van pulled into the street. The man looked at the name on its side and scanned his list. There! Terry Cooper. Thank God, he breathed. He stubbed his cigarette out, wound up the window, and got out of the car.

'Excuse me, sir,' he called to a grubby and tired Terry Cooper, who was walking up the garden path to number 65 carrying a large bag of plumber's tools. Terry paused. The man walked over to him, and pulled out a plastic wallet.

'My name's Marlowe,' he introduced himself. Improbably apt, but it was in fact his name. The snag was with his first name, which he would have liked to have been Philip, but which was instead Norman. He had tried adopting Philip, but his Mum, with whom he lived, refused to call him anything other than "Norm" and the attempt had failed. Norman Marlowe flashed an identity card bearing his photograph at the young man. 'I'm a private detective,' he said. Eight years of snooping had not diminished the pride with which he announced his profession.

'Oh yeah?'

At that moment the front door opened and a middle-aged lady in an apron appeared on the threshold.

'What's up, Tel?' she asked.

'Dunno, Mum. This chap says he's a private detective.'

'Yes, madam, that's right. May I ask you a few questions, sir? It will only take ten minutes.'

'What's he done?' asked Mrs Cooper sharply.

'Nothing, as far as I know. He may have been a witness to something, that's all.' Terry looked at his mother and shrugged.

'You'd better come in, then,' said Mrs Cooper, standing back and opening the door wide.

•

PROOF OF EVIDENCE OF
TERENCE JOHN COOPER

I live at 65 Drapers Lane, London E10. I am a plumber. On the evening of 21 June 1963 I went with the rest of the darts team from the "Rising Sun" public house in Leyton to a public house in Greenwich called The Victory for a darts match with the "Victory's" ladies team. The match was at eight o'clock, and we arrived just before.

I went into the public bar where the match was to be held, but I felt ill and left after a few moments to go to the toilet which is outside in a separate building, situated in the corner of the carpark. The only cubicle was occupied, and I was about to be sick. I vomited just outside the toilet block. While I was still there recovering, I heard a man approach the car behind which I was crouching. The car was a silver Austin Princess. I believe it was a man because of his heavy tread, and the fact that I could see beneath the car that he was wearing heavy black shoes, like those worn by a policeman. I noted that his trousers were of heavy dark material, either blue or black in colour. This person came to the very car where I was and opened the boot. There was then a thump, as if something heavy was being placed inside or moved around in the boot. The boot lid was then closed again.

I did not notice where the man came from, but I am reasonably sure that he went towards the pub after closing the boot.

I am prepared to give evidence if requested.

PROOF OF EVIDENCE OF WILLIAM McCREADY

In June 1963 I was a student at a college in Catford, and obtained part-time work as a barman at The Victory Public House, Greenwich. I was on duty on the night of Friday 21 June. That night there was a private party in the upstairs room, and I was asked to keep an eye on the room, bring down used glasses and bottles, and empty the ashtrays.

The party actually began sometime after lunch. Most of the guests were young men, and later in the evening young women too. During the evening, while I was upstairs clearing glasses, a gentleman in a suit came upstairs. He looked quite a lot older than the other guests, which is why I remember him. I thought at first that he had come upstairs by accident. He was expected however, and he took a drink and sat at a table. I heard his name mentioned once or twice, and I think it was Robinson, or something like that. I continued to watch him because he seemed so ill at ease and out of place. No one seemed to talk to him much. I can say for certain that he did not leave the bar until about twenty minutes later, when some police officers came in and asked him to go downstairs to the car park to look at his car. I did not see him again after that. The rest of the people came upstairs again, and the party continued as before.

I am prepared to give evidence if requested.

COMMENTS OF HAROLD ROBESON ON THE CROWN'S FURTHER EVIDENCE

I admit that I am the principal shareholder in Prince Estates (1960) Limited which itself is the controlling shareholder in Overbrooke (G.B.) Limited. Prince Estates (1960) Limited also owns shares in a number of other property companies. In total, Prince Estates (1960) Limited and all of its subsidiary companies own around two hundred residential properties in and around London, most of which are in the Guildford area. Many of the properties are purchased for development or as capital assets, but some are given to agents to let before the company is ready to deal with them. It may well be that the robbers rented premises owned by one of my companies, but that is a pure coincidence. I have no dealings whatsoever with the letting of the premises, and all of the details are dealt with by the agents. Had I been involved as alleged by the police, I would certainly not have been stupid enough to allow the robbers to use a property with which I was connected.

Mr Lyall has been a client of the firm for many years, and in addition to his criminal cases, the firm had conveyed houses for him and dealt with other non-contentious business on his behalf. It is entirely possible that I might have mentioned that one of my companies owns properties in Surrey. So far as the withdrawal of cash is concerned, as director of Prince Estates (1960) Limited I entered into a contract to purchase some land at Holmbury St. Mary, Surrey, from a company called Ross Farm Management Limited. The sale was part of a chain of buyers and sellers, and Prince Estates (1960) Limited entered into a contract race for this land. In an effort to secure the sale, I agreed to pay cash. The contract (herewith) shows that exchange was due to take place on 13th December 1962 and on exchange we were to pay £1,600. I withdrew the two sums of money from the account in the previous week for this purpose. The only reason I made the withdrawal in two parts was because I was nervous at carrying such large quantities of cash around with me.

Withdrawals of large sums of cash are not unusual in the normal course of the company's business, especially when properties are being converted or renovated. Many subcontractors and tradesmen require to be paid in cash. I produce herewith further bank statements relating to the account of Prince Estates (1960) Limited from which it will be seen that other similar withdrawals were made in the six months before this robbery, and one or two were made afterwards also. I also produce a schedule prepared by the accountants of Prince Estates (1960) Limited which shows all the properties under development at that time.

So far as the statement of DS West is concerned, Appendix

2 shows that over 26,000 notes made up the £84,155 returned to Mr Lyall following his acquittal. It is to be assumed that Mr Lyall would have spent some of that cash in and around London, and it is perfectly possible that I picked one banknote up innocently. More likely however is that Lyall paid me that £10 directly. I was Lyall's solicitor, and he paid me for his legal representation in cash. It is therefore not surprising that I would have in my position at least one note from the cash found at his home.

•

Charles felt something warm and wet behind his knee. He lifted the Robeson papers, pulled up the bedclothes, and looked down his naked body. Sally had been asleep, curled up like a cat, entirely submerged under the covers.

'Nice snooze?' he asked. 'I don't know how you can sleep under the covers like that. Don't you get hot and sweaty?'

She licked his leg again, the tip of her pink tongue making a little circle of damp. 'Don't you like hot and sweaty?' she asked. She uncurled herself and rose to her hands and knees. She crawled up Charles's body, deliberately dragging her breasts across him as she moved upwards. She reached his chest and straddled it, her hands on either side of his head, swinging her breasts gently so that her nipples grazed his nose and lips.

'I take it I'm not going to be able to carry on reading?' asked Charles.

Sally didn't answer but continued with her swaying motion, her nipples hardening. Charles opened his mouth and licked each nipple as it went past. His hand reached blindly outside the perimeter of the bed and dropped Robeson's case papers onto the bedroom floor.

'Okay,' he concluded, returning his hands to the warmth under the covers and cupping her buttocks.

•

Sally slipped into Charles's bathrobe and padded into the kitchen to make something to eat.

Charles turned onto his front and, leaning out of the bed, gathered the papers and his thoughts following the interruption.

He wasn't concerned about the £10 note. Robeson's explanation was perfectly plausible, indeed likely. But the property trail was more worrying. It wasn't unheard of for cash to be used to purchase land, especially during a contract race, but it was unusual. And the use of Robeson's property could easily have been a coincidence. But the two factors taken together...?

He was still frowning with concentration when Sally returned from the kitchen, put a tray on the floor, dropped the bathrobe and jumped back into bed.

'Christ, it's cold in there!' she said, cuddling up to him.

'Then put some clothes on.'

'I thought you preferred me without any, Charlie. The naked slave girl unable to leave the harem.'

'Yes,' he said distractedly, leafing through the additional evidence.

'What's so interesting?' she demanded, pulling the

Instructions out of his hand. 'This again?' She turned to Charles, concerned. 'Why are you so worried about this case? You never used to be like this at Chancery Court.'

'I know. But he's managed to get under my skin. I don't normally dwell on whether or not my clients are guilty – that's not my decision. But every now and then you get a case where you're certain that the police have made a mistake, and that the man in the dock is innocent, and I worry more about those. I met him in con. I expected not to like him, and I found I liked him a lot. I listened to what he had to say and I thought, "Yes, I believe you". He didn't try to persuade me, either. Since then, in only a few weeks, he's saved my practice and enabled me to stay in Chambers, and he's been exceptionally kind to my family.'

'How's that?'

'Oh, he got Dad into a private hospital for some tests, when he'd have had to have waited for months on the N.H.S. We're still awaiting the results. Now, not only do I believe what he's told me, but I feel indebted to him.'

'So he's innocent. Where's the problem?'

'It's this evidence. This is turning into a grudge match between Robeson and the bent officer in the case, a chap called West. He's really working hard to get a conviction. And he may succeed – largely because he's not afraid to bend the rules.'

'Which is something *you* can't do.'

'Exactly. Everyone in this game – on both sides – breaks the rules constantly, while I'm fighting with one hand tied behind my back. Oh, fuck it!' and Charles threw the papers off the bed and back onto the floor. He leaned over Sally's torso and reached down to the tray on the floor by her side of the bed. 'Yum,' he declared, coming up again with a bagel in his hand. His shoulder brushed her breasts on the way and he grinned. He took a large bite of smoked salmon and cream cheese and traced the outline of the breast nearest to him with his free hand.

'For a nice Jewish boy,' he said, grinning and with his mouth full, 'heaven is a bagel in one hand and a warm boob in the other.'

chapter 14

Charles pushed open the doors to the robing room at the Central Criminal Court. It was good to be back. This was his first full trial at the Old Bailey for months. Charles placed the red cloth bag containing his robes on the table and undid the white rope drawstring. There were several barristers in the robing room vying for places in front of the mirrors, fiddling with collar studs, tying white bands around their necks, adjusting wigs and chatting about cases. One or two had turned towards the door as Charles entered but as he stood at the table taking off his tie and collar he noticed a definite reduction in conversational volume levels. One old barrister with whom Charles had been on nodding terms for several years turned his back. Two barristers on the far side of the table with whom Charles used to eat lunch in Middle Temple Hall every now and then inclined their heads towards one another and whispered conspiratorially. Charles definitely heard the word "bent".

'If you have anything to say about me, Tony,' said Charles across the table, 'have the courage to say it to my face.'

The temperature in the robing room suddenly dropped to below zero. The barrister addressed picked up his brief and Archbold, the criminal practitioner's Bible, and walked out of the robing room without a word.

Charles completed changing into his court wear, silence ringing around him.

•

'Are you Harold Joseph Robeson?' asked the clerk of the court.

'I am,' replied Robeson in a firm voice.

Robeson stood in the dock of Court 1 of the Central Criminal Court, the Old Bailey. The enormously high-ceilinged courtroom was wood-panelled, with small windows set high in the walls. Across the well of the court, high above him, sat the Recorder of London under an enormous carved pediment. To Robeson's left sat two banks of jurors and to his right, crammed into insufficient space, a score of reporters and other onlookers. Below him, in the well of the court, sat Charles and the other barristers.

From his position beneath the judge the clerk read from the indictment.

'You are charged on this indictment with an offence of conspiracy to rob, contrary to common law. Particulars of the offence are that between the 1st day of March 1962 and 31st day of December 1962 you did conspire with Kenneth Lyall, Peter Simons, Raymond Papier and persons unknown to rob the South African Gem Corporation of a quantity of diamonds worth £945,000. How do you plead, guilty or not guilty?'

'Not guilty.'

'You may sit down.'

'Yes, Mr Stafford,' said His Honour Judge Pullman QC. Charles knew Pullman well. He had had a formidable reputation as a prosecutor when at the Bar. He had been on the bench for over ten years and, having been promoted swiftly, was now the most senior judge sitting at the Old Bailey. He had seen it all, which went some way to explain why he was irritable and impatient with the advocates who appeared in his court. That and because, as Charles had warned Robeson, he was an utter bastard.

Marcus Stafford rose to his feet with an audible effort. He was immensely fat, his wing collar flattened and splayed outwards by his multiple chins. He was often to be heard hissing and wheezing as he perambulated his enormous bulk round the corridors of the Old Bailey, where most of his practice was conducted. Charles had done battle with the other barrister on several occasions. Some barristers were delightful opponents, no matter how hard-fought the case might be, and Charles would look forward to a fair fight and a pint afterwards. Some were less congenial, and kept their dealings with their opponent to the minimum required. But Stafford was something else; he made no attempt even to be civil, and seemed to take pleasure in being as rude as professional courtesy would allow. When forced to speak directly to Charles, he adopted an air of distain.

Charles had wondered if it was his working class origins or his Jewishness which Stafford found so unpalatable.

This morning they had passed one another on the stairs and even though Charles was sure Stafford had seen him, the latter had made no eye contact and forbore even his usual curt nod. Yet when he stood to address the jury in opening, his round rosy face creased into an apologetic smile and his voice took on the regretful tones of a man whose distasteful duty it was to reveal to the jury the seamier side of life.

'Members of the jury,' said Stafford, adjusting his pince-nez, and hooking his pudgy thumbs into the pockets of his waist-coat, 'in this case, I appear for the Crown, and the Defendant is represented by Mr Holborne, who sits nearest to you.' Charles noted that the usual appellation – "my learned friend" – was omitted. He was thus neither learned in the Law, nor Stafford's friend.

Charles looked up from his papers and smiled generally in the direction of the jury. Now was not the time to establish eye contact with them individually.

'My purpose now,' continued Stafford, 'is to give you a brief outline of what the Crown's case will be. I shall give you a framework into which you can fit the evidence when you hear it. You must not forget however that what I say is not evidence. You will decide this case, in accordance with your oaths, on what you hear from the witness box and what is read as agreed evidence to you, and not from what I say.'

The problem with Marcus, thought Charles, was that his Billie Bunter persona was so benign, and he was able to present himself as so scrupulously fair a prosecutor, that juries warmed to him immediately. What was more, his appearance was so extraordinary that one was apt to forget the incisive mind that lay behind the piggy eyes.

'The defendant, Mr Harold Robeson, is a solicitor, ladies and gentlemen. And, as you will no doubt hear in greater detail from Mr Holborne in due course, a man of exemplary character. A solicitor of the Supreme Court. A man who sits on numerous charitable boards. A man who has, in the past, been a pillar of the establishment. It is all the more sad therefore that I have to tell you that the Crown say he fell from grace, and became involved in a criminal enterprise with one of his own clients, a man named Lyall. You may have read in the newspapers that Mr Lyall was himself tried for a robbery in which slightly less than one million pounds-worth of diamonds were stolen. And you probably know that he was, in due course, acquitted. That does not concern you. You do not know what evidence the Crown had to offer against that man. You do not know what influenced the jury's minds in that case. You must therefore put it out of your minds entirely. What alone concerns you is whether this man, Harold Robeson, entered an agreement with Lyall and the others to commit the crime. And I shall tell you now, because it is of prime importance, that if you are anything less than sure of Mr Robeson's guilt, you must acquit him, for in all criminal cases, the Crown have to prove a man's guilt, and they have to prove it to the highest of standards: so that you are sure. Nothing less will do.'

Charles groaned inwardly. The jury were following Stafford's every word. Every now and then a jury member would turn and look at Robeson in the dock, as if examining an exhibit.

'The robbery itself was carried out on 21st. December 1962. In it, a man – a security guard – was blown up and crippled for life. It is not suggested that Mr Robeson participated in the actual robbery. That task was reserved for the other men named in the indictment, and others, who have not to this day been caught. The Crown however says that Mr Robeson provided the funds for the robbery to take place. Specifically, he paid for two cars, a Wolsey and Ford, to be lawfully purchased, and unlawfully used, as getaway cars. The Crown also says that he was present at the house that the robbers used before and after the robbery. He was there when the jewels were being valued, in the background, an éminence grise watching over the proceedings.'

That was a misjudgement, thought Charles. You do not quote French to a jury composed of honest burghers of Westminster and the City. The common touch was required.

'That house, you will hear, was owned by a company. When you look to see who owned the shares in that company, you find another company. And when you look to see who owned the shares in that second company, you come to the accused. He interposed a number of "screens" between himself and the house, but when you strip away those screens, the Crown will without a doubt satisfy you, so you are sure, that he controlled that house.

'Finally, and of the greatest importance, a gun, proved to have been used in the robbery itself, was found later in the back of this accused's car. So, if you accept the evidence, you will see that he was involved before the robbery in its planning, he has a connection with the weapon used to steal the diamonds and he was present immediately afterwards in the division of the spoils. The Crown cannot call evidence of the actual making of the conspiracy, the moment of criminal agreement, but they ask you to look at the evidence of what was done in pursuance of the agreement, and to

conclude from that, that agreement *there must have been.*'
He turned to the judge. 'With my Lord's leave, I shall call
the evidence.'

'Certainly Mr Stafford.'

'My Lord, the first few witnesses are to be read.'

'Very well. Members of the jury,' said the judge, turning
to the jury benches, 'the Defence have seen the evidence that
the Crown proposes to adduce, and have said in the case of
the witnesses who follow, that they agree the evidence and
have no questions for the witnesses. Therefore, there is no
need for them to attend, and their statements will be read
to you. The evidence has exactly the same force as if it were
given by the witnesses personally.'

Charles listened with half of his attention as the clerk
of the court read the statements of the two car dealers, the
neighbour of the house in Surrey and the security guard.
He had no questions for any of them.

'The next witness is to give evidence, my Lord,' said
Stafford. 'Call Peter Millard.' The estate agent entered
court and gave the oath.

'Your name is Peter Millard?' asked Stafford.

'Yes.'

'At the end of 1962 did you work for an estate agency
called Country Estates trading from Windlesham in Surrey?'

'I did.'

'What was your job with that firm?'

'I bought and sold properties on behalf of clients. I also
acted as a letting agent for some clients.'

'Do you know of a property called "Staplecroft",

Orchard Lane, Lower Barnsthorne?'

'I do. We used to let that cottage on behalf of a client called Wilson.'

'Did you ever deal with that property for anyone else?'

'Yes. Professor Wilson sold it to a company called Overbrooke Properties, or Overbrooke G.B. – I can't remember which.'

'Do you remember when that sale took place?'

'I think it was before the man with the scar came to rent it.'

'Tell us about the man with the scar.'

'Well, it was in December 1962, a week or two before Christmas. He telephoned and asked about properties in the village. We only had one on the books actually in that village, that was "Staplecroft". He made an appointment to see it and we met at the house. He took it.'

'Can you describe the man?'

'He was tallish, heavy build, with long dark hair and a bad scar running down his forehead and cheek. I can't remember which cheek.'

'Did you have any dealings with the man after that?'

'Not really, no. He paid in full before the letting. He dropped off the keys and collected his deposit at the end. That was it.'

'Did you see him drop the keys off?'

'Well, no, not actually. I was told by someone in the office that he'd –'

'Stop there Mr Millard,' commanded the judge. 'The rules of evidence do not permit you to say what others told you. Just stick to what you yourself saw or heard.'

'Certainly. I'm sorry.'

'Thank you, Mr Millard,' said Stafford, resuming his seat.

Charles rose. This would be the first time the jury heard him speak. He smiled at the witness. 'The man with the scar did not ask for the house by name then?'

'No.'

'He asked for houses in that village.'

'Yes.'

'So, had your firm had other houses on its books for that village, he might easily have ended up with a different house altogether?'

'I suppose so.'

'One owned by someone else?'

Millard shrugged. 'Yes.'

'Thank you. Just one other matter, Mr Millard. You said in your evidence that the sale from Professor Wilson to the company had occurred before this man came to rent the cottage.'

'Yes?'

'Are you sure about that?'

'Pretty sure.'

'Is it possible you have made a mistake?'

'Possible, but I don't think I have.'

Wonderful, thought Charles. That's all I need: a reasonable witness. 'Do you remember making a statement to the police?'

'I do.'

'Would you accept from me that in that statement you

told the police officer that you were not certain whether the sale to the company occurred before or after the enquiry from the man with the scar?'

'If that's what my statement says, then I do accept it, yes.'

'So it is possible that the enquiry came before the sale to the company?'

'Yes.'

'And if that were right, at the time of the letting, the owner of the property would have been Professor Wilson, and not Overbrooke (G.B.) Limited.'

'That is correct.'

'Thank you, Mr Millard. I have no further questions, my Lord.'

Always be polite to witnesses, thought Charles. The jury likes it, and it is much more effective when you have to get nasty.

There was no re-examination and the judge had no questions.

'The next witness, my Lord, is Declan Mahoney. Page three in my Lord's bundle of Additional Evidence,' said Stafford, ever helpful.

'Thank you,' said the judge, giving him a friendly smile.

'I have told my learned friend,' said Charles, rising to his feet, 'that he may lead this witness. There is no dispute about his evidence.'

'Thank *you*, Mr Holborne,' said the judge, smiling at Charles, who could not decide if the smile was a trifle less warm in his case or whether it was his imagination.

The clerk from Companies House gave evidence exactly

in line with his statement, Stafford simply leading him through it and getting him to agree with all he suggested. Stafford sat down five minutes later, curious to hear what questions were to be asked by Charles. Charles rose.

'Your evidence Mr Mahoney, in a nut-shell, is that Mr Robeson controls Overbrooke (G.B.) Limited and thus, at some time, this property called Staplecroft?'

'Yes. Through another company called Prince Estates (1960) Limited.'

'Would you have a look at these please?' asked Charles, handing a bundle of papers to the usher. 'My Lord there is a separate bundle for your Lordship and one here for my learned friend.' Charles handed those too to the usher.

'Now, Mr Mahoney, you will see that these are all searches of the records kept at Companies House.'

'Yes.'

'They are searches in respect of a further eight companies. All seeking information as at 1st December 1962.'

The witness counted them. 'That's right.'

'The Memorandum and Articles of Association of each company have been included, do you see? Am I right in thinking that they are all property companies?'

Mahoney leafed through the documents. Charles had made sure they were in order and divided into separate companies. He didn't want the number of documents to hold up the flow of his questions.

'They all appear to have been set up to deal in properties, yes,' replied Mahoney.

'Will you look through the register of shareholders in

each case? And will you confirm for the jury that Mr Harold Robeson is named as a shareholder in each?'

'That is right.'

'The annual accounts of companies have, normally, to be filed at Companies House too, do they not?'

'With some exceptions, yes. All these companies would have to file returns.'

'If you look at the copy annual returns with each search, you will be able to see what assets each company had.'

'Mr Holborne,' interrupted the judge. 'This could take all day. This evidence is not contentious. Why were steps not taken to agree it before the trial so that time could be saved?'

The reason was that Charles wanted this evidence given by a live witness. Evidence given from the box was always more powerful – and remained longer in the memories of the jury members – than a bland admission or a statement read by the court clerk. Charles was trying to make a point that was of slim value at best; he wanted therefore to make the most he could of it. However, that reason was not one that would appeal to His Honour Judge Pullman QC. On the other hand, he was not allowed to lie or mislead the court.

'My Lord will see that the dates on the searches differ but if I can take you to the summary sheet at the end – '

'Oh, just get on with it,' snapped the judge testily.

Charles turned back to Mahoney. 'The documents in your hand include the auditors' reports in respect of each company. If you look at them, you will see that in December 1962 these eight companies between them owned one hundred and seventy-eight residential properties.'

Mahoney paused and flicked through the documents, counting the number of properties. 'I accept that, yes.'

'And Mr Robeson had as much connection with them, as he did with the properties owned by Overbrooke (G.B.) Limited?'

'How can this witness answer that?' demanded the judge. 'You needn't answer that,' he directed Mahoney. Charles was content to change subjects. The point was made, whether Mahoney answered or not.

'One further matter please, Mr Mahoney. Let us assume for the moment that Mr Robeson did own this property, or at least controlled the company which owned it.'

'Yes.'

'And let us also assume that Mr Robeson was party to the robbery and was looking to provide the robbers with a property from which to work.'

'Yes.'

'Can you think of any reason why he would want to *let* the property to the other robbers, when doing so made a witness of Mr Millard and a paper trail to be found by the police? Surely he would simply have handed the keys to the robbers?'

'I can't answer that.'

'No, Mr Holroyd,' intervened the judge. 'He can't. That's a matter for submissions by Mr Stafford and by you at the appropriate time.'

'As your Lordship pleases.' said Charles, sitting down.

Stafford rose again. 'I have no re-examination, my Lord. Has your Lordship any questions? No? Then I call Roger

William Duncan, please,' he said, adjusting his spectacles. The banker entered the court, bearing a heavy file of papers.

'Again,' said Charles, half-rising, 'the witness may be led.'

'I'm grateful,' replied Stafford.

The witness was sworn, and ran through his evidence regarding Robeson's withdrawals of cash. Charles rose to cross-examine.

'You have produced the bank statement of Prince Estates (1960) Limited for the month of August.'

'I have.'

'Do you also have in your file the statements for other months?'

'I have the statements from the date the account was opened until the present time.'

'Good. Please look at, say, September 1962. There are large cash withdrawals in that month are there not?'

'There are. They range from five hundred pounds to... about twelve hundred.'

'Similarly, in October and November?'

'Yes. There are four – no five – withdrawals, ranging from six hundred pounds to seventeen hundred and eighty pounds.'

'Let's have a look at the period after the robbery, in January 1963. There is a withdrawal of two thousand one hundred pounds is there not?'

'Yes, on the 11th. And, to save you the trouble, Mr Holborne, there are similar withdrawals in February and March.'

Charles smiled his thanks. 'Thank you Mr Duncan.' He

was confident that he'd established that it was not unusual for the company to withdraw similar sums of money as those allegedly used to purchase the cars.

To Charles's surprise Stafford rose to re-examine. 'Have you looked at any of the other statements, apart from the ones Mr Holborne has dealt with?'

'Yes, I have done a thorough analysis of the transactions on the account.'

'And what have been your findings?'

'Well, there is indeed a substantial number of large withdrawals in the six months before December 1962 and in the three months thereafter. But the account was operated for four years before that, and the pattern did not exist then, nor indeed after March 1963. The withdrawing of large sums of cash seems to have been a short-term phenomenon.'

'Thank you. Does my Lord have –'

'There is one further matter,' volunteered the banker.

'Yes, Mr Duncan. What is that?'

'I have also analysed the other side of the account, the credits. Although there were a number of large withdrawals in the period there were also many more, smaller, deposits. Very nearly the same amount was in fact paid in as went out. The difference is about one thousand five hundred pounds.'

Stafford frowned theatrically as if he had not grasped the point. 'So are you saying that there was a lot of *apparent* movement, but no actual movement of funds –'

Charles leapt to his feet to prevent an answer. 'My Lord, that's a leading question, and in any case the conclusions to be drawn from the evidence are matters for the jury, not for this witness. Furthermore, this witness can only say that there was a balance of deposits and withdrawals; he cannot say if the money came from the same sources.'

'He doesn't say there was a *balance*, Mr Holborne,' responded Pullman. 'He says that there was a difference of about one thousand five hundred pounds – a sum *very* similar to the cost of the two vehicles used in the robbery. In other words, that sum was in fact drawn out and not replaced, isn't that right, Mr Duncan?'

'That is right, my Lord.'

'Just pause there and let me make a note of that,' said the judge, making sure the jury had not missed the point. 'Now, Mr Holborne,' said the judge, smiling like a shark, 'what was your objection?'

Charles repeated himself. The judge considered the point for a second, and then, grudgingly, agreed. 'I think that must be right, mustn't it, Mr Stafford? The conclusions to be drawn from Mr Duncan's evidence are for the jury to decide.'

'I don't press the point, my Lord,' replied Stafford with an expansive gesture. He didn't need to. 'Does my Lord have any questions?'

'No, thank you.'

'Avram Goldstein, please,' said Stafford.

Charles rose. 'Before the witness is brought in, my Lord, there is an application I should like to make.'

'Do you want the jury to leave?' asked the judge.

'Well, it is a matter of law, and therefore for your Lordship to decide, but it may be stated in a sentence, and I have no objection to the jury remaining.'

'Very well.'

'I should like permission for Mr Robeson to come out of the dock and sit beside my Instructing Solicitor behind me. The reason is this: as my Lord knows from reading the papers, this witness's identification is crucial to the Crown's case. It was made in unusual circumstances and I submit that your Lordship should in due course direct the jury that great care must be taken concerning it.'

'Well?'

'If the witness comes into court, and sees the man in the dock, when asked to describe the man he saw on the night he may be tempted, even subconsciously, to describe the man he can see in front of him. I therefore ask that Mr Robeson may be able to sit behind me for a short period while the description is being given and cross-examined if necessary. He's been on bail and the chances of him trying to escape from a full courtroom are, my Lord might agree, insignificant.'

'What do you say about this, Mr Stafford?' asked the judge. 'It's certainly an unusual application.'

'It is unusual my Lord, although I have encountered it before. My Lord will be aware of the recent cases where mis-identification has led to wrongful convictions, and the Crown would be very anxious to avoid that occurring in this case. I agree that your Lordship can probably discount the risk of Mr Robeson attempting to escape and, as I understand Mr Holborne's application, he will be returned to the dock in only a few minutes. On balance, the Crown is neutral; it's a matter for your discretion.'

'Well, Mr Holborne, I've dealt with hundreds of identification cases, and never heard this application before.'

'That may be because I have not appeared before my Lord on this sort of case. It is an application I make quite often in identification cases.'

'Well, I'm not inclined to grant – '

'Please forgive me for interrupting, but what your Lordship does not know is the nature of the defence in this case. I am not able to tell my Lord about it at this stage, but *in fairness to the Defence*, if the Crown have no objection, I must ask that your Lordship grant the application.'

As he used the words "fairness to the Defence" Charles looked at the jury. This was why he was perfectly happy for the jury to remain in court while he made the application. In his experience pro-prosecution Judges were occasionally embarrassed into fairness by the presence of the jury. Whether that reasoning was right in this case or not, Pullman relented.

'Yes, very well. I shall rise for five minutes in any event.'

'Court rise!' called the clerk.

The court rose, and the jurors filed out to their jury room. Charles saw Robeson beckoning him and slipped over to the dock.

'Why's he risen?' he asked.

'He's a smoker. He probably just wants a cigarette.'

chapter 15

'You're doing well, Charles,' said Robeson. Robeson was now sitting behind Charles in the solicitors' bench.

'Not really. This is just early skirmishing. We're picking up the odd point here and there, but they're insignificant compared with what's to come. I'm irritated about that banker. I should have asked for all the statements before I waded in.'

'No, it's not your fault. I left it to the accountant to sort out, and I didn't check them myself. I didn't know he'd only picked out the statements that helped.'

'What do you say about this point, the balancing entries in the account?'

'Of course there's going to be money going in; we're running a business. What do you think we do with the rents? So far as the last six months are concerned, we took a policy decision to be much more aggressive in property purchasing. The big boys can always beat our offers when it comes to a tasty property, so we decided we'd offer cash instead. That decision was taken in June or July 1962. It didn't really work, so we abandoned the policy in March 1963. There's nothing sinister about it.'

'Fine. You can deal with that in chief. Let's concentrate

on Goldstein. Are they here?'

'Yes.'

Robeson signalled to one of his clerks sitting next to the door. The man rose swiftly and disappeared outside for a second. He then re-entered with another man and directed him to Robeson. The man was about fifty years old, with greying hair. He came down the aisle and sat next to Robeson.

'Charles,' said Robson, 'let me introduce Bill Summers. He's an outdoor clerk in our Beckenham office.' Charles shook his hand. 'Do you think he'll be alright?' asked Robeson. 'He doesn't look anything like me.'

'No, but he's the about the same age and build. That's all I want. I'm not into pulling stunts. I just want to see how good Goldstein's description is, without him having any help from seeing you alone. If he's been primed to pick you out, they'll have made sure he's seen a recent photograph anyway. Where's Norman?'

'Here he comes now.'

Norman Marlowe approached them from the back of the court. He shook hands with Robeson, who he appeared to know well, and sat down on the same bench on the other side of Robeson. He was in fact thirty years younger than Robeson and quite different in appearance but Charles wanted Robeson lost in a crowd. There were now three men sitting behind Charles on the solicitors' bench, all wearing similar suits.

'The judge is coming back in, gentlemen,' announced the clerk. The door to the jury room opened and the jurors filed back into their seats.

There was a knock on the judge's door, the usher called 'All rise!' and the judge entered. 'Yes, Mr Stafford,' he said, once the court had settled.

'Thank you, my Lord. The Crown calls Avram Goldstein.'

The dock officer moved to one side in the dock, and opened the door that led down to the cells.

'Bring him up,' he called.

There was a jangling of metal and Goldstein was led up into the court handcuffed between two prison guards. They had allowed him to wear his own clothes while giving evidence, as he was in a suit rather than prison clothing. As always he wore a skull cap on his head. The three men manoeuvred their way around the dock and filed out. Goldstein was taken to the witness box.

'Religion?' asked the usher, apparently oblivious to the Jew's hair, beard and head covering.

'Jewish.'

The usher handed him a copy of the Old Testament and a printed card. 'Take this in your right hand and read the words on the card.'

Goldstein read the oath in a strong Eastern European accent, his voice faint and halting.

When he had finished he glanced around the court nervously. Charles noticed that he paid particular attention to the public gallery.

'Your name, please?' asked Stafford.

Goldstein looked round sharply at his interrogator.

'Avram Shimon Goldstein.'

'Your occupation?'

'Jeweller. I was a jeweller.'

'Where?'

'I had premises in Hatton Garden.'

'What is your present address please?'

He lowered his voice. 'Camp Hill Barracks, Isle of Wight.'

'You must remember to keep your voice up, Mr Goldstein. Camp Hill Barracks is, I think a prison, is it not?'

'Yes,' shouted Goldstein, inappropriately loudly, staring fixedly at the side of the witness box. Charles deliberately kept his attention on his notes. He didn't want to make eye contact with Goldstein yet or risk him spotting Robeson sitting directly behind him.

'I want to ask you about a night in December 1962. Do you remember any night that month on which someone came into your shop late?'

'I do.'

'Who came in?'

'A man called Kenny Lyall.'

'Do you remember the date?' asked Stafford.

'No, but it was between Christmas and the New Year. He'd been a customer for some time.'

'What time of the day was this?'

'Late afternoon. Before the Sabbath.'

'Keep your voice up, Mr Goldstein. Was he alone?'

'No. He had another man with him.'

'What sort of man?'

'Just a man.'

'A big man, small man, thin man, fat man?'

'He was big. In his thirties maybe. He looked like a boxer – broken nose and suchlike. He didn't speak.'

Stafford turned to look at the jury before asking his next question. Their attention was fixed on Goldstein. 'What did Lyall and this man want?'

'They wanted me to do a valuation.'

'Is it usual for customers to come in like that for an immediate valuation?'

'It happens. He, Lyall, had asked me some months before if I'd do a valuation for him. I'd agreed. It was part of my job.'

'Did he tell you what he wanted the valuation for?'

'The first time he mentioned it, he said it was because he was being offered jewellery to pay off an old debt, and he didn't know if it was worth anything.' Goldstein's voice was now much firmer. Charles noted that he was now volunteering information rather than answering as shortly as he could. He was becoming more confident.

'What did he say when he came in on that December night?'

'He wanted me to do the valuation that night.'

'Where? In the shop?'

'No. He said the jewels were somewhere else, and that I had to go with them then.'

'"*Had*" to go?'

'He was very insistent. He was offering me more and more money. He got angry when I kept saying no. He said he'd hold me personally responsible if he lost out because of it.'

'Did you agree to go?'

'Not for a while. It was a Friday evening. I was due at home. But in the end I went because I was scared. I thought it was easier to go than not to go.'

'Where were you taken?'

'I can't tell you. He blindfolded me as soon as we left the centre of London. It felt like a long journey though.'

'What car did you go in?'

'I don't know. I don't really know one car from another.'

'What, if anything did you notice about your destination?'

'Well, I can't be sure, but I thought that it was in the country, as there was wind in the trees, and very little traffic.'

'What happened when you arrived?'

'I was guided into a house and straight up some stairs. The blindfold was taken off. In front of me was a desk and on the desk were diamonds.'

'Did you value the diamonds?'

'I did.'

'Did you realise that they were stolen?'

'By that time I had guessed that there was something wrong with them.'

'You are now serving a prison sentence for assisting Lyall and others in the retention or disposal of the diamonds.'

Again Goldstein's voice dropped to almost a whisper. 'Yes.'

'Now, Mr Goldstein, did you see anyone in that house?'

'Kenny Lyall was there.'

The judge and both counsel glanced sharply at Goldstein. He knew who it was he was there to identify. Was the answer evasive, or just ingenuous?

'Anyone else?' asked Stafford smoothly.

'The driver. I never heard his name.'

'Anyone else?'

Goldstein paused. He looked around the court again, as if seeking an escape. His forehead was shiny with sweat. What the hell is he so worried about? wondered Charles. And who is he looking for?

'Yes. A man.'

'Can you describe the man?'

'He was never in the light. It's very difficult.'

'Well, do your best, Mr Goldstein.'

'He was middle-aged. Wearing nice clothes.'

'Colour of hair?'

'I'm not sure. Grey I think.'

'Build?'

'Normal. Not thin, not fat.'

'Colour of eyes?'

'I don't know. I never saw.'

'Can you say anything more about him?'

'No. Not really.'

'Did you ever see that man again? After that night?'

Goldstein gulped air like a drowning fish and blurted out his answer. 'Yes. When a policeman came to see me in prison. He showed me some photographs, and I picked the man out.'

'If I were to show you the same photographs, do you

think you would be able to pick him out again?'

Charles had no alternative but to jump up to prevent the answer being given. 'I object, my Lord. This is in effect a dock identification, which is prohibited. Further, this case has been widely covered in the media, and who knows how many times the accused's face has appeared in the papers or on television? How do we know that any identification done today is of the man seen that night, as against the man all over the daily papers?'

'Yes,' replied the judge. 'Mr Stafford, in all the circumstances, it would be best not to ask the witness to see the photographs again. The officer will give evidence of who was picked out.'

'Yes, my Lord. In that case, I have no further questions.'

'It's five to one,' said the judge. 'You may cross-examine after the short adjournment, Mr Holborne. Mr Goldstein, you will be taken down in any event, but you are still giving evidence, and I must tell you not to speak to anyone at all about this case until your evidence is completed. Do you understand?'

Goldstein nodded.

'Very well. Members of the jury, we shall adjourn until five past two. I shall give you a direction now that will apply throughout the rest of this trial: do not discuss the case with anyone outside your number. Your families will no doubt be very curious as to what you're doing, but please resist the impulse to tell them anything, as once you start, it's very difficult to stop and to prevent them making some comment. The decision to which you come must be uninfluenced by what others say. Five past two, please. Mr Robeson will be on bail as before until further order.'

'All rise!'

The defence team sat still until Goldstein had been taken in handcuffs across the court, back into the dock and down into the cells.

Robeson leaned forward to touch Charles on the shoulder. 'What are you going to do for lunch, Charles?' he asked.

'I don't know. I've got to make a phone call to find out how Dad is; his test results came in this morning. After that I think I'd just like to have a bite to eat on my own, if you don't mind Harry. I'd like a quiet think about what's coming up next.'

'Yes, of course. We'll be in the public canteen if you need us.'

Charles made his way up to the robing room, sought a telephone and asked for an outside line.

He dialled his parents' number. Millie answered. 'Mum? It's Charles. Well, what do they say?'

'Oh, Charles!' she replied, and burst into tears. Charles could hear her wailing, even though her hand was held over the mouthpiece. The noise grew suddenly louder, and another voice spoke.

'Charles? It's Sonia. You Mum's too upset to speak at the present.'

'What's going on?'

'Well, your father does need an operation. I don't really understand it, but they say he has a blockage in or near the left side of his heart. The doctor said he's all furred up like an old radiator.'

'Is he in danger?'

'I don't know. The doctor told us, but I can't remember most of what he said. He said that there was a risk that your father he might die during it. Your mother went to pieces and I had to take her out of the room. David's spoken to them since on the telephone, and he understands what's going on. He'll be here later.'

The telephone was taken back by Millie, as it was her voice Charles heard next. She was a little calmer.

'Oh, Charles, I don't understand it. A month ago he was fit and well, and all of a sudden he's dying.'

'Don't talk like that, Mum, he's not dying. He needs an operation. Do you know when's he got to go in?'

'As soon as there's a space.'

'What? You mean he has to wait?'

'Of course. Up to three months.' She began to cry again. 'He'll die before then. I know it.'

'No he won't. Just calm down, Mum. Everything's going to be fine. I'll sort something out. He won't have to wait three months. But, I've got to go now. I'll come round this evening and we'll talk about it. Okay?'

'Okay.' Her voice was no more than a whisper. ''Bye.'

Charles no longer felt hungry. He paced about the robing room for twenty minutes and then, because he had nothing better to do, he went down to sit outside the courtroom. He sat on a bench in the Great Hall with his eyes closed for a while, feeling a knot in the pit of his stomach, and trying to relax. He'd been there for a quarter of an hour when somebody in front of him coughed.

'Excuse me,' said a woman's voice.

Charles opened his eyes. A woman with dark eyes stood before him, a scarf covering her hair. Her face looked drawn and pinched and she had heavy rings under her eyes. She was unmistakably Jewish.

'Excuse me,' she repeated, 'but I'm trying to find the right court, but I don't know the name of the case. I told the man on the door and said he thought I should try here.'

'What sort of case are you looking for?' asked Charles, conscious that the question sounded odd.

'My husband is giving evidence today for the police.'

Mrs Goldstein? he wondered. Was that who Goldstein was searching for in the gallery? 'What's your husband's name?'

'Avram Goldstein.'

'Then this is the right court,' confirmed Charles.

'Thank you.' She walked away a few paces and then returned. 'Am I allowed to go in?'

'Yes. But you'll have to go round to the entrance in Warwick Street to get into the public gallery. And you'll need to be early to get a seat; it's been very crowded.'

She nodded, her pale face expressionless, turned and walked across the black and white polished marble towards the doors.

chapter 16

'All rise!'

The Recorder of London entered, bowed to the barristers' benches and resumed his seat. At the same time the clanking of chains and steel doors could be heard from below the empty dock as Goldstein was brought up. Everyone else in court had sat down by the time the jeweller was in place, but Charles had remained on his feet.

'Mr Holborne?' said the judge, inviting Charles to start his cross-examination.

Before Goldstein had time to settle or focus on his interlocutor, Charles fired his opening question. He wanted Goldstein's attention on him and on nothing else in the courtroom.

'Do I take it, Mr Goldstein, that you did not want to go with Lyall that evening to value his diamonds?'

Goldstein drew a deep breath, as if about to shout, but then answered simply, 'I did not want to go.'

'You're not saying that you went involuntarily?'

'Well, I didn't want to go. There were two of them in the shop, both big men.'

'Did they force you into the car?'

'No.' Goldstein spoke with his head down, making no

eye contact with Charles. 'Did they actually touch you in any way?'

'No.'

'Did they carry any weapons?'

'I don't know; maybe.'

'Did you see any weapons?'

Goldstein shook his head, his long curly sidelocks swaying. 'N ... no.'

'Did they tell you they *had* any weapons?'

'No.'

'Did they threaten you?'

'Not in so many words.'

'Well, in *what* words?'

'Lyall told me that he would be very sorry if I did not go. That he would hold me responsible if he lost out as a result.'

'Did you know that he was a criminal?'

'No.'

'So you knew nothing of any reputation he might have had?'

'He was just a customer.'

'So, this ordinary customer comes in with a friend, and asks you to do a valuation which you do not want to do. He does not coerce you in any way, but just says he will hold you responsible if he loses out. You're saying that that frightened you so much that you went against your will?'

'You don't understand,' replied the jeweller, pleading in his voice. He looked at Charles directly for the first time. 'You had to be there. I felt as if I had no choice.'

'Did you plead guilty to handling these diamonds? Or were you found guilty after a trial?'

'I was found guilty.'

'Did you defend the charge on the basis that you had been forced?'

'Yes.'

'But the jury trying your case rejected that defence?'

'I don't know.'

'Mr Goldstein, they found you guilty, right?'

'Yes.'

'Did you give evidence in your own defence?'

'Yes.'

'On oath?'

'Yes.'

'And they didn't believe you.'

Goldstein stared rigidly at his hands, clasped together on top of the witness box. 'They didn't believe you, did they? Are you going to answer me, Mr Goldstein?'

Goldstein looked intensely uncomfortable but didn't respond. The judge turned and stared at him. Charles let the profound silence in the courtroom lengthen for several seconds. The scene was utterly still, with every eye fixed on the miserable Jew.

'Well,' continued Charles finally, his voice softly breaking the spell. 'Let's move on.'

Charles could have insisted on an answer – and Pullman would have demanded it on pain of contempt of court if he *had* insisted – but Charles was satisfied. Goldstein's performance and his demeanour spoke more powerfully than any further answer.

'What did they offer you?'

'At first, £200.'

'£200? To value some jewels? That's equivalent to the average man's wage for … what? … about three months?'

'There were a large number, it meant going a long distance, and it was out of hours. On the Sabbath.'

'So you thought £200 was a fair price?'

'I suppose so. Not unfair.'

'Did you accept it?'

'No. I told you, I didn't want to go.'

'He then offered you £300 did he not?'

'Yes.'

'And you accepted?'

'Because, as I said, I was frightened.'

'You were frightened at £200 too, weren't you? Why did the offer of another £100 suddenly allay your fears, Mr Goldstein?'

'It didn't. I was still frightened.'

'But you thought it might be worth being frightened for £300, eh?' There was a sprinkling of laughter in the court.

'No.'

'You had the presence of mind to demand £100 in advance, did you not? And the balance? What of the balance?'

'At the end, as they dropped me off, Lyall gave me a diamond.'

'How much was it worth?'

'I don't know.'

'That's a lie, Mr Goldstein. You had just valued them all. In your statement to the police you claimed that it was worth £500.'

'Maybe.'

'Do you want to see your statement?'

'No.'

'It was worth, by your own estimate, £500?'

'Yes,' he hissed.

'So you were paid the equivalent of £600 for your work. What's your annual income, approximately?'

'About £2,000.'

'So almost a third of your year's income for one evening's work. And what happened to that diamond?'

'I sold it.'

'What did you do with the money?'

'I bought some furniture for my home.'

Charles paused. When he spoke, he lowered his voice and spoke slowly. 'Are you still telling this jury that you were forced into going? Or isn't it that you were bought?'

The court fell totally silent, awaiting the answer. Charles looked at the jury with satisfaction. The attention of all of them was riveted to Goldstein. One or two of them looked as if they had bad smells under their noses. They don't trust him, thought Charles.

'I believed at the time that I was forced.'

'There was no main light on in the bedroom where you examined the diamonds?'

Goldstein looked perplexed for a moment, unable to comprehend the sudden change of tack. Then he realised that Charles had changed subject, and sighed. The jury also relaxed, shifting in their seats. 'That is right,' he answered, his voice betraying relief at a simple statement with which he could agree.

'So the only light was from the desk lamp.'

'Yes.'

'Pointing to the desk.'

'Yes.'

'So the rest of the room would have been in virtual darkness.'

'Well, it was not well lit.'

'Did you ever speak to the man you later identified?'

'No.'

'Did you ever shake his hand?'

'No.'

'Were you ever introduced to him?'

'No.'

'So did you ever meet him face to face?'

'Not really. I saw him as I stood up and went out of the door. He had been standing behind me watching me work.'

'And you then went down the stairs.'

'Correct.'

'Did you ever see him again?'

'Not in person.'

'So how long was he in your sight for?'

'A few seconds. Ten maybe.'

'Just imagine you are in the room, about to stand up. Start counting for us in seconds, out loud please, and stop when you would have gone through the door.'

Goldstein shrugged, but did as he was asked. 'One… two…three…four…five…six…stop.'

'So your identification is based upon a six-second view of someone in shadows?'

'Yes.'

'How can you be sure it was the same man as the one you saw in the photograph?'

'I am sure.'

Charles whirled round and stared at Goldstein's wife in the gallery. Goldstein's eyes followed Charles's. Charles spun back towards the witness. The effect on Goldstein was if he'd been electrocuted. He was rigid, his eyes and mouth wide open, staring at his wife. I knew it! thought Charles in triumph. It *was* she who he was so anxious about.

'Really sure?' asked Charles.

Goldstein opened his mouth to speak, and moved his lips, but no sound emerged. 'Mr Goldstein?'

Goldstein wrenched his eyes from his wife for a second to flash a glance at Charles. His face was a picture of despair.

'Mr Holborne,' interrupted the judge, 'who is that lady in the gallery?'

'I believe her to be this witness's wife, my Lord.'

'What is she doing there?' thundered the judge, suspecting foul play.

'I am not sure, my Lord, other than watching the case.'

'Stand up, madam!' commanded the judge. Up in the public gallery Mrs Goldstein stood. All heads turned and all eyes in the court fastened on her. 'Are you here under any sort of pressure?'

'Me? No, sir, not at all,' she answered, bewildered.

'Then what is going on? I demand to know what is going on!'

'Nothing, sir … my Lord. I came to watch my husband give evidence. I haven't seen him for months. That's all.'

Charles watched the judge's face. Pullman was plainly convinced something *was* going on, and would have loved Charles to have been at the bottom of it, but he seemed undecided as to what to do. He stared alternately at Charles and Mrs Goldstein.

'Very well. Carry on Mr Holborne.'

'I was asking you, Mr Goldstein, if you could be sure.'

'I don't know … I don't know anymore … maybe … maybe not.'

'Is that your wife up there?'

He nodded without looking up at her.

'Your nod cannot be recorded on the transcript, Mr Goldstein. Please answer.'

'Yes,' he said softly.

'When did you last see her?'

'Two, three months ago.'

'And your children? How many do you have?'

'Four.' His voice was almost whisper.

'Do you miss your family?'

'Yes, of course I do,' he answered with longing.

'And when are you due for parole?' asked Charles conversationally. 'I don't know.'

'Has anyone told you that by giving evidence you might improve your chances of parole?'

'Well … I don't know.'

'What do you mean you don't know? Has someone told you or not? You must know if someone's spoken to you about it.'

'It has been mentioned.'

'Who by?'

'I can't remember.'

'Who by?' demanded Charles sharply.

'I tell you I can't remember.'

'Was it Sergeant West, the officer who took your statement?'

'I don't know. Maybe. I can't remember.'

'Your statement was given to the police long after you were convicted, is that right?'

'Yes. I was in prison.'

'How did it come about that you saw the police again?'

'I don't understand.'

'Sergeant West is a busy policeman in the Metropolitan Police. He doesn't travel from London to the Isle of Wight on the off-chance that someone wants to talk to him. So how did you and he make contact?'

'He came to see me.'

'At your invitation?'

'No.'

'So, what did he say when he came to see you?'

'I don't remember.'

'You must have talked about the robbery?'

'I suppose so. He asked if I thought I might be able to identify the man at the house.'

'And he showed you a picture of Mr Robeson, didn't he – before the formal identification process – and told you to pick him out.'

'No. He did not.'

'I suggest that's a lie.'

Goldstein shook his head, and began an answer, and then Charles looked up at Mrs Goldstein.

Goldstein also looked up. His voice faltered. He mouthed the word "No" but no sound emerged.

'Speak up!' commanded Charles.

Tears welled in Goldstein's eyes, and he silently shook his head.

'Your services were bought by Lyall, Mr Goldstein, and I suggest they've been bought today. You never saw Mr Robeson at that house, did you?'

Goldstein stared at Charles, willing him, pleading with his eyes, for Charles to stop. 'Did you?' repeated Charles.

'I don't know any more.'

'The truth is, you can't be sure *who* you saw on that night, can you?'

'No,' he conceded, the word emerging like the last breath of a dying man.

'No,' repeated Charles, softly. Charles looked at the judge. 'May I take brief instructions, my Lord?'

'Yes.'

Charles turned and whispered generally to the men sitting behind him. 'I don't think it's necessary to take the risk of an identification. He's been so badly damaged, the jury'll never believe him.'

'No!' whispered Robeson, urgently. 'Go ahead with it.'

'My strong advice is not to. It's immensely risky. Why take the risk when there's no need?'

'Charles, I was never there. If he's starting to tell the truth, he can't pick me out! Go for it!'

'He can pick you out – from having seen your photo – either then or in the papers since. Don't do it, Harry!'

'You have my instructions, Charles,' insisted Robeson curtly.

Charles shrugged, and turned back to the court. 'Thank you, my Lord. Now, finally, Mr Goldstein, describe for the jury the man you saw that night in the shadows.'

Goldstein shook his head. 'I can't,' he replied, his voice flat and his shoulders slumped. He was beaten.

'You can't?'

'No, I can't.'

'Do you see any man in court who you recognise from that night?' asked Charles, crossing his fingers behind his back, but underneath his robes.

Slowly Goldstein raised his head. His eyes were red and moist, and his face glistened with sweat. He looked around the court, at the judge, at the jury, and the barristers and other lawyers sitting in the benches around Charles, and, finally, at the public gallery. Then, with an almost imperceptible smile he faced Charles and replied. 'No, I do not.'

'Thank you. I have no further questions.' Charles realised that he too had been sweating while waiting for the answer.

Goldstein lifted his face towards the public gallery and smiled weakly at his wife. She smiled back at him. Stafford declined to re-examine, and Goldstein was led back down the stone steps to the cells.

'I shall rise for five minutes,' said the judge. 'I should like to see counsel in my room.' He stormed out of court.

'What's this all about?' asked Charles of Stafford.

'No idea. But if I had to guess, I'd say his Lordship believes you've been up to skullduggery. As do I.'

'Well, I haven't.'

'Really?' replied Stafford, disbelieving.

'You know me, Stafford. When have I ever been anything other than scrupulously straight with you?'

Stafford slipped his pens back inside his jacket pocket and picked up his blue counsel's notebook. 'I don't know you at all, and I don't want to. You lot are all the same,' he said, and sidled his enormous bulk out of the barristers' benches.

chapter 17

'Are you ready, gentlemen?' asked the court clerk.

'Yes,' replied Charles and Stafford together.

'Follow me, please.'

The clerk led the way up the steps beside the judge's bench and opened a door in the wall behind his seat. Charles found himself in a large carpeted corridor with paintings on wood-panelled walls. He followed the clerk and Stafford around a couple of corners and down a short flight of stone steps. The clerk turned and motioned for the barristers to wait. She knocked on an oak door and waited.

'Yes?'

The clerk put her head into the room. 'Counsel to see you, Judge.'

'Bring them in.'

The clerk opened the door wide and the barristers entered. Judge Pullman was sitting at his desk still in his robes but with his wig on the desk beside him. He was smoking an untipped cigarette.

'Sit down, gentlemen.'

Charles and Stafford drew chairs from the walls into the centre of the room and sat facing the judge.

'Now, Holborne. Would you mind telling me what the

hell's going on?'

Charles shook his head and shrugged. 'I haven't the faintest idea, Judge.'

'Really?' asked Pullman icily, his tone exactly like that of Stafford moments before. 'I don't know about you, Stafford, but it looks to me very much as if that Jew was under some sort of pressure. Extraordinary display. That was a man in fear if ever I saw one.'

'That was my impression, Judge,' affirmed Stafford.

'No doubt about it. Let me make myself clear, Holborne,' Pullman continued, jabbing his cigarette in Charles's direction, 'I don't like gamesmanship. I will not have my court turned into a circus, is that clear? I know all about your history – assaulting that police officer, burglary and so on.'

'I was framed by an escaped convict for murder and I faced the gallows,' replied Charles, in as level a voice as he could command. 'There was a full investigation by the police and my Inn. I have never faced charges.'

'That proves nothing. Anyone practising in this court knows how cheaply police officers can be bought.'

'What?' said Charles, standing. 'Are you suggesting – '

'Sit down, Holborne!' ordered the judge. 'Unless you want me to hold you in contempt!' Charles drew a deep breath and resumed his seat.

'Maybe I can't prove you were behind that scene in court, but I warn you: if I catch even a whiff of any more tricks, there *will* be charges. And not just to your Inn!'

'I had no hand whatsoever in what just occurred between Goldstein and his wife,' said Charles through gritted teeth, his black eyes flashing with unconcealed hatred towards the judge. 'It was clear to me that Goldstein was very scared of *something*, but I had no idea what. I'm still not sure. I saw him looking nervously towards the gallery when he started his evidence, but I couldn't understand what was bothering him. At the end of the luncheon adjournment I was approached by a woman in the Great Hall who asked if I could tell her where her husband was giving evidence. She said her husband was Goldstein. I directed her to the public gallery. I have no reason to disbelieve what she told you: she just wanted to see him. I've never seen her before in my life. I just played a hunch. You saw the reaction when he realised she was in the gallery.'

Pullman squinted at Charles through his cigarette smoke, evaluating him. He delicately spat a flake of tobacco out of his thin lips where it landed on his blotter, and turned to Stafford. 'What do you say?' he croaked.

'I have never seen anything like it before, Judge. It is difficult to put out of one's mind the accusations made only a few months ago against Holborne or, for that matter, his race. He and Goldstein share a common heritage, and we're in no position to know what might have passed between them which wouldn't have been noted by a gentile. Having said that, I can't *prove* what Holborne says is untrue.'

Pullman snorted at Stafford's credulity. 'And what do you suppose Goldstein found so terrifying about his wife? Unless of course, she was acting under some sort of threat, and was only there to remind him.'

'I may be able to suggest something,' volunteered Charles.

'Well?'

'He's a *hasid*, a strictly religious Jew. For him to lie on oath would be a very serious matter.'

'And what's his wife got to do with that?'

'I'm not sure. I'm just guessing, but he would hesitate before perjuring himself on the Old Testament before a Jewish witness.'

Pullman snorted again. 'I'm not satisfied with that. Stafford, as soon as he's finished giving evidence, ask the officer in your case to speak to the woman. I want to see a statement from her dealing with her presence here today. I want the officer to speak to you afterwards and tell you if, in his opinion, she's acting under duress.' He turned to Charles. 'I shall review the position then. You may go. I shall return to court immediately.'

Charles and Stafford filed out. Stafford glanced at Charles. 'You bastard, Stafford,' whispered Charles.

'One more comment like that, Holborne, and I'll see you're struck off for unprofessional conduct – whether the judge takes action against you or not.'

The two barristers continued in silence down the hushed corridor, passing thick oaken doors that led to the judges' benches in the other courts. For a split second Charles fantasised about the damage he could wreak on the English judiciary with this degree of access, three minutes, and a machine gun.

As they approached the door leading back into Court 1, Charles said: 'If I were you, I'd make sure DS West was accompanied when he speaks to the wife.' He spoke lightly, as if it was a throwaway comment.

Stafford looked across at Charles. 'Why should I do that?'

'Well, it's your call, but you heard the judge's comment about corrupt police officers. If I had "Tricky" West as the officer in *my* case, and a judge already suspicious about witnesses being put under pressure ... Well I'd be protecting my back, that's all. I'd want a third party present during the interview.'

Charles watched the fat man's brow furrow, and as he opened the door and stepped into Court 1 next to the judge's leather seat, he permitted himself a small smile.

The two barristers resumed their seats and watched the jury file in. Robeson beckoned to him but before Charles could move the judge entered. Charles leaned towards Robeson's clerk. 'Tell him not to worry, and I'll explain later,' he said.

Stafford scanned his papers.

'Yes, Mr Stafford?' asked Pullman.

'Yes, my Lord. The Crown calls Detective Sergeant West.'

The sweaty sergeant entered and strode to the witness box. He'd finally succumbed to his wife's nagging and, in celebration of Robeson's arrest, had bought himself a new suit, one more commensurate with his increased girth. Nonetheless the tie around his short, red neck, tightened only the moment he had entered court, still made him look distinctly uncomfortable. He took the Bible firmly in his hand and raised it to shoulder height. He gave the oath in a clear voice without faltering, staring fiercely at the jury as if daring them to disbelieve that his evidence was anything but the truth, the whole truth and nothing but the truth. He gave his name, rank and number without being asked, turned to the judge and said: 'My Lord.'

'I shall be asking you, Sergeant,' started Stafford, 'about events occurring on the evening of 21 June 1963. Will you need to refresh your memory from any notes?'

'I may, my Lord. The notes were made on the same evening, back at the police station immediately after the accused's arrest. That was the first opportunity I had to make them. The matters were fresh in my mind at the time.'

'Very good, officer,' said the judge. 'You may refresh your memory from the notes if you require.' West took a pocket book from his jacket and opened it.

'Where were you at approximately 7 p.m. that evening?'

West consulted his notebook. 'At 7.06 p.m., my Lord, I was on duty in plain clothes with Detective Constable North and acting Detective Sergeant Walker in an unmarked police car in Brewers Street, Greenwich.'

'What was your purpose there?'

'My Lord, we had been engaged in a surveillance operation on Mr Harold Robeson, who we had reason to believe was involved in the robbery of the South African diamond consignment in December 1962.'

Charles realised that West was an accomplished witness. Although being asked questions by Stafford, he turned to direct each answer to the judge and he watched Pullman's pen carefully to make sure that he wasn't giving his answers too fast. By the end of the trial, when the judge summed up, every word of West's evidence would be there to be recited again to the jury.

'What did you do when you arrived there?' asked Stafford.

'We parked the car and in due course entered The Victory public house. Once there we went to the public bar. We waited there for a few minutes, and then as a result of information received we went upstairs to a room where there was a private party in progress.'

'What happened upstairs?'

'I identified the accused and asked him to accompany us to his car which was parked in the car park of the public house.'

'Did the accused agree to go with you?'

'He did, my Lord. In the car park I asked him to unlock the boot of his silver Austin Princess car, registration number 238 AJK, which he did.'

'What happened then?'

'I saw a long dark object in the boot. I reached in and found it to be a shotgun.'

Stafford turned to the bench behind him where a young man was holding out to him a gun wrapped in a plastic sheet. Stafford took it and handed it to an usher.

'Just look at this please, Sergeant.'

West took it and unwrapped the plastic. He looked carefully at the gun and identified the label tied to its stock. 'That is the gun, my Lord.'

'Let that be exhibit 1,' said the judge.

'I then asked the accused if the gun was his, and he replied "No it is not. I have never seen it before." I then arrested the accused at 7.48 p.m. and cautioned him, to which he made no reply.'

'What happened to Mr Robeson after that?'

'He was taken to West End Central police station.'

'Were you involved in this matter any further?'

'Yes, sir. I was present later that evening when, at 10.05 p.m. Mr Robeson was interviewed.'

'I think we can take this quickly, Sergeant. Is it correct that Mr Robeson declined to answer any questions at all, as was his right?'

'That is correct, my Lord.'

'What did you do with the shotgun?'

'I attached that label to it, and passed it to the forensic science laboratory for examination.'

'Thank you, Sergeant. Now, one last matter: were you present when the accused was given bail at this court in July?'

'Yes I was.'

'And were you involved in returning the accused's property to him which had been seized on his arrest in Greenwich?'

'Yes.'

Stafford dealt with the £10 note found in Robeson's wallet very briefly, simply leading West through the contents of his supplemental statement. The light touch he deployed indicated to Charles that Stafford placed no great reliance on that evidence.

'Wait there please,' said Stafford, as he concluded the examination in chief. He sat down.

Charles rose. 'I take it therefore, Sergeant, that your presence at The Victory Public House was not an accident?'

'No sir. As I have explained, we were there as part of an investigation.'

'So if I suggest to you that you told Mr Robeson to come downstairs and look at his car because there had been a report of someone tampering with it, you would deny it?'

'No, sir.'

'You *did* tell Mr Robeson that someone had been tampering with his car?'

'Yes, sir.'

'And who was that?'

'No one, to the best of my knowledge, my Lord.' West turned to the judge and smiled. 'There was a very boisterous party in progress upstairs, at which there were a number of known criminals. I felt that it might be unwise to raise the real nature of our visit in all the circumstances, so I decided to give an innocuous excuse to persuade the accused to come downstairs without causing any alarm.'

The judge smiled. 'Yes, Sergeant, I understand. Very sensible.'

'Thank you, my Lord.' West turned to face the jury and smiled at them, to make sure that they, too, thought that he had been very sensible.

'So,' continued Charles, 'you deceived Mr Robeson as to the reason he was required downstairs?'

'Yes, sir. An innocent deception, I felt.'

'To the best of your knowledge, no one did interfere with Mr Robeson's car?'

'I can tell you for certain sir, that no one did interfere with it.'

'How can you tell us that?'

'Because there was someone observing the vehicle throughout.'

'Why was that?'

'Because I didn't want it to be driven away by Mr Robeson, did I?'

West looked at the jury again, inviting them to join him in his amazement at such a stupid barrister. One or two of the jury members smiled slightly.

'Yes, Mr Holborne. That does appear to be obvious, does it not?' asked the judge.

'If my Lord says so. And who, Sergeant, was conducting the observation?'

'DC North, my Lord.'

'And DC North remained outside for the entire period, is that right?'

'That's right. Until we went upstairs to see the accused.'

'Why was it necessary for anyone to wait outside? You knew Mr Robeson was upstairs; why not go straight up and get him down? That way, no one had to wait outside to ensure that his car didn't move.'

'That's effectively what we did.'

'No. That's not so, Sergeant. You arrived at the pub at 7.06 p.m. according to your earlier evidence, but you did not arrest Mr Robeson until 7.48 p.m. You waited for some considerable time.'

West grinned mischievously. 'Well, to tell you the truth,

sir, unprofessional as it may sound, we stopped long enough to have a drink. That was the only reason for the delay.'

'You stopped for a drink? Before making an arrest of this importance?'

'I've been a policeman for almost twenty years, my Lord. I've arrested many men – women too, for that matter – on charges every bit as serious as this.'

'This wasn't the first time you had had dealings with Mr Robeson, was it?'

'No sir.'

'He practises in the field of criminal law, doesn't he?'

'I believe so.'

'You *know* so. He's defended in many important criminal trials.'

'I expect so, my Lord.'

'In particular, he represented Kenneth Lyall, the man alleged to have been one of the robbers in this very robbery.'

'That is right.'

'Mr Lyall was eventually acquitted of that charge.'

'Yes.'

'And you were not happy about that, were you?'

'It's part of the job, sir. My job is to get the evidence to put before a jury. Then it's up to the jury to decide.'

'You thought he was guilty didn't you?'

'I did, my Lord, or else I wouldn't have charged him with it, but the jury didn't agree.'

'And you had to pay back to him eighty-five thousand pounds odd that you had found and seized from his home – money that you thought were the proceeds of the crime.'

'That's right, my Lord. The jury acquitted him, and so that money was his. Or so I was advised.'

'That must have been galling. Having to hand back all that money, tenner after tenner?'

'As I said, my Lord: part of the job.'

'That's very reasonable of you, Sergeant,' said Charles with heavy sarcasm. 'But Kenny Lyall was not the first man to be acquitted after you had thought he was guilty.'

'Nor the last, I expect, my Lord.'

'Nor was he the first to be represented by Mr Robeson?'

'I expect not.'

'Mr Robeson has defended in prosecutions in which you have given evidence on a number of occasions.'

'I really wouldn't know, my Lord. I don't keep tally. Policemen, sir, are generally too busy catching criminals,' and here he nodded towards the dock, 'to keep scores.'

'I suggest to you, Sergeant, that this was one arrest where you would not stop to have a pint before getting your man. This was something of a "grudge match".'

'You can suggest what you like, sir. It was just another job.'

West stood in the box, his hands held behind his back, and rocked slightly on his heels. He was putting on a good performance, and he knew it. 'Besides,' he added, almost as an afterthought, 'at the time, I didn't know that the accused was going to be arrested. I didn't know what might be in the boot of his car.'

Charles snapped back immediately. 'Then what on earth were you doing there?'

West suddenly looked slightly uncomfortable, but he recovered well. 'We were there as a result of information received.'

Charles paused. If he asked West what that information was he was certain to get an answer damning to Robeson. West had hardly missed an opportunity to put the boot in, the references to the villains at the party, the nod towards the dock when speaking of "criminals". At the same time, the risk of not going into West's "information received" could be as great. The jury would already be wondering what had brought the police to the pub.

'You told us that the interference with the car was a ruse to get Mr Robeson downstairs without any fuss.'

'Yes.'

'So you must have had a reason to ask him to open his boot?'

'Yes.'

'Your "information received" was that there would be a gun in the boot?'

'Not quite, no.'

Charles paused to consider carefully the framing of his next few questions. 'I don't propose to ask you the identity of your informant.'

'I wouldn't give it to you anyway,' replied West, no longer smiling. 'Unless, of course, I was ordered to do so by my Lord.'

'But it must be right, that the police receive a great deal of information from such people.'

'That is right, my Lord.'

'Some of it very reliable information, and some of it less so. I expect you've had tips which turned out to be precisely correct, and tips which turned out not to be correct at all.'

'Yes, my Lord.'

'Some sources can be relied on, others cannot.'

'All sources are variable, my Lord. Some are more variable than others.'

'And you have to be very careful about how you act on these sources.'

'Indeed.'

'They may have their own motives for informing.'

'They all do. Money, mostly.' There was some laughter at that. West had recovered his lost confidence.

'They may perhaps want to settle scores.'

'That's possible.'

'Those working in the criminal courts, policemen, barristers, judges, they can easily make enemies in the course of their work.'

'I suppose so.'

'As can solicitors.'

West's expression changed as he realised Charles's direction.

'If you're trying to say that this information was unreliable because it was given by someone with a grudge against Mr Robeson, sir, you're wrong. I don't know if the person has a grudge or not. But the information was right. The shotgun from the robbery *was* in the boot.'

'So that *was* your information? That the shotgun was in the boot?'

'Not quite. We were told to be there by a certain time, and that the accused would be there and that we should look in the boot.'

'Just be there and look in the boot?'

'Yes.'

'That was pretty slim information on which to mount an operation involving so many police officers. Why did you go?'

'Because I thought the information was reliable.'

'Did you pay for it?'

'No.'

'Did you know who it came from?'

'I didn't take the message.'

'That's not what I asked you. Did you know the name of the alleged informant?'

'No.'

'Why then did you think it would be reliable?'

West began to look more uncomfortable. The jury were watching him closely now. 'I ... don't know sir ... a hunch I suppose.'

Charles laughed. He spoke with as much derision as he could command. 'You had a hunch that a respected solicitor might just be carrying round in the boot of his car the shotgun used in a robbery committed by an ex-client of his seven months before? Is that what you're saying?'

'Yes. Well, I had a hunch that the tip might be worth following up.'

'A police officer – not you – receives an unsolicited message from an unknown source, that this respected solicitor will be at a certain public house at a certain time, and that you should go and look in his boot. And that was enough for you?'

'Yes.'

Charles shook his head in disbelief. 'And, based upon this *hunch* of yours, how many busy officers did you involve in this operation, Sergeant?'

'Five.'

'Five people, on the basis of that tip?' asked Charles incredulously.

'Yes.'

'Then, I'll ask you again, Sergeant: isn't the truth of the matter, that this was indeed a very important "collar" for you? You *wanted* Mr Robeson.'

'A bent solicitor is a dangerous animal, my Lord. It's far more important to catch him than the criminals he helps.' This time the urbane and reasonable voice had a distinct edge of anger in it.

'So, now we're getting there, Sergeant West. Now we see some of your true feelings about Harold Robeson.'

'Please save your speeches for the right time, Mr Holborne,' interrupted the judge.

'I apologise, my Lord. It is right, is it not, that your feelings about catching Mr Robeson were not exactly indifferent?'

'I was not indifferent, no. I think he's a very dangerous and clever criminal – '

Charles interrupted him. 'Less of what you think, please Sergeant! Speeches for the Crown are made at the end, and then by counsel. As you have already said: it's for the jury, and not for you or I to decide.'

'Mr Holborne!' protested the judge.

'My Lord?'

'I will tell witnesses what they can and cannot answer! Your direction of the witness is quite improper.'

'I apologise again to my Lord if I have acted improperly. What this officer thinks of Mr Robeson is, in my submission, irrelevant.'

'That may very well be, but in my experience it is for the judge – not defence counsel – to prevent witnesses answering questions. Do not test my patience any further.'

Charles took a deep breath and started again. 'Sergeant West: you have told us that you were engaged in surveillance of Mr Robeson. May I take it that that surveillance began before the tip about the car boot?'

'We were keeping an eye on him, yes.'

'When did that start?'

'I can't remember exactly. Before that evening anyway.'

'And what happened to prompt such surveillance?' It was a dangerous question, as Charles only suspected, and did not know, the answer he was likely to receive.

'We received some evidence.'

'The evidence of Avram Goldstein?'

'That's right,' replied West, frowning.

'You took Mr Goldstein's statement from him in prison on 7th. June.'

'If you say so, sir.'

'So, the position is that Mr Robeson first becomes a

suspect when you see the statement of Avram Goldstein?'

'That's correct.'

'Mr Robeson will say, if asked about this, that your surveillance of him began about a month before Lyall was eventually acquitted,' asserted Charles. 'He was being followed by your men during Lyall's trial. Long before you obtained Goldstein's evidence.'

West looked at the ceiling as if ransacking his memory. 'No …' he said slowly, 'I don't think that can be right, my Lord. I don't know the exact date when our surveillance of this accused started, but I don't think it was as long ago as that. But I'd need to check the records at the station.'

Charles decided to change subject. He was venturing into unknown waters and he didn't want to give West the opportunity to make up some other "information received" which he couldn't rebut.

'By 7th June Goldstein had been serving a prison sentence for some months.'

'Yes?'

'Why did you suddenly decide to see him then?'

'I went with another officer who was to show him some photographs.'

'Why did you decide to see Goldstein *then?*'

'Because I accompanied the inspector. The rules require that someone showing photographs should not be part of the investigation. He had nothing to do with the case.'

'You're still not answering my question. This inspector from a different police force – someone who knows nothing about your investigation – would not have decided to go and see a serving prisoner for no good reason. Someone had to ask him to go. That someone was you, was it not?'

'I don't remember, my Lord. It may have been.'

For the first time, His Honour Judge Pullman's patience with West showed a frayed edge. 'The point being made, Sergeant, is that you, or another officer, made the decision to go and see Goldstein. You're being asked why.'

West now looked distinctly uncomfortable. 'I really can't remember, my Lord.'

'Between Goldstein's conviction and 7th June 1963,' continued Charles, 'Lyall was tried twice.'

'Yes, that would be right.'

'You didn't think of calling Goldstein to help the prosecution convict Lyall?'

Stafford rose to interrupt. 'That is not a matter that can be commented on by this witness. The decision who to call and who not to call would have been made by the Crown in consultation with counsel, and is protected by legal professional privilege.'

'I shall rephrase the question, my Lord,' conceded Charles. 'Did Mr Goldstein give evidence in either of the two trials against Lyall?'

'No. I don't believe he did.'

'Do you remember speaking to Mr Goldstein between the time of his conviction in March, and when you went there in June with another officer to show him photographs?'

West didn't answer but stared at the ceiling, apparently deep in concentration. Charles persisted.

'It's simple enough, Sergeant: did you visit Goldstein at

the prison before this occasion?'

'I can't remember, my Lord,' concluded West, with a shrug. 'I don't think so.'

'Surely you would remember if you had visited the man in prison at the Isle of Wight. That's not exactly part of your "patch" is it? It would mean a special trip, wouldn't it?'

'Yes, it would, my Lord.'

'Well then, did you go to the Isle of Wight before this occasion to obtain from Goldstein a statement regarding Lyall's involvement?'

'I don't think so, but other officers may have done. I'm part of a large team.'

'Have you ever seen any other statement made by Goldstein?'

'I can't remember ever seeing one,' he answered.

'Very well. So, for months, during the course of which the police brought two unsuccessful prosecutions against Lyall, you didn't think to speak to Goldstein, who could have identified not only Mr Robeson but also the ringleader, Mr Lyall. Correct?'

'Yes, my Lord.'

'Nonetheless, within a couple of days of Lyall's final acquittal, there you are, digging away at Mr Goldstein, looking for evidence against *Mr Robeson*, Lyall's lawyer.'

'I did interview Goldstein, yes.'

'You've already admitted that you weren't indifferent to Mr Robeson. I suggest that it went much further than that. This was something of a crusade, wasn't it?'

'If you mean that I wanted to catch a dangerous and

clever criminal, then yes. I did. "Crusade" is your word.'

'You thought he was a criminal because of the outcome of Lyall's trial!' shouted Charles.

'Amongst other things. If you want to know the truth, I think he fixed that jury!' The words echoed round the court.

'Is that right?' replied Charles softly. 'Well, I'll come back to that in a moment. But it's clear now isn't it, Sergeant: you're not quite so indifferent to the verdicts of juries as you pretend, are you? You weren't satisfied with their verdicts in Lyall's case, so you decided to put the matter right?'

'I decided to make a further investigation.'

'To right what you considered to have been an injustice?'

'It's always an injustice when a crime is committed, and a criminal escapes.'

'Indeed. From your point of view, Sergeant West, you felt that the system had failed in the case of Lyall, and you were going to try to ensure that it didn't happen again.'

'Yes – no! I started an investigation, that is all. As a result of that investigation I came to a conclusion. Not the other way around.'

'Let us summarise your evidence so far, please Sergeant. At first you tell us that Lyall's acquittal did not affect you. "Part of the job" you said. Now you admit that you felt an injustice had been done, by Mr Robeson, and you decided to see if you could get evidence on him. Why did you feign indifference at the outset of your evidence?'

'I suppose because I thought it was irrelevant to this case.'

'What was irrelevant?'

'My suspicions that Robeson fixed the jury.'

Charles knew he was being diverted off the point, but it was important to deal with the allegation of jury rigging before West referred to it yet again. 'Alright, let's deal with that now, shall we?' he said. 'Have you a single shred of evidence that the jury was fixed by anyone?'

'Well, Lyall was acquitted.'

Even before the words had finished echoing around the court, West realised that he'd made a dreadful error. His face flushed, and his eyes darted about him.

'I beg your pardon?' asked Charles, incredulously. 'A man is acquitted, so the trial must have been fixed? You have scant regard for what the twelve men and women of the jury thought,' said Charles. He pointed to the jury. 'I suppose you'll say that *this* jury's been fixed too, if they're sufficiently independent of mind to acquit Mr Robeson?'

Several members of the jury stared in open hostility at West. The judge turned again to look at him.

'I'm sorry, my Lord. That didn't come out the way I meant it. I felt that he was acquitted against the weight of the evidence. Many of us thought it.'

'Perhaps, Sergeant, the jury did not accept some of the police evidence,' suggested Pullman wryly.

Charles raised an eyebrow. Even Pullman was beginning to have his doubts about West. 'The fact is,' resumed Charles softly and with regret in his voice, 'you were so incensed at the result of the earlier trials that you went straight to the prison, and you put pressure on Goldstein to give evidence against Mr Robeson. Isn't that right?'

'It is not. He signed that statement of his own free will.'

'We have seen him give evidence this morning. Can you think of any reason why he might have felt under pressure?'

The judge again looked up from taking his notes and scrutinised West. 'No. None.'

'Did you mention parole to him when you saw him?'

'Not at all. That would have been improper.'

'I'm not suggesting that it would have been correct to do it; I'm suggesting that you knew it was improper, but you did it nonetheless.'

'Well, you're wrong, sir, my Lord. I would not do such a thing.'

'Did you see Goldstein before he was shown the photographs?'

'I had to. I had to tell him what we were there for, and introduce the other officer.'

'So you told him you were about to show him some photographs including that of Robeson?'

'Certainly not. I told him that the officer was helping our enquiries into the robbery, and that he would explain the procedure. I didn't mention the photographs at all.'

'And that's all you said?'

'That's all.'

'So it would have taken a minute at most.'

'Probably.'

'Where was the other officer during that minute?'

'I can't remember. He was probably with us. I can see no reason why he would not have been.'

'You told Goldstein precisely who he was supposed to pick out, didn't you?'

'I most certainly did not.'

'Let's pause again, shall we, to review your evidence. You tell us that it was your understanding that Goldstein could identify not only Mr Robeson, but Lyall as well. Indeed, he knew Lyall well. Correct?'

'Yes, my Lord.'

'Yet during two trials of Lyall, at which the police failed to obtain convictions, you did not go to speak to Goldstein about it.'

'That is right.'

'And no statements from Goldstein exist prior to the one you obtained in respect of Mr Robeson; thus we may infer that no one else took a statement from him about it either.'

'I suppose so.'

'Yet within days of Lyall's final acquittal, which you consider was caused by Mr Robeson's fixing of the jury, it suddenly comes into your head to ask Goldstein about *Mr Robeson's* part in the affair, months after the robbery was committed.'

Charles looked down at his papers, and paused. He felt everyone in court waiting for him to speak. When he did, he didn't look at West, but at the jury. It was an old trick, and one he found cheap, but he had to make them think about his next point.

'When did you receive your alleged tip-off? On that Friday?'

'It was not an "alleged" tip-off. It did occur. And I received it about a week before. It may have been received at the station a day or so before then.'

'Did you not think it an extraordinary coincidence that within as little as a fortnight of seeing Goldstein in prison, someone contacted you with information about Mr Robeson's car?'

'I did, yes. I thought someone might have been told that I'd been to Camp Hill and decided to assist the investigation.'

'I suggest to you, Sergeant, that this entire story of a tip-off is complete nonsense. You never received any such thing.'

'I did sir. At least, I didn't, but I was informed that a message had been left.'

'I suggest that you were so incensed by the acquittal of Lyall, you decided to take matters into your own hands. To that end you went and saw the hapless Goldstein, and bullied him into concocting a false identification of Mr Robeson. With that in your hand, you planted the gun in Mr Robeson's car, and arrived with several other officers, already certain of what you'd find.'

'That is an outrageous suggestion, my Lord. I never put any pressure on Goldstein and I'd never seen that gun in my life until I found it in the back of that Austin.'

Charles paused, watching the jury as they digested West's rebuttal. There is always a moment during the course of a witness's evidence when the court's impression of them seems to crystallise. It doesn't emanate solely from the jury, although they are the most important arbiters, but somehow from everyone in the courtroom. The jury, judge, barristers – even members of the public – all contribute to it. It's like an invisible electrical charge in the air. A good jury advocate can sense it, that moment, when the balance in the minds of the listeners slowly sinks to one side or the other: do I believe this man, or do I have doubts?

Charles watched the faces of the jury members, all with eyes fixed on Detective Sergeant West. He saw frowns and hesitation, and he was satisfied. One jury member even looked across at Charles and made eye contact, always a good sign.

'Now, one last matter if you please Sergeant. The tenner you claim to have found in Mr Robeson's wallet. Mr Robeson was Lyall's solicitor, when Lyall was tried for his part in the diamond robbery, was he not?'

'That's right, my Lord.'

'Do you know any solicitor who works for free?'

West laughed, as did several other people in court including, Charles noted with satisfaction, most of the jury members.

'I suppose it's possible, my Lord, but I've never come across it,' replied West.

'So it wouldn't surprise you if Mr Lyall paid Mr Robeson for his legal services?'

'No.'

'And it wouldn't be surprising if a man like Mr Lyall, a professional criminal, paid his bills in cash rather than in any more formal way.'

'No.'

'So one entirely innocent explanation for the fact that the accused had a £10 note in his wallet which could be traced to Mr Lyall, is that it was part of the proper and lawful payment by a client to his solicitor.'

Charles could see from West's face that he was reluctant to answer in the affirmative but he had no choice. 'I suppose that's right.'

'At the end of Mr Lyall's retrial, when the court directed his acquittal, someone had to return the money seized from Mr Lyall's house. That someone was you, was it not?'

'It was, my Lord.'

'And you personally had to count out over £84,000 in bank notes before handing the money over?'

'Yes.'

'And in fact it wasn't Mr Lyall himself to whom you handed the cash, but his solicitor, Mr Robeson?'

'Yes. All but a couple of hundred pounds.'

'Thank you. So, again, another perfectly honest way in which that £10 could have found its way into Robeson's wallet.'

'I suppose so.'

'Thank you Sergeant. Just one last point on this subject, if I may: it's a normal part of a custody officer's duty to go through the belongings of all arrested persons, and list them, is it not?'

'Yes, that's right.'

'And it's important to list everything, or else there'll be disputes afterwards and the officer could get into trouble if it was alleged that he'd lost or misappropriated an item of property.'

West had guessed where Charles's line of questioning

was heading. 'Yes, of course. But the desk was extremely busy at Greenwich Police Station that night. It was a Friday night and the place was full of arrested drunks and football fans. The desk sergeant was trying to deal with half a dozen different arrests at the same time. It wouldn't surprise me if he accidentally missed the £10 note when it was tucked into a small compartment in the wallet.'

Charles had been on the point of suggesting that West had planted the note, but on consideration of the policeman's answer thought better of it. He had no evidence to support his assertion, merely a hunch, and the cross-examination so far had reduced the importance of the banknote so completely that Charles decided that it was unnecessary to pursue the point further.

'Thank you, my Lord, I have no further questions,' said Charles, resuming his seat.

The judge closed his notebook. 'It's five minutes to four, Mr Stafford. You may re-examine tomorrow morning. Sergeant: you are in the course of your evidence. Please do not speak to anyone about the case in the meantime.'

'I'm sorry to interrupt, my Lord, but I have no re-examination of Sergeant West, and it would assist me greatly if I could speak to him over the adjournment. There is the matter your Lordship mentioned in chambers.'

'Yes, I understand. So be it. You may stand down, Sergeant. Members of the jury: remember the warning I gave you about discussing this case with anyone outside your number.'

'Court rise!'

chapter 18

Robeson was required to stay in the dock until the jury had departed. Finally, the dock officer opened the gate and allowed him to descend into the well of the court. Charles had remained in his place while the court emptied, collecting his papers.

'Well done, Charles,' said Robeson, coming up behind him.

'No. If you think about it, we didn't get very far with him.' Charles took off his wig, and ran his fingers through his flattened hair. 'Yes, he looked shifty, but all we got out of him was his conviction that you're guilty. And his failure to see Goldstein earlier can easily be explained on the basis that he simply missed a trick.'

'Who's being called first tomorrow?'

'Either DC North or DS Walker. Then the identification inspector, followed by the ballistics man. Then you.'

'Do you think I'll be giving evidence tomorrow?'

'Probably.'

Charles felt Robeson's hand on his arm. 'What's up, Charles? You look very down.'

'Oh, it's nothing about the case. Bad news about my father.' He continued tying up his case papers.

'Tell me.'

'The test results are in. He definitely needs an operation, and it looks more serious than we thought. And there's a long waiting list.'

'I see.'

'And this time, the cost to have it done privately is more than a grand.'

Robeson turned Charles round to face him. Charles looked at the solicitor's face for the first time and saw genuine concern.

'That needn't be a problem you know, Charles.'

Charles drew a deep breath. 'I can't ask it of you Harry. When I was at the hospital with Dad last time, I asked the anaesthetist. With the surgeon's costs, hospital fees, convalescence and the anaesthetist himself, and assuming no untoward problems, about £1200.'

'Two years ago, Charles, I've no doubt you could've written a cheque for that without even speaking to your bank. Believe me, I'm better heeled than you ever were! That sort of sum won't break me – '

'Yes, but – '

'But nothing. You're half way through the most important case of *my* life. I need to be confident that you're relaxed and on your toes. So, leaving aside the fact that I like you – and your parents for that matter – it's in my own interests to help you out. I may even be able to set it off against tax as a business expense,' he joked. He put his hand up to stop any argument. 'Nothing you can say will change my mind, so don't waste your breath. I'll speak to the hospital tonight.'

Charles looked at Robeson, took his hand, and gripped it for a moment. He felt his eyes sting with tears and he had to wait a moment before he could rely on his voice. 'You're under more stress than most people ever have to cope with, and I'm coming to *you* for help.' He shrugged awkwardly. 'I just don't know how to thank you.'

Robeson held Charles's gaze, and his hand. 'Win the case, my boy. Now,' he said breezily, clapping Charles on the back, 'I could do with a drink. Have you time?'

'No, thank you. I've work to do for tomorrow, and I've got to go to Mum and Dad's.'

'Fair enough.' Robeson picked up his briefcase. 'See you tomorrow. And cheer up. You're going to win. I have faith in you.' He waved, and left.

Charles balanced his wig on top of his case papers and his copy of Archbold, and turned to leave.

'Hang on, Charlie,' came a woman's voice from the back of the court. Charles spun round. 'Sally? What on earth are you doing here?'

She came up to him. Charles had a quick look around, and kissed her on the lips. They walked together up the aisle of the now deserted court to the swing doors.

'I was here for a "tea party" with a load of other clerks trying to fix a couple of cases, and I thought I'd pop in and listen for a few minutes. How's it going? Here let me get that,' she said, reaching for the door handle.

'Not too bad. We did a fair bit of damage to the jeweller I told you about, and Tricky West certainly lived up to his nickname. An awful lot depends on that plumber.'

'He looked awful to me.'

'Who?'

'That sergeant.'

'Yes, but unfortunately you're not on the jury.'

'Don't worry, Charlie. I was watching them. They were interested.'

'Interested isn't convinced.'

'Patience. You're not half way through the case yet.' Charles halted. 'Erm…Sally?'

'Yes?' she said with a smile, anticipating him.

'I've got to go to my parents' for a while, and then I've an hour or so of preparation for tomorrow, but, after that – '

'Yes. The answer's yes. Mum went to Wales to visit her cousin yesterday. Just had a hysterectomy, and needs a hand round the house. There nothing like someone even more ill than her to buck up my Mum. So, if you give me the keys, I'll warm the bed up.'

'Wonderful. I'm in love.'

'No, you aren't. But it's nice of you to think so. Now, I've got to run. See you later.' She stood on tip-toes, kissed him on the nose and ran off.

•

'Take a seat, gentlemen.'

Sergeant West took the armchair in the corner of the room. The solicitor sat at the desk facing that of Marcus Stafford so that he could take notes. Stafford squeezed into his leather seat which groaned slightly under the assault.

There was a knock at the door, and a man's head appeared. 'Oh, sorry, sir, I didn't realise you were back,' apologised Stafford's clerk.

'That's okay Henry. We've need a short con about today's case. Any chance of some tea?'

'I'll try, sir, but Bob's checking the list and the phones are going like mad.'

'Well, don't worry about it then.'

'May I just get a brief from your desk, sir?'

'Yes. Which one?'

'The GBH at Chelmsford, *Saddler*. I'm afraid it's in tomorrow.'

'Shit. Who's going to deal with it?'

'I don't know yet. Things are very busy tomorrow. It may have to go out of Chambers, I'm afraid. Anyway,' he said, picking up the brief, 'I'll leave you to it.'

The door closed behind him.

'Now,' said Stafford. 'Firstly, did you speak to Mrs Goldstein?'

West shook his head. 'Sorry, sir, but she'd already left court by the time you asked me. I sent a squad car to her home, but there was no one in. I'll try again this evening.'

'Pity,' replied Stafford. 'But send someone else this evening, as you're going to be busy.' He leaned forward on the desk, the leather chair protesting alarmingly. 'I'm not saying we're in bad shape, but things are not going as well as I'd have liked. Holborne's substantially watered down the connection between Robeson and the house, and the evidence relating to the bank account is not as clear as I'd have liked, even at this stage, before Robeson starts explaining his withdrawals, which he's bound to. He'll certainly be able to muddy the waters enough to render the evidence neutral. Goldstein's next to useless – ' and he glanced at West, who looked studiously at the pattern in the carpet, ' – and that really only leaves the gun.'

He paused. 'Now, Sergeant, with the exception of a couple of completely daft answers, you didn't do *too* badly under cross-examination. But I'm not happy to leave the evidence as it is. I want to come back to what we were discussing last time. Richard,' he said, addressing the solicitor, 'do you have that bundle of company documents Holborne produced.'

'Yes,' replied the other, handing it across.

'Hmmm,' said Stafford as he leafed through it.

'If you're thinking what I think you're thinking, sir, it would be impossible in the time available,' said West.

'I'm not so sure about that, Sergeant. Look: finding a residential property to work from is easy. They really didn't need it at all – it just tied up a loose end. But they *had* to have somewhere to do the painting. You can't paint two vans in Gas Board livery in the middle of the street. Someone would be bound to ask questions. So, they had to have a garage. Somewhere where they knew they wouldn't be disturbed. Where the landlord's friendly. If Robeson is guilty – '

'Oh, he's guilty,' interrupted West.

' – then somewhere in these 178 properties, I'll bet there's one with a garage, stables, or an outhouse of some description that was used as a paint shop. We've just got to find it. The task's been made a lot easier with Holborne's list here.'

'In a day?' asked Richard.

'Yes. Maybe two, if we're lucky.'

'Like I said, it's impossible,' repeated West.

'No. Difficult, yes, but not impossible. Work on a radius of, say, five miles of "Staplecroft". I can't believe they'd have gone much further afield than that – it would've caused too many logistical problems. That'll probably cut out seventy-five per cent of the properties. Then get an ordnance survey map and have a look at the ones that remain. If they're terraced, mews or suburban semis, you can forget them – too small. We're looking for a farm, a warehouse, something like that.'

'Right,' said West, standing up, and holding out his hand for the bundle of documents. 'I'll get cracking.'

'Fine. And, Sergeant,' added Stafford, 'if you find it, I'll need a further statement from you and from the Scenes of Crime chap, for service on the Defence.'

•

'Sally?'

'Yes. Where the hell are you, Charlie? What time is it? Jesus, it's almost eleven. I fell asleep.'

'I'm sorry. I'm in Chambers. I just got back from Hendon. Look, I'm going to be a while yet. There's some papers here I've got to sort out tonight. Do you want to give it a miss?'

'You don't learn, do you, Charlie? Why do you think

Henrietta was so bloody unhappy? The people around you always take second place to your job.' There was silence at the other end of the line. 'Oh, I'm sorry, Charlie. I shouldn't have said that.'

'No, you should. And you're right. And I *am* sorry. But it so happens I've not been working. I told you, there were things I had to discuss with my family. My Dad's quite ill.'

'Is he? You didn't say. What wrong with him?'

Charles drew a deep breath. 'It's complicated, and I don't understand, all of it but it's to do his coronary arteries. He needs an urgent operation.'

'Oh, blimey,' replied Sally, the Cockney slipping out. 'Now I feel really bad. Look, I can probably wait a bit longer if you want. But if you're still going to be a while, I think I will go home, if you don't mind. I might as well sleep in my own bed and have a clean blouse to put on in the morning.' There was a pause and Charles heard her lift the phone as she walked across the bedroom. 'Oh, sod it! My knickers are still soaking. I washed them out and put them on the radiator to dry –'

'The radiator's broken – '

'Really?' she replied, with heavy sarcasm. 'Okay, that decides it. I'll see you tomorrow.'

'Okay. I'll give you a call when I'm back from court. Goodnight.'

''Bye.'

She hung up and Charles settled down to work.

About twenty minutes later Charles heard the outer door to Chambers creak open. He had left the hall in darkness and he listened for the light switch, but heard nothing. It was obviously not a member of chambers. He held his breath, and then heard the light pad, pad of footsteps coming down the corridor. He turned his own lamp off and stood up, tip-toeing to the door of his room. The footfalls got closer, reached the door, and went past.

'Can I help you?' Charles asked, turning on the light as he spoke.

Sally had just passed his door in the darkness, and leapt round, her face white. 'Jesus Christ, Charlie, you scared me half to death!'

'What on earth are you doing creeping about my chambers in the dark?'

'Trying to get these back to you!' she hissed, holding up his front door keys. 'Or would you have preferred to sleep here tonight? I couldn't find the bloody light switch,' she explained.

'Oh, thank you. Come in a second.' He led the way into his room.

'This is cosy,' she said, putting her bag down and perching on his desk. 'Curtains and all. Do you share?'

'Yes, with Peter Bateman, my old pupil. He moved with me, remember?'

'Oh, of course. I didn't realise you were still sharing with him. Look you'd better take these before I forget,' she said, offering him the keys. He went up to her and put his arms round her neck. He kissed her on the lips. She dropped the keys on the desk by her side, and put her hands round the back of his neck.

'Sorry I couldn't make it,' he said softly.

'Yes, well, you don't know what you missed.'

'I do,' he said, kissing her neck. 'That's why I'm so sorry. What did you do about your knickers?'

She took her arms from him and reached behind her to her bag. She delved in, coming up with a plastic bag. 'I borrowed this from your kitchen,' she said, holding it up. 'They were too wet to put in my pocket. The bra too.' Charles could see her damp underwear folded neatly inside the bag.

'Which presumably means….' he said, sliding his hand up her thigh to be met with soft warm fuzziness.

Sally sighed deeply. 'Oh, Charlie…' she said, putting her arms back round him and letting her legs move apart.

She let him touch her for a few seconds, her face nuzzling his neck. Then she gripped his wrist firmly and extracted his hand.

'OK. That's enough of that,' she said firmly. 'Don't start what you can't finish.'

'Who said I can't finish?' he whispered in her ear.

'What here?' she asked, incredulous. 'On your blotter?'

He stepped back from her. 'Don't move!' he ordered. 'Just don't move!'

She heard him run down the corridor and then the two outer doors slammed. He ran back into the room, closing the door behind him. He approached her again, putting his arms round her.

'God, are you serious?'

'Why not?'

'But this is silly, Charlie. You've got a perfectly good flat and a nice double bed three hundred yards from here.'

'I know,' he said, licking her neck, his tongue travelling up to her left ear. He felt her shiver.

He slid her skirt up her thighs with one hand until it was bunched around her waist. 'But what if someone comes in?' she said, putting her arms round his back.

'They won't.' His hand moved to her left breast and, through the cotton of her blouse, found her nipple. He caressed it through the material and felt it harden under his touch.

'But what if they do?' she asked quietly, reaching down with both hands to his fly.

'I'll think of something,' he whispered, taking her earlobe in his mouth.

She undid his trousers and they fell to his ankles. Her warm hand snaked past his underpants and went straight to him.

'Oh God,' he moaned.

'You ever done this before?' she asked. 'In Chambers, I mean.'

'No.'

She shifted her weight so that she was sitting right on the edge of the desk, and opened her legs wide, hooking her ankles behind him. With one hand on his erection, and another on his shirt-tail covered buttocks, she pulled him into her.

'I bet you look a sight from behind,' she giggled, but his hips had started moving back and forth, and Sally no longer felt like talking.

chapter 19

'Detective Constable North, please.'

The detective christened by Robeson as "Fil" entered court. Now that Robeson could observe him more carefully, he was reminded even more strongly of an anglepoise lamp. DC North was very tall and very skinny, with thinning sandy hair. Robeson guessed that he had shot up at school before his peers, giving him a lifelong self-consciousness about his height, and which in turn caused him to walk slightly bent at both hips and neck. He was about ten years younger than West. He took the oath and gave his name, rank and number in a quieter voice than had his sergeant. It turned out that he had not made up any notes of his own concerning Robeson's arrest. He had instead read Sergeant West's notes, and signed them as correct. He was given permission to use the same notes if he needed them, although he didn't appear to want them, as they were left unopened on the lectern in front of him.

He answered questions simply, without elaboration, and his evidence in chief was almost identical to that of West. Charles didn't bother to take a note of his evidence, but simply watched him. In the fifteen or more years that Charles had been in practice, he had developed a keen eye for untruth. Like everyone, he could be taken in by a good liar, but he had learned to trust his sixth sense. That sense told him now that North was, by and large, more honest and less evasive than Sergeant West had been. Charles looked at the jury. They were following his quiet voice carefully. And they liked him.

Stafford sat down.

'Yes, Mr Holborne,' said the judge. Charles rose.

'The "Compass Team". Isn't that what you're called?'

North grinned and looked slightly embarrassed. Oh, yes, thought Charles. They'll like you. This will have to be done carefully.

'That's right, my Lord. We're called that sometimes.'

'Why?' asked the judge.

'Well, officers West and North, you see, my Lord.'

'Oh, I follow. Yes, carry on.'

'Have you been part of the same team for long, officer?' asked Charles. 'Two years.'

'And you get on well?'

'Very well, sir.'

'I guess you have to trust one another implicitly.'

'Of course. There are times when your life depends on that.'

'Do you trust Sergeant West's intuition?'

'Yes, I would say so. He's an experienced policeman.'

'Even when his orders are a bit of a pain?'

'I'm sorry, but I don't follow you.'

'Well, there must have been times when he thought he was onto something – relying on his intuition – and you've wondered if it was all a bit of a waste of time.'

North grinned. 'Occasionally, perhaps.'

Charles smiled at him conspiratorially. 'Perhaps when he had you and a colleague following Mr Robeson all over London, it felt a bit like that.'

'A bit,' conceded North, still smiling.

'Which you and another officer were doing for several weeks before your trip to The Victory?' asked Charles.

'Yes, my Lord.'

North's admission that Robeson was under surveillance long before Goldstein was interviewed was an important concession, but Charles decided to hold it up his sleeve for a few minutes more.

'Did you by any chance accompany Sergeant West on his visit to the Isle of Wight to see Mr Goldstein?'

'No, I didn't.'

'But I assume that you would have seen the statement that resulted from that trip?'

'Yes. Or I would have been told about it.'

'It would have been a major break in the case?'

'It would have been important.'

'And before that, what evidence was there against Mr Robeson?'

'I don't think I'm qualified to answer that, my Lord.'

'You were part of the team investigating Mr Robeson, were you not? You'd have to have known what evidence there was against him to be able to do your job, surely?'

'In broad terms, yes, but Sergeant West had the file most of the time. If there were any briefings, I would have been there. For the most part, I did as I was told.'

'Let me ask it in this way: are you aware of any evidence that you, the police, had against Mr Robeson before Goldstein's statement was obtained?'

'Not specifically.'

'Yet you have told us that you and another officer kept Mr Robeson under surveillance for several weeks before Goldstein's statement came into existence.'

DC North hesitated, realising that he had been led into a trap, but unsure exactly what it was. 'Yes,' he replied hesitantly.

'So Mr Robeson was the subject of investigation well before your team had any evidence from Mr Goldstein.'

'That would be right.'

'Indeed you were following him during the course of Lyall's second trial?'

'Yes, my Lord.'

Now Charles looked across at the jury to see if they had spotted the discrepancy with the evidence of DS West. Two or three of the jury members made eye contact with him, suggesting to Charles that they had.

'You were unaware of any evidence against Mr Robeson, yet DS West had you and another officer running around London following the solicitor engaged in the defence of Mr Lyall.'

'I wouldn't have put it that way, but we did have him under surveillance at that time, yes, my Lord.'

'Thank you. Now let's return to the night of Mr Robeson's arrest. What was your understanding of what the "Compass Team" was doing at The Victory that night?'

'We were going to arrest Mr Robeson,' he said, nodding towards the dock.

'To arrest him?'

'That's how I understood it.'

'Not just to question him and see if there were grounds for an arrest?'

North hesitated. 'No, at least not as far as I was aware. I understood that he was to be arrested. That's why we had all the entrances and exits covered.'

'Was there a briefing before the police left the police station?'

'Yes there was.'

'And who gave that briefing?'

'Detective Inspector Wilkinson partly. Mostly Sergeant West.'

'And who was it who said that the purpose of the visit was to arrest Mr Robeson?

'I can't remember. I would guess it was Sergeant West, but I may be wrong.'

'Thank you.' Charles paused to look again at the jury. Several more jurors returned his glance. 'Now, then, we've heard about some information that was received and which prompted the arrest. Were you the officer who received it?'

'No.'

'Were you told of it?'

'Yes, I was, my Lord.'

'And what were you told?'

Stafford raised his huge bulk from the bench. 'I object to

that question, my Lord. The answer is hearsay.'

'Yes, it is. Isn't it, Mr Holborne?' asked Pullman.

'No, my Lord, with respect, it is not. I do not solicit the answer so as to prove that the words allegedly spoken were true – just the contrary; my case is that they weren't in fact spoken at all, and in any event they would have been false. It is the officer's state of mind that I am concerned with, and for that I need to know what information he had.'

'Yes, very well.'

'What were you told?'

'Just that we were to be there and look in the boot of Mr Robeson's car.'

'Do you know who took this message?'

'I don't. Sergeant West told me about it.'

'Do you know of any officer who claims to have heard of this message from any source *other* than from Sergeant West?'

'No.'

Charles changed his tone and smiled as he asked the next question. 'I gather you were the odd man out, the one not invited inside for a drink?'

North looked puzzled. 'I don't know what you mean, sir.'

'Oh,' said Charles, feigning surprise, 'didn't the other officers go into the pub for a drink, while you waited outside?'

'I certainly waited outside, my Lord, but I'd be very surprised if the others had a drink.'

'Why? That would be unlike Mr West would it?'

'Most unlike him,' replied North vehemently. 'Particularly on such an important operation.'

'I see. This was an important arrest, then?'

'Of course. A man was crippled on that robbery.'

'Not the sort of arrest to be taken lightly?'

'No.'

'Not the sort of arrest that could be deferred for a quick pint?'

'With five men and two cars tied up? The arrest of a well-known solicitor?'

'Well then, can *you* explain to me what the delay was for? The delay between arriving at the pub, and actually speaking to Mr Robeson?'

'I don't know. I was told to wait outside and keep an eye on his car, that's all. You'd have to ask Sergeant West.'

'I did. He said he stopped for a pint.'

North frowned, thought about the information, and then shrugged.

'Did you watch the car throughout?' asked Charles.

'Either I, or other officers, did, yes.'

'You mean that you were not outside for the entire time?'

'No. I came inside to report once. And once Sergeant West relieved me, so I could … erm … relieve myself, if you see what I mean. It was quite a chilly night in that car park.'

The jury laughed, and the tension broke. Charles waited for silence before continuing. 'So, there was a period during which Sergeant West was guarding the accused's car?'

'Yes. Only for about five minutes, though.'

'And he would have been on his own out there in the car park?'

'I guess so.'

'And after you returned?'

'Well, it was then that we went upstairs to find Mr Robeson.'

'The waiting ended then?'

'Yes.'

'After Sergeant West's period guarding the car?'

'Yes.'

'Thank you, officer. I have no further questions.' Charles sat down, pleased.

Stafford rose ponderously to his feet. 'I have one or two further questions for you, officer,' he said. I guessed you might, thought Charles to himself. 'Where was the Austin Princess parked in relation to the road?'

'It was in the far corner of the car park. I'd say, about forty yards from the road.'

'I assume you arrived at the pub in a vehicle?'

'Yes.'

'And where was that parked?'

'In the road.'

'How far from the Princess was it parked?'

'Sixty to eighty yards, I suppose.'

'Whose car was it?'

'It was an unmarked police car.'

'I'm sorry, it's my fault. Who used the car normally?'

'I did. With Sergeant West.'

'How long were you away from the Princess, when you went to the lavatory?'

'No more than three minutes.'

'In that time, would it have been possible for someone to

have gone from the Princess to the police car, and back again?'

Charles looked up sharply. He had taken the trouble to go to the public house to understand the layout perfectly, and the fact that Stafford asked the question suggested to him that Stafford had not taken the same trouble. Had he done so, he wouldn't have asked the question.

North considered the question and after a pause gave precisely the answer Stafford didn't want. 'There would probably have been time, yes, my Lord. It would depend on whether they knew where they were going, I suppose. The car park was quite dark, and the Austin Princess was away from the road.'

'Thank you, officer. Does my Lord have any questions?'

'No, thank you.'

Charles watched the jury as North walked out. It was notoriously difficult to anticipate a jury's views, but Charles was confident they'd taken the point. West had clearly been building a case against Robeson long before Goldstein's statement came into existence. And he'd known that he was going to arrest Robeson even before he left the police station, which could only mean that, despite his denials, he *had* to have known what would be in the boot of the Austin before he even looked. Further, and this was an unexpected bonus, he'd had the opportunity to plant the gun while North was in the toilet. It was always much easier to allege impropriety against one officer than a conspiracy involving several. Charles was relieved that he'd not had to suggest *North* planted the shotgun; he doubted the jury would have believed it. When North's evidence was added to West's obvious anxiety to even the score with Robeson, the Crown's case began to look decidedly shaky.

Charles felt someone tug his gown from behind. He turned to see Robeson's clerk holding out a piece of paper to him. Charles opened it and read:

"There's a Mr. Cooper outside. He's been waiting all day and wants to know when he's going to be needed."

Charles whispered to the clerk. 'What's he doing here? He won't be needed until tomorrow at the earliest.'

'Mr Robeson organised the witnesses. He told Cooper to be here today.'

'Okay. Tell him I'm very sorry, but he won't be required until tomorrow, at, say 2 p.m.'

'Okay. But he's not going to be very happy about it. Apparently his father's not well. He wants to go to the hospital.'

Charles thought for a moment, pondering the coincidence. Then he stood.

'My Lord, a matter has arisen which requires my attendance outside court. I wonder would your Lordship consider rising for five minutes to enable me to sort out the problem?'

'Very well, Mr Holborne. I should think that the jury would enjoy a short break. Five minutes.'

The judge rose and while the jury filed out Charles went outside with the clerk. Sitting facing the door of the court was a young man in a suit. He looked worried and the pile of cigarette butts by his feet bore testament to a long wait.

'Mr Cooper?' asked Charles.

'Yeah?' replied Terry, getting to his feet and grinding

out his current cigarette.

'My name's Charles Holborne,' said Charles, offering his hand, which Terry shook. 'I'm the defence barrister, and I'm afraid it's my fault you've been called to give evidence. Look, I gather you've got a problem which means you need to be somewhere else.'

'I'm sorry an' all that, but me Dad's been taken poorly. He's got emphysema, and it's suddenly got worse. I'd really like to be with me Mum at the hospital.'

'I really do understand, because, funnily enough, my father's very ill at the moment too. I'm very sorry you've been brought here today, but things have taken longer than anticipated. If you're released now, could you come back at two o'clock tomorrow afternoon? I'll do my best to ensure you're away within a couple of hours.'

'Can you guarantee it?'

'No, I'm afraid I can't, as it's not within my sole control. Normally the defendant gives evidence before his witnesses, but I shall ask for special permission to call you first so that you can get away. How does that sound?'

'Alright. As long as I don't have to come back again. I don't want to be difficult, you understand – I want to help if I can – but it's me Dad, y'know?'

'I understand perfectly. I'll see you again tomorrow at two.'

'Righto. 'Bye, then.'

Terry Cooper rushed off towards the exit, anxious to get to the hospital as soon as possible. He didn't see the man that had been standing behind one of the statues discard his newspaper, and hurry after him. Nor did he see that man signal to another waiting just outside the main entrance. So preoccupied was he that he failed to notice the two of them follow him all the way to St Paul's Underground Station and thence to the London Hospital.

•

'I'll be back in a tick!' called Terry from the door of his van.

Mrs Cooper waved from the front door of their terraced house, and stepped wearily inside. She'd spent the whole day at her husband's bedside and she was exhausted. She'd had no time to make tea and so Terry had offered to pop down to the chippie and get fish and chips. She went straight to the kitchen and put the kettle on.

Terry drove the mile and a half to the fish shop, named the "Peking Dragon Fish Shop" since the Ho family took over a few months back. The addition of Chinese food to the menu didn't seem to have affected the quality of the cod and chips. Indeed, as far as Terry could tell, they were rather better than they had been when Mr Tibbs had been the owner.

He came out of the shop juggling two bags of food, two cans of shandy, a packet of cigarettes and his van keys, and didn't see the two men waiting for him, leaning arrogantly against his van.

They walked straight up to him and, each grabbing an arm, propelled him backwards.

'Heh!' protested Terry, but a sudden hard blow struck him in the stomach, completely winding him. Terry dropped his purchases and gasped for breath as the men dragged him backwards around to the far side of the van and into the shadows. He felt himself slammed up against the side of the van.

'Now, sonny,' said the man to his right, still gripping him by the upper arm, 'you listen to me, and you listen carefully. You do *not*,' and the man cuffed him hard across the face with the back of his free hand, 'want to give evidence, right?'

Terry was still trying to inflate his lungs, although with rather more drama than his state required. He allowed his arms to sag slightly.

'Are you listening to me?' asked the man. He repeated his previous sentence, punctuating each word with a slap. 'You ... do ... not ... want ... to ... give ... evidence.'

Terry heaved his arms apart, throwing the man to his left off balance. For a second the grip on his left arm slackened and he wrenched it free. He swung it hard at the man to his right. Terry was right-handed and it was a ham-fisted blow, but he was a strong young man, used to heavy work, and it connected hard with the other's chest, and pushed him away. Terry's other arm came free and he threw one good punch at the man who had done the talking. It landed with a satisfying crunch on the other's nose, and blood spurted onto Terry's jacket. Terry turned to locate his other attacker just in time to see an arm rise and fall. He felt an excruciating pain in his temple as a cosh landed on his head. The ground rushed up to meet him.

He was conscious of blows and kicks to his body and head, but they seemed to come from miles away and didn't hurt him. After a while they too stopped, and Terry remembered no more.

chapter 20

'Call Inspector Bathington!'

It was shortly after lunchtime on the following day. The statement of the ballistics expert had been read as agreed evidence; Charles did not dispute that the shotgun found in Robeson's boot was the same one as used on the robbery. Detective Constable Brian Walker (who, for reasons Charles didn't comprehend, Robeson insisted on referring to as 'Denis') had also given evidence, but to little effect. He'd been another member of the police team at The Victory, but he'd remained outside the pub by the public bar entrance throughout until the group descended from the party, at which time he joined them in the carpark but said, and apparently heard, nothing. He claimed not to have known the purpose of the visit as he'd missed most of the briefing. He maintained he'd been "volunteered" as he entered the police station and told to come along and make up numbers.

Robeson was convinced that he was lying, but if so, Charles had made no impression on him. The one essential piece of evidence that Charles had been able to get out of him was that Robeson had not left the upper room of the pub from the moment at which the police officers entered, until he went out to the car park in their company.

Inspector Bathington was to be the last prosecution witness. He was the officer who had shown Avram Goldstein the album of photographs, including that of Robeson. He strode into court, a big, upright man in the uniform of the Hampshire Constabulary, indeed, the first uniformed witness the jury had seen.

Charles had given permission to Stafford to lead him through his evidence, and it was therefore only five minutes before Charles rose to cross-examine.

'I understand from your evidence, Inspector, that you had nothing whatsoever to do with this case until the day on which you showed Mr Goldstein that album of photos?' asked Charles, pointing to the album.

'That's right.'

'Who was responsible for making up the album?'

'I was.'

'How did you go about that?'

'I keep a large number of photographs as part of my duties, and I went through them to find eleven others of similar types of men.'

'Eleven others?'

'Yes. Sergeant West provided me with a photograph of the accused, and I had to find eleven others to go with that one to form this album. I try to find others of a similar type so that the suspect does not stand out.'

'When did you do this?'

'I can't tell you exactly. A couple of days before we saw Mr Goldstein in prison.'

'You had never met Mr Goldstein before?'

'That is correct.'

'Did you have any idea what the case was about?'

'A brief outline. I didn't concern myself with it very much. I had other duties at the time.'

'And when you arrived at Camp Hill Prison, what happened?'

'I arrived shortly before DS West. When he arrived we were shown to an interview room, and I went through the formal procedure according to this form.'

'Yes, you've already been through that with us. So you just walked in, plonked the album in front of Goldstein, and started with your first question?'

'No, of course not. Sergeant West went in and explained the purpose of our visit, and then I started the process.'

'You waited outside?'

'Yes, I think so. But not for long.'

'Twenty minutes?'

'Good heavens, no. Nearer ten.'

'So Sergeant West had a ten-minute private conversation with Mr Goldstein?'

'It was a few minutes. I wouldn't like to be precise about its length.'

'Did Sergeant West tell you that he would speak to Goldstein alone first?'

'Yes, he did.'

'Did he tell you what he wanted to say to Goldstein?'

'Yes. He wanted to tell the man that I was there with an album of photographs, and to tell him that I would conduct the identification.'

'And that took ten minutes?'

'Five, ten. Something like that.'

'Thank you, Inspector. I have no further questions.'

'Unless my Lord has any questions for Inspector Bathington, that is the case for the Crown,' said Stafford.

'I have no questions, thank you. Yes, Mr Holborne?'

'I have an application, my Lord, to call a witness out of turn. A Mr Terence Cooper has been waiting to give his evidence for two days now, and his father is quite seriously ill in hospital. He naturally wants to get away as soon as he can. I have asked my learned friend if he would have any objection to Mr Cooper giving his evidence before that of Mr Robeson, and he has none. Would my Lord permit me to call Mr Cooper first?'

'You have no objections, Mr Stafford? Have you seen a medical certificate?'

'I have not, my Lord, but I have been given details of Mr Cooper's father's illness, and it has been confirmed by telephone that Mr Cooper senior was admitted to the London Hospital by ambulance two days ago. I therefore have no objections to the Defence application.'

'Very well, Mr Holborne. You may call your witness first.'

'Thank you, my Lord. Mr Terence Cooper, please.'

All eyes in the court followed the usher as she walked up the aisle to the swing doors. She could be heard outside calling Terry's name. She did so on three occasions and then returned.

'No answer, my Lord.'

Charles whipped round to Robeson's clerk. 'Where the fuck is he?' he hissed.

The clerk shrugged. 'I don't know. He wasn't there at 2 o'clock after lunch, but I assumed he was just a couple of minutes late. I've not been out since.'

'Mr Holborne?' asked Pullman.

'My Lord?'

'If he's not here, I suggest you call your client in the normal manner. That will give your instructing solicitor time to make enquires.'

'Yes, my Lord. In that case –'

Charles was cut short by the door behind him opening, followed by a sharp intake of breath from the jury who, unlike counsel, could see the door from their seats. Charles turned around again. Terry Cooper walked up the aisle towards the front of the court. His head was bandaged so that only a small part of his scalp was visible. His face was swollen, both eyes blackened, the right one completely closed. His lower lip was split and the black string of a suture trailed over his chin. His left arm was in a sling. So astonishing was his appearance that judge, jury and counsel watched open-mouthed as he made his slow way to the witness box. He climbed the two steps in obvious discomfort, and waited there patiently.

The judge found his voice first. 'Mr Cooper?'

'Yes,' replied Terry, his voice muffled and his articulation impaired by his swollen jaw and stitched mouth.

'I can't believe, Mr Cooper that you're fit to give evidence. I thought that it was a relation of yours who was ill.'

'It is. My Dad.'

'But then – '

'This happened last night. I want to give evidence.'

He said it with such grim determination that Pullman, who had been ready to refuse to proceed, was taken aback. 'Why? Surely you should be in hospital?'

'Maybe, but *after* I've given evidence.'

'Mr Holborne?' asked the judge, seeking assistance.

'I knew nothing of this, my Lord. And I agree, Mr Cooper does not look fit, and I wouldn't dream of calling him in this state … but if he insists …?'

The judge shrugged. 'Very well. Usher, get him a chair so he can sit – '

'I don't want a chair, thank you.'

The judge sighed. 'Then proceed with the oath.'

Terry took the New Testament in his right hand, but he was unable to take the card bearing the oath in his left. The clerk took the card and read it line by line, with Terry repeating each line a quiet, muffled voice.

For the first time in Charles's memory, Stafford spoke to him without being spoken to first. He leaned over to Charles and whispered. 'I assure you, if *that* was done by anyone on the Force, I swear, heads'll roll.' Charles nodded, and turned to address Terry.

'Could you give us your name and address, please?' Terry did so.

'And you're a plumber, is that right?'

'Yes. I have me own business,' he replied, a measure of pride apparent through the muffled speech.

'Mr Cooper, what on earth has happened to you?'

'Last night, two men. They beat me up. Told me not to give evidence.'

'They did *that* to you?' asked the judge.

'Yes. I reckon, well, if they'd do this to stop me from giving my evidence, it must be pretty important. So I thought I'd better come along. There was a right barney at the hospital, I can tell you, but I discharged meself – for the minute anyway. I'll get a taxi back to hospital when I'm done.'

'Can you tell me who these men were?' asked the judge.

'No, sir, I can't. I'd never seen 'em before. The police have shown me some pictures, but I ain't identified them yet.'

'I see. Well, Mr Holborne, you'd better get on with it and let Mr Cooper get back to hospital. I shall require a full investigation into this matter, Mr Stafford.'

'Of course, my Lord.'

Charles drew a deep breath. 'Mr Cooper, do you know The Victory public house in Greenwich?'

'Not well, but I know it.'

'Have you ever been there?'

'Once.'

'Do you remember when that was?'

'It was a Friday night in June. That's all I can tell you. Quite a chilly night, I remember.'

'What were you doing at the pub?'

'I was there for a darts match. I was the captain of the darts team from my local in Leyton.'

'What time did you get there?'

'The match was from 8 o'clock. We got there about ten to fifteen minutes before that.'

'Did you actually play darts?'

'In the end, yes.'

'Why do you say, in the end?'

'Well, I was taken ill, and the match was delayed.'

'How were you taken ill?'

'The match was about to start; I suppose it was about five to eight.' He paused. Speaking was obviously difficult. 'I suddenly felt sick. Well, actually, it wasn't sudden, 'cos I'd been feeling a bit dickie for most the afternoon. But it suddenly got worse, and I had to make a dash for it.'

'A dash where?'

'To the toilet.'

'Where is the toilet in The Victory?'

'In an outhouse in the corner of the car park.'

'So you went outside?'

'Yeah. But there was only one cubicle.'

'And?'

'And there was someone inside.'

'So what did you do?'

'Well, it was pretty urgent. There was a sink, but it was bunged up, paper towels floating in it, you know. So I looked around for somewhere else to be sick. I got as far as the doorway, but knew I wasn't going to be able to hang on, so I just made it behind some car.'

'Were you sick?'

'Slow down, please, Mr Holborne,' instructed the judge. 'I want to get a full note.'

Charles stopped and held up his hand to prevent Terry from speaking further. The judge being interested in a Defence witness: a good sign. He watched while the judge caught up with his handwritten note, and proceeded only when Pullman looked up.

Charles repeated his question. 'Were you sick?'

'Very.'

'Do you know by what car it was you were sick?'

'Not at that time. It was just big and shiny. Silver, I thought. But later on I saw that it was an Austin Princess.'

'I'd like to deal with it in order, so we'll come back to what happened later in a moment. Did you actually throw up on or near the car?'

'On, I'm afraid. I'm very sorry,' he said, looking at the judge. 'I would never have done it if I'd had any choice, but I couldn't help meself.'

Charles looked across at the jury. All of them were leaning forward in rapt attention, straining to hear Cooper's soft muffled voice. There are times during a criminal case when someone gives evidence in so patently an honest and open fashion that it shines through all the other dross. This was one of them. This young man, with absolutely no axe to grind and merely a sense of what was right, was giving the jury the truth, the whole truth and nothing but the truth. God bless this honest, and very brave, East End plumber, thought Charles.

'And how long were you by the car?' continued Charles.

'Maybe five minutes? I felt really ill. Me legs went, and me 'ead was spinning.'

'While you were there, did anything happen?'

'What do you mean? About the bloke?'

'Tell us about the bloke.'

'Someone came up to the car while I was beside it. I thought it was the owner, and I was pretty worried, 'cos I'd made a good mess of his wheel. Wheel arch too, I reckon. I was still retching, like, so I just kept me head down.'

'What did this man do?'

'He came up to the car, and opened the boot.'

'What then?'

'I heard a thump. As if something heavy was being put in, or moved around in the boot. Then the boot closed and the man went away.'

'Could you tell which direction he went in?'

'I thought that he went back to the pub. He certainly didn't go towards the road, or else he'd have gone the opposite way. He might even have tripped over me.'

'Can you help us as to what this person looked like or what he was wearing?'

'No, not really. He had quite a heavy tread, so I'm sure it was a man. I don't remember seeing any clothes except a pair of shoes.'

'And what were they like?'

'Dark, quite sturdy. I can't say any more than that.'

'What happened then?'

'I felt a bit better after a while. The air was cool, so I stayed out for a couple more minutes to make sure I wouldn't throw up again, and then I went back into the darts match.'

'Did you play darts?'

'Not immediately. I was waiting to play, when there was a bit of a commotion outside in the car park, and people began going to the windows and the door. I went to have a look too. There was a crowd of people exactly at the spot where I'd been ill. I thought there was going to be trouble about me damaging the car.'

'Did you see then what sort of car it was?'

'Yeah. It was the same one – an Austin Princess.'

'Did you see what happened then, outside, I mean?'

'No. I was called back to the board for my throw.'

'What did you do after that?'

'Nothing. Except get beaten at darts by a girls' team.'

The jury laughed, and even Judge Pullman permitted himself a smile. 'Thank you, Mr Cooper. Please remain there for a while.'

Marcus Stafford rose.

'So it was just chance that you happened to vomit over that particular car?'

'Yes.'

'Why didn't you use the lavatory?'

'I've already explained. It was occupied.'

'Are you sure?'

'Positive. The locks on them often don't work or are broken off, right? So I never like to push at the door in case you … you know … barge in on someone. So I had a quick dekko under the door first, to make sure.'

'Why didn't you wait for a few seconds to see if the occupant came out?'

'Well, for one thing, I was desperate, and for another, he

weren't going to come out in a hurry.'

'How on earth do you know that?' asked Stafford with some irritation. 'Did you ask him?'

'No, but I could see. His boots were, like, pointing towards me, and his trousers were round his ankles. I guessed he'd be there a while.'

'Boots?'

'Yes, boots, or heavy shoes. Black they were.'

Charles cursed inwardly. According to Terry's proof of evidence the black boots had been worn not by the occupant of the toilet, but by the man approaching the car. He's mixed them up! Then a thought occurred to Charles. He turned back to the point in Terry's statement where the occupant of the toilet was dealt with. There was no mention of any of this. It did not appear that anyone had thought to ask about the occupant of the toilet or his footwear. Maybe he was *not* wrong. Hadn't North said he'd gone to the toilet? There might have been police shoes under the door *and* under the car!

Stafford decided to change tack. 'Forgive me for asking, Mr Cooper, but what had you drunk that night by the time you went out to the lavatory?'

'Nothing. I'd had a pint bought for me, but only had a sip of it before I went out.'

'Nothing at all?'

'No.'

'What about at lunchtime? A couple of pints at the pub?' he suggested, essaying a conspiratorial grin.

'No,' replied Terry, clearly aggrieved at the suggestion.

'I never drink when I'm working.'

'Well,' said Stafford sternly, all twinkle extinguished, 'you might like to help us as to the reason for your sudden illness.'

'I can't tell you. Maybe what I had for lunch. I got something from the shop next door to where I was working.'

'Are you often ill like that?'

'Never before, at least as far as I can remember, and never since.'

'I understand from what you said before that you were quite doubled up.'

'I was.'

'In pain?'

'Yeah.'

'We all no doubt know how unpleasant it can be when we're sick. It makes your eyes water, your belly hurt?'

'Yeah.'

'And that's what happened to you?'

'Yes.'

'And in the middle of this someone approaches where you are crouching?'

'Yes.'

'Someone by whom you would rather not be seen?'

'Yes.'

'So you get your head down.'

'Yes.'

'The car park was dark, was it not?'

'It was, yes.'

'It would be fair, would it not, to say that your ability to see accurately what was happening in the car park was quite limited, by your position, your discomfort, and your wish not to be seen?'

'Yes, it would be fair. But the light was behind this person as they came from the pub, and I am certain that they came to the car I was by.'

'How?'

'Because the car moved slightly as the boot was slammed shut. So I know that it was the same car as I was by.'

'Very well. But what about that car? At the time, you thought just that it was a silver car?'

'Yes.'

'Did you count the number of silver cars in the car park?'

'No, of course not.'

'It is possible that there were several?'

'I suppose so.'

'Indeed, there might have been more than one in that part of the car park?'

'Maybe.'

'All you can say is that you vomited on, or near a silver car?'

'Well…'

'And that after a few minutes, a crowd gathered in the same area of the car park, around a silver Austin Princess.'

'They did – '

'But you can't be sure that they were the one and the same, can you?'

'I can.'

'But how? You didn't take the number of either car. If

there had been two similar cars in that area of the car park, you may have been ill by one, and the crowd gathered by the other.'

'I don't think so. The crowd was exactly where I'd been.'

'You didn't go outside though.'

'No, but – '

'And you were watching from a brightly lit pub, through a crowd of interested people, all looking out, into a dark car park.'

Terry looked concerned. His swollen face contorted into a frown, and he looked at Charles sorrowfully, as if to apologise for being unable to disagree. Charles avoided his eye. He didn't want the jury thinking that he'd been coaching the witness. Furthermore, Stafford was doing a good job of discrediting the evidence of Charles's star witness, and he was anxious to prevent either Terry or the jury seeing that he was concerned.

'Isn't is possible that, after all, you vomit over Car One, and see people crowd round Car Two? That would mean that whatever was put in the boot of Car One had nothing to do with this case. Isn't that right?'

'I suppose so. It's possible, but I don't think it's likely. I was certain at the time that it was at the exact same spot.'

'But now you're not so sure?'

'Well, the way you go on, I begin to wonder.'

'Thank you, Mr Cooper.'

Stafford sat down again, and looked pointedly at the jury box.

'Any re-examination Mr Holborne?' asked the judge,

but Terry forestalled anything Charles was about to ask.

'Can I just say something?' asked Terry. 'If I saw nothing to do with this case, why did anyone bother to do *this* to me? Eh? *Someone* obviously thinks I've seen something important, or they wouldn't kick seven bells out of me to prevent me giving evidence.'

Charles saw several members of the jury nodding their heads vigorously in agreement. You little darlings! he thought. They believe him.

Unnoticed by anyone in court, a slim young man in an Italian tailored suit and gold rings on all his fingers slipped out of the public gallery. At almost exactly the same moment, and for the second time that afternoon, the swing doors behind the dock burst unexpectedly open and Sergeant West appeared. He scuttled down to the barristers' benches, a crumpled piece of paper clasped in his hand. He was hot and sweating, and his face bright red, but the look of triumph on his pudgy features was unmistakeable. He thrust the paper under Stafford's nose and whispered to him. The entire court had watched his entrance, and there was an uncomfortable silence. Stafford became aware of it after a few seconds. He halted West's furious flow with a raised hand, and looked up at Judge Pullman. Charles saw that Stafford's face too was altered. His earlier expression had given way to a barely-suppressed grin.

'I do apologise to your Lordship for this hiatus. A matter has just been brought to my attention that is of the greatest importance in this case. I shall have an application to make, which would best be done in the absence of the jury.'

chapter 21

THE QUEEN vs.
HAROLD ROBESON
NOTICE OF ADDITIONAL EVIDENCE

TAKE NOTICE that in addition to the evidence of the deponents whose names appear on the back of the Indictment, the Crown intends to rely on the statements of the witnesses attached hereto.

Statement of Jonathan Peter West
Occupation: Detective Sergeant
Address: COO8, West End Central Police Station

I refer to the list of properties owned by Overbrooke (G.B.) Limited and Prince Estates (1960) Limited in December 1962 prepared by the Defence in this case. Of the properties listed there, fifteen fell within a radius of five miles of Staplecroft, the property used by the robbers before and after the robbery. Of those, eight were, or included, premises large enough for large vehicles to be stored. Over the last 24 hours, together with other officers, a search has been conducted of those eight properties. The third such property, called The Ridings, is a

*livery stable in the village of Lower Barnsthorne. I produce
an ordnance survey map of the area from which it may be seen
that although no roads connect The Ridings to Staplecroft,
there is a bridle path which leads from the livery stable to the
back of the houses of which Staplecroft is one. I investigated
the bridle path and found that it is in the position indicated
on the plan. The Ridings includes several outbuildings in one
of which I found markings of paint on the walls and floor.
I called for SOCO Leavis from the Surrey Constabulary,
who had been one of the SOCO's originally to investigate
the robbery, to come to The Ridings and there I watched
him remove flakes of paint from the walls and floor of the
outbuilding*

Signed D.S. West

Statement of Frederick Leavis
Age: Over 21
Occupation: Scenes of Crime Officer
Address: Guildford Police Station

*On the 21st. December 1962 I was one of a team of Scenes
of Crimes Officers attached to the Robbery Squad
investigating the robbery of a quantity of diamonds from the
South African Gem Corporation at Brighton Road, Coulsdon,
Surrey. At the scene of the robbery I found abandoned two
vans painted in the livery of the Gas Board. I examined the
vans and came to the conclusion that they had been spray
painted recently. I took samples of the paint on each van, and*

*placed them in separate containers which I labelled "FL 1"
and "FL 2" respectively.*

*I was today requested by Detective Sergeant West to
attend at a property named The Ridings, Lower Barnsthorne,
Surrey, livery stables with a number of outbuildings. One such
building is used to store agricultural machinery. At the far end
of this building I found evidence of paint spraying. The walls
and floor had marks indicating that a spray gun had been used
in close proximity to them, and in the north-east corner of the
building I found four empty paint canisters, which I produce as
exhibit "FL 3".*

*I took scrapings of paint from the walls, and have been able
to extract small quantities of paint from the empty canisters.
A full analysis of the paint is awaited from the forensic science
laboratory, but from my examination of it, it appears to be
indistinguishable from the retained paint flakes "FL 1" and
"FL 2".*

*It is my opinion based on this evidence that the two mock
Gas Board vans were painted in the outbuilding at The
Ridings, Lower Barnsthorne, Surrey.*

Signed Frederick Leavis

'What the fuck are we going to do?'

It was the first time Charles had seen Robeson look
really frightened. He paced up and down the cell in the
bowels of the Old Bailey his brow contracted into a frown.
Ominously, the judge had directed that he remain in
custody for the duration of the short adjournment while
the new evidence was considered. He threw himself onto

the wooden bench, and stared morosely at the cell wall. It may have been the dim light of the cell, which emphasised the lines and creases in Robeson's face, but Charles thought for the first time that he looked his years.

'Well, firstly,' said Charles, 'Stafford's got to obtain leave to re-open his case. Also, this evidence isn't definite; it's only a provisional conclusion. Green paint is green paint, and bear in mind that colours fade over time. What might look the same now might not have looked the same months ago.'

Charles paced as he talked, speaking more quickly as he warmed to his theme. 'So he has to have a full scientific evaluation by the laboratory – which means that he'll need an adjournment. I suggest we deal with those applications first. If and when he's successful, we'll consider what we should do. Do you know any paint experts?'

Robeson didn't appear to be listening. He launched himself from the bench and went to the steel door, his hands on the bars of the wicket.

Charles reached out and touched his shoulder. 'Harry? Harry? Listen, I know this is worrying, but you've been amazingly resilient so far. Don't go to pieces now. You're almost home and dry. Harry? What on earth's wrong with you?'

The solicitor sighed deeply. 'Nothing. Just coming to terms with it.'

'Coming to terms with what?'

'Charles, I reckon if this evidence goes in, I'm sunk.'

'Nonsense – '

Robeson held up his hand. 'Don't tell me nonsense!' he interrupted furiously.

'Why? asked Charles, perplexed.

Robeson smiled grimly, and shook his head. 'Let's just wait for the judge's decision, eh?'

'That's better.'

Charles squeezed the other's arm in affection. 'Come on,' he said gently. 'Terry Cooper was a winner. The whole thing's falling into place. We've established that West had the motive and the opportunity to plant the shotgun and put pressure on Goldstein. Terry's evidence – and the state of the poor bloke – they sew it up. You must have seen the jury; they loved him.'

'Do you think so?'

'Sure of it. *This*,' said Charles, holding up the two new statements, 'is hardly proof that you entered into an agreement to rob.'

Charles looked at the older man, wishing he could dispel his worries. He realised then how much Harry Robeson had come to mean to him in the last few weeks. He was no longer a client – indeed he had ceased to be that within a very short time of their meeting – he was a friend. Charles cared for him far more than would have thought possible a month before.

'Come on. Let's see what Stafford has to say about this.'

Back in court, Marcus Stafford had much to say.

'My application, my Lord, is to re-open the Crown's case so as to lead this evidence. I accept that the proper time for calling it would have been during the course of the

Crown's case. But the task of finding all the companies with which Mr Robeson had a connection in December 1962, and identifying those companies which owned property in Surrey, would have been virtually impossible.

'I do not say "impossible", but almost so bearing in mind the resources available to the police. In my submission this was not evidence that the Crown could reasonably have called before now.

'Since we were provided with the list, every effort has been made to investigate the properties on it as quickly as possible. As a result, the Crown has discovered yet another link between Mr Robeson and the vehicles used in the robbery. The force of the evidence, should the jury accept it, is immense. Whereas it may be contended that the connection with the other property was mere coincidence, a link with two properties cannot be. And if it transpires that the paint is the same as that used to mock up the gas board vans, the link with the robbers is indisputable. It now appears that Mr Robeson controlled not only the property used by the robbers before and after the robbery, but also the property used by them to disguise the vehicles.'

'I see,' said Pullman. 'Tell me, I have a discretion do I not, as to whether or not to permit the evidence to be given?'

'You do, my Lord.'

'Do you agree with that, Mr Holborne?'

Charles rose to his feet. 'Yes, I do my Lord, but I don't accept that your Lordship's discretion should be exercised in favour of the Crown.'

'I will hear you in a minute.' Charles resumed his seat. 'Is there anything else you would like to say, Mr Stafford?'

'Yes, my Lord. The new evidence falls within a very narrow compass and can be considered in a matter of minutes. Although I should not oppose a defence application for a short adjournment – say, overnight – to consider their position, the late reception of this evidence will, in my submission, cause no prejudice. It is of course of the greatest importance to the case, and this is a very serious charge. The interests of justice must require that all relevant evidence be placed before the jury if at all possible.'

Stafford sat down. 'Mr Holborne?'

Charles rose again. 'I have, I think, four submissions, my Lord. Firstly, I rely on the general rule that all evidence the Crown wishes to adduce should be given before the close of their case.

'This is a very old case in the sense that there have already been two trials, the first at which Goldstein and others were found guilty and sentenced and, the second, the unsuccessful retrial of Lyall.

'Secondly, your Lordship should not accept the Crown's submission that it wasn't reasonably possible for the connection between the two properties to have been discovered before now. We're told that The Ridings is only a hundred yards from Staplecroft! The police will have conducted house-to-house enquires as a matter of course once Staplecroft was identified. Such enquiries should certainly have revealed this information, without the necessity for the "virtually impossible" investigations at Companies House. So the supposed difficulty of making Companies House enquiries is a red herring.

'Thirdly, and perhaps most importantly, my learned friend is not only seeking to re-open his case, but it is he who is, in reality, forced to seek an adjournment. The evidence of Mr Leavis is only provisional. As I understand it, he will need to send the paint to a laboratory for full analysis. A visual inspection merely tells us that the paint is the same colour, not that it's the same paint.'

'Mr Stafford?' interrupted Pullman. 'Is this right?'

'If my Lord grants the application, I shall need to take instructions to find out if Mr Leavis has the expertise required to undertake any further tests. I suspect however that he hasn't. If that's right, I shall apply for further time for a full chemical analysis.' He turned and saw West nodding reluctantly. 'Yes. my Lord. That appears to be the case.' He resumed his seat.

'And,' continued Charles, 'who knows how long that will take? Once that's been done, and the final results given to the Defence, it must then be open for me to have an expert instructed on behalf of the Defence to verify or challenge the findings. That will certainly take days, if not weeks.'

'Weeks, more likely,' commented the judge.

'As my Lord, says, weeks, more likely. What's to happen to the jury in that time? They've heard all the evidence in this case save that of the defendant. They've heard it all within the last two days. It's fresh in their memories now, but they can't be expected to keep it in mind for weeks on end during a prolonged adjournment. And your Lordship cannot in any case order the sequestration of a jury for weeks on end; their deliberations would almost inevitably be tainted after weeks of reading newspaper reports.

'Finally, there's the prejudice to Mr Robeson. He is a man of exemplary character, facing trial on a most serious criminal charge. His personal and professional life are in tatters already, but they face complete destruction if he is convicted. The strain of this case has been immense, as I'm sure my Lord can imagine. Is he to be required to wait for an indefinite period while the Crown get their tackle in order for a second bite at the cherry? I submit that that would be most unfair.

'The Crown obviously considered the evidence they had at the outset of this trial and decided it was sufficient to secure a conviction – or they wouldn't have proceeded. They should be required to take their stand on that evidence. In all the circumstances, I submit that the application would cause substantial injustice to Mr Robeson; it would render the trial process flawed; and it ought not be granted.'

Judge Pullman looked at Stafford again. 'Anything else, Mr Stafford?'

'No, my Lord.'

'Then, in my view, it would not be proper for me to permit the Crown to re-open their case at this stage.'

Charles turned round and winked at Robeson. The solicitor smiled broadly at him.

'I think,' continued the judge, 'that Mr Holborne's submissions are well-founded – particularly with respect to the necessity for the trial to be adjourned for an indefinite period. If the evidence regarding the paint was said to be conclusive, that is, if it showed that the paint was clearly the same, I might be of a different view. But it is conjecture only. It looks the same, but it might not be – and we shall not know until after a full analysis; maybe not even then. I'm not prepared to interrupt this trial, for what may be a prolonged period, on that uncertain ground. Now ...'

Pullman was interrupted by his clerk, who turned and spoke quietly to him.

'It appears, gentlemen, that there is an urgent application to be made in another case and as our jury is out, I've been asked if I'll deal with it. I'm told that it will only take five minutes. Will you forgive me, please? Mr Robeson can go down for the present.'

chapter 22

'Charles, that was brilliant!' Robeson's face had altered completely since the last time he was in the room. His cheeks were flushed and his eyes shone. He was elated. He clapped Charles on the back. 'Brilliant!' he repeated.

'No it wasn't.'

'Well, you've saved my skin, Charles, that's for sure! We're going to win.'

'I did nothing of the kind, Harry. Even had Stafford been given leave to put the evidence in, we'd have come up with something. But I think you're right: we're pretty much home and dry. I was never too worried about the paint evidence.'

'Really? Why not?'

'Well, the paint might have been quite different on analysis. Even if it wasn't, for all we know it might be very common …'

Charles stopped in mid-sentence. Robeson was lighting up a cigar, grinning from ear to ear, shaking his head.

'Why are you shaking your head?'

'Forget it, Charles. Let's just say I'd *never* have agreed to a chemical analysis.' He sat on the bench and crossed his legs, wreathed in cigar smoke, and winked at Charles. Then his attitude changed and he became serious. 'Any last points about my evidence?'

'No, just hold on, Harry. I want to know what you meant.'

'No, you don't. Believe me, Charles, you don't.'

Then, only then, did Charles appreciate what Harry was saying. He stood in the tiny converted cell and stared at Robeson, his mouth slightly open.

'You did it?' Charles spoke softly, the words a question, but one to which he suddenly knew the answer. 'You're saying you did it. I don't believe it.'

In his turn Charles began pacing up and down, oblivious to his client, trying to assimilate the information, to slot Robeson's implicit confession into the Crown's evidence and see how it fitted. Robeson watched him warily. Charles suddenly stopped and spun on his heel, his finger pointing at Robeson.

'Wait a minute! The shotgun. Terry Cooper wasn't lying; I'd stake my life on it.'

'No, he wasn't.'

'So the gun *was* planted?'

'What do *you* think? What the hell would I be doing driving around with that bloody gun in the back of my car, seven months after the job?'

'Well, then?' asked Charles, uncomprehending.

'I have been wondering when one of you two clever barristers would work it out,' replied Robeson with ineffable smugness. 'If the police had had possession of that shotgun, don't you think they'd have used it against Lyall? Come on Charles, think about it. The police never recovered the shotgun.'

'Then who...wait a minute ... if the police never had it, then the robbers would ... Lyall! Lyall planted it!'

'Either him or one of his Firm, that's my guess. I suspect it was his lads who did Terry over, too. That was a mistake, as it turned out.'

'But ... but ...' Charles stared at Robeson, lost for words. 'But why? Why should he do that? If you and he were in on it together?'

'Hah! Money! I sometimes wonder how often criminals fall out over the money – because there's certainly no honour among thieves. Of course, he had his way in the end. I'm no hard man.'

'Then I still don't understand. Why go to all this trouble?'

Robeson took a deep breath and looked hard at Charles, weighing him carefully.

'Look, something happened during the job – ' Robeson waved his hand dismissively through the cigar smoke, ' – you know nothing about it – but something happened, you see?' He saw Charles was still frowning. 'Someone *died*, Charles. A neighbour. The police thought she'd had a heart attack and that it was a coincidence – but it wasn't.'

Charles put up his hand to protest but was cut short. 'Yes, I know, there's nothing about it in the case papers. I learned the truth from one of the others. I thought it gave me a cast-iron insurance policy. I couldn't believe that Lyall would touch me – I could've had him hanged, understand? Apparently I was wrong. I guess he couldn't resist the temptation to get rid of someone with a hold over him. All he had to do was contact Tricky West and tell him to be at The Victory at the right time. I'd have assumed West was behind it. And *that* explains why West had to wait before arresting me: he was waiting for the gun to be put in the boot. Quite an unholy alliance that.'

'So you *did* do it,' repeated Charles. 'You bastard.'

'I'm admitting nothing, Charles,' said Robeson, no longer smiling, 'but don't get upset. You've done a first rate job – I knew you would.' He stood and approached Charles. 'With a bit of luck my evidence will be completed by –'

He got no further because Charles pushed him violently in the chest, throwing him back to the bench onto which he fell with a thump. Robeson stared up at Charles, shocked.

'How could you?' asked Charles, still in disbelief. 'How could you, Harry? You lied to me.'

Robeson looked up from where he sat, taken aback by Charles's violence. He tucked his silk tie back inside his jacket.

'Don't be a child, Charles. Lied to you? Don't most of your clients? You're not fussy, are you? You just put forward their stories, and leave it up to the jury. And very often you know bloody well that they're guilty.'

'I do not!'

'Alright,' he conceded, 'then you suspect it. It comes to the same thing.' Robeson sneered at him. 'You barristers give yourselves such airs and graces! You stand there in court, robed in your professional ethics as if the dirt you deal with every day, day in, day out, never touches you. You think you all have such clean hands! I swear to God, there may not be many bent briefs, but I prefer the company of those few. At least they're not hypocrites!'

He got to his feet again and came so close that Charles could feel his spittle on his face as he spoke. 'How many times have you been a willing party to miscarriages of justice, eh? That's how you boys make your reputations, isn't it?' He turned his back on Charles, and sat down again. 'You sicken me. You're like a whore complaining of being raped.'

'No, Harry, you're wrong. I believe in what I do. I believe in integrity – straight dealing – abiding by the rules.'

'Really? Then you're just naïve. We live and breathe in a swamp of filth, you and I. The Krays, the Richardsons, Tricky West, the Filthy Squad – even half the judiciary – they're all as bad as one another! Corrupt right through. This is just a game to them.'

'Well, it's not a game to me. I may have grown up in your swamp, but I got out of it. I'm a member of an honourable profession, and – .'

Robeson interrupted. 'Then you're a bigger fool than I took you for. Do you really think that by playing by your toff colleagues' rules those bastards will ever accept you? Face it Charles: you're an East End Jew-boy with a bit of a past, and they'll never let you forget it!'

The anger seemed to desert Robeson momentarily and when he spoke again he sounded exhausted. 'None of that matters right now. For me it's simple: I'm fighting for my life. How long do you suppose I'll last inside?

I'm facing fifteen years; I'll never live to see the end of it.'

'But all that crap you gave me at Brixton, why bother with that, eh? I would'verepresented you without any of it!'

'Yes, maybe, but how well? You believed in me, and you fought for me as if I wasinnocent.'

Charles shook his head in amazement. 'You really are a calculatingbastard.'

Robeson threw back his head and laughed heartily. 'Thankyou.'

'I mean it, Harry. You used me. You used me to practise a deception. I thought we were friends.'

'Oh, dear, Charles. You're sounding like a schoolboy. I hope we *are* friends. I know Sally does, too.'

'What?'

Before he could answer there was a knock on the door and a prison office put his head round the door. 'You're wanted back in court, gentlemen. The judge is waiting to continue.'

'We'll be right there,' said Robeson breezily, standing up and straightening his tie.

'Wait a minute!' commanded Charles. 'Tell His Lordship that something has arisen, and I must have a further five minutes. Tell him I'll explain then.'

'Well, he's waiting in court, sir, so I think you'd better come and ask him yourself if youneed some time.'

'Tell him!' shouted Charles. 'I shall not be up for five minutes, d'you hear?'

The prison officer's eyes widened in astonishment.

He hesitated for a second and then disappeared. Charles turned on Robeson.

'Sally? What are you talking about?'

'Sally. Your ex-junior clerk? The one you've been seeing, for want of a better word.'

'Sally?'

'Yes, Charles, *Sally*. My daughter.'

Charles felt as if he were in a dream. 'Sally's your daughter?'

'Yes. She didn't tell you then? I'm surprised; I thought she would.'

Charles shook his head slowly, his eyes wide. 'You're breathtaking, Harry. You even had your daughter screw me, to make doubly sure I was on board. Oh, God!' Charles slapped his forehead as he remembered. 'And Dad's hospital fees. My God, you're unbelievable!'

'Well, now, don't give me too much credit, Charles,' Robeson said with a smile, 'Sally may well have something to say about – '

He got no further because Charles punched him hard, with all the considerable weight of his body, full on the jaw. Robeson collapsed like a stack of cards onto the floor of the cell. He lay still for a moment, and then stirred. He looked up at Charles, feeling his chin. Charles stood over him, fists ready.

'Take it easy, Charles, I'm not getting up again. I'm not sure how many of those I can take.'

There was movement at the door and two prison officers stood there.

'What the hell's going on?' asked one of them. He looked from Charles to Robeson and back again.

'Nothing, officer,' replied Robeson. 'Just a little dispute about … tactics,' he said with a smile. 'Do you think I might stand up now, Charles?'

Charles relaxed his fighting stance, and stood back. Robeson stood up and brushed off his jacket.

'The judge has given you five minutes, sir,' said the other officer. 'Although he was not best pleased, and wants an explanation.'

'Thank you,' said Charles. 'Will you leave us for a minute please?'

The two men hesitated but Robeson nodded and the door was closed again. Charles was aware that he'd heard no footsteps and guessed the prison officers were standing outside the door in case there was further trouble. He waited a few seconds before speaking, and the men moved off.

'Well, Harry. What now?'

'I'll tell you. I'm going upstairs to give evidence. Then I'll listen to your storming speech for the defence and, as long as nothing unforeseen occurs, I shall be acquitted. Then I shall get on a plane with a few belongings and a little nest egg that I've converted into universal currency, and with a little help from some friends I shall disappear. London may not be terribly conducive to my health for a while. Kenny Lyall's a vindictive man. Not to mention Sergeant West.'

'No,' replied Charles softly.

'No, what? You think Kenny Lyall is *not* a vindictive man?'

'I mean "No" to all of it. You're not giving evidence, Harry. I'm not calling you.'

'You can't stop me, Charles. Look,' he said, placating, 'you can square your conscience. You never knew until now, right? You don't actually *know*, even now. You've done your job with clean hands and an unsullied heart. Not a soul can blame you.'

'You're right: I can't stop you. But I'll have no part in it. You may have contempt for barristers generally and me in particular, but *I* have certain standards, things that *I* believe in, that *I* live my life by. And it maybe naive, childish, even meaningless for someone like you, but I believe in justice. That's why I do the job. Because I feel I'm doing something worthwhile, something that's decent, that'll last. And I won't allow myself to be used to pervert it; not for you, not for Sally ...' and here he paused, '... and not even for Dad.'

'What are you going to do?'

'Well, the first thing will be to tell the judge that I'm professionally embarrassed. I can't call you to give evidence which I know will be perjured.'

'That's tantamount to telling him that I've confessed.'

Charles looked him straight in the eye. 'Yes.'

'You can't do that, Charles.'

'I can and I will. You know as well as I what my professional rules dictate. I cannot knowingly allow myself to be used as an instrument of your perjury.'

'But the jury will know. You must at least make a speech. If I agree not to give evidence, you can do at least that, surely?'

'No. On your instructions I have made a scurrilous attack on the police who were, for once, innocent of any wrongdoing. I've even suggested that a particular officer planted that gun, when you knew full well he did nothing of the sort. How can I make any speech now, when I know the entire basis of the case I've run was a lie?'

'But if you suddenly disappear, the jury'll guess what's happened. Barristers don't leave their clients half way through trials ....'

'Indeed. That's a risk you should have considered first.'

'This must be in breach of your professional rules.'

'It isn't. It's my professional rules which give me no choice in the matter. And if you disagree, then report me.'

'You fucking hypocrite!' spat Robeson. 'You didn't give a fuck about professional ethics when *you* were up against it! From what I read you broke into buildings, deceived people, even assaulted one or two! Well, my life is no less at risk than yours was then.'

'Yes, but there's a difference: I was trying to clear my name when I was innocent. *You're* guilty – and manipulating me to avoid the consequences. What's more, I asked no one else to do my dirty work. You want to deceive the court: fair enough, you do it. But not with me.'

'You do realise the danger you're putting yourself in?' threatened Robeson.

'Danger?'

'You know who I work for. The Krays have a great deal invested in me. I've represented them, members of the Firm, their dodgy doctor – all of them – for years. It's a cliché but I *do* know where all the bodies are buried. The twins want me on the outside, not rotting in some prison. One of the Firm has been in court every day of the case, haven't you noticed? And have you seen Ronnie when he doesn't get his way?'

'So you're threatening me that if I don't continue to represent you, I'm in personal danger?'

Robeson shrugged. 'I'm just saying there are bound to be consequences.'

Charles stared at Robeson, his eyes narrowed dangerously. 'Is that it? Anything else to say? Any last cards you want to play?' Robeson didn't answer. 'Very well.' Charles turned and opened the door. 'Officer!' he called.

'What are you going to do?' asked Robeson.

'Exactly as I said. I'm going straight to Pullman's chambers to tell him that I'm professionally embarrassed.'

'What about me?'

'You're no longer my problem, Harry. You may be able to persuade the judge to give you a re-trial. I doubt it, though. My advice is to plead guilty. Tell the judge that you simply couldn't bring yourself to lie on oath. Say anything you like. I don't care.'

Charles made to go. Robeson grabbed him by the upper arm. 'What about Sally? Don't you care about her?'

Charles eyed him icily. 'Let go of me, or I shall beat the living daylights out of you here and now.'

Robeson let go. Charles stared at him for a further moment, and then swept out.

chapter 23

Charles marched into court and demanded to see Pullman in chambers. Stafford raised an interrogative eyebrow at him but Charles simply shook his head. Stafford was going to insist on an explanation but he saw the thunderous look on Charles's face and decided for once to let events take their course. A minute later the clerk came into court to take them into Pullman's chambers. The clerk led the barristers along the red carpeted corridor, knocked on Pullman's door, and opened it wide for the barristers to enter. The Recorder of London was sitting behind his desk. He rose, stubbing out a cigarette.

'This better be – ' he started.

Charles interrupted. 'I apologise, Judge, if I've appeared rude, or if my behaviour has seemed bizarre, but … extraordinary as it may seem this late in the case, while in the cells my client has put me in the position that … I cannot continue to represent him.'

Pullman stared at Charles in surprise and sat down slowly. 'Good heavens,' he exclaimed quietly. 'At this stage? The man must be mad. I thought he had every chance of getting off.'

'So did I.'

'Then what's he playing at? Is he hoping for a retrial?'

'No, that's certainly not it. I'm sorry, but I really can't explain it, Judge.'

'I understand. Take a seat, gentlemen.'

In fact, Pullman had misunderstood. Charles's inability to explain was not due to any professional constraints but because he still couldn't believe that Robeson had committed forensic suicide. Charles didn't think the point worth clarifying.

'And you are quite sure that you cannot continue to represent him?' asked Pullman.

'Quite sure.'

'Well, Stafford, what are we to do?'

'I think that's a matter for you, Judge. We can either proceed without Holborne or we could discharge this jury and start again with different counsel.'

'Very well. I shall come into court and you, Holborne, had better make your application to be relieved of further conduct. I'll then hear what Robeson has to say, and make a decision.'

Charles and Stafford returned to court. Judge Pullman entered a moment later.

'I am grateful for the time given to me, my Lord,' started Charles when the court had settled. 'I regret however that as a result of certain events that occurred during the adjournment, I find myself professionally embarrassed. It is with the greatest reluctance that I must therefore ask to be discharged from further representing Mr Robeson.'

There was a moment of profound silence in the

courtroom as the observers absorbed the implications of Charles's statement. Then, like the rumblings of a distant storm, a muttering began, and newspaper men began scribbling furiously. Conversations erupted throughout the public gallery and on counsel's benches.

'Silence in court!'

'Are you quite sure, Mr Holborne?'

'I regret, my Lord, that I am.'

'Then of course I must discharge you. However, would you please remain in court for the moment?'

'Of course.'

'Now, Mr Robeson,' said Pullman. 'Do you have anything to say about this?'

Robeson stood upright in the dock. Charles turned and looked up at the solicitor. He saw that Robeson's chin was red and sported a very obvious swelling. He wondered, with surprising indifference, whether the judge would be able to see it across the well of the court and might even accuse Charles of beating Robeson into submission.

Robeson smiled at the judge. 'Yes, my Lord. May I ask for the indictment to be put again?'

'I beg your pardon?'

'I want the indictment to be put again.'

Pullman looked staggered. 'Mr Holborne, did you anticipate this course?'

'Not at all, my Lord.'

'Mr Robeson, you are unrepresented at present, and I am reluctant to allow you to take such a course without legal advice. Do you wish to apply for a short adjournment?'

'No, thank you. I don't need legal advice. I've been a Solicitor of the Supreme Court for longer than your Lordship has been at the Bar or Bench, I daresay. So I know what I am doing, my Lord.'

'Be that as it may, I'm not happy with what's occurred. You are under no obligation to alter your plea because of Mr Holborne's difficulties.'

'I appreciate that. But there's nothing that any counsel could tell or advise me that would change my mind. I do not wish to be represented further. I have decided to alter my plea.'

'Well, if that is what you want.'

'It is, my Lord.'

'Very well. Let the indictment be put again.'

The clerk of the court rose. 'Harold Joseph Robeson, you stand charged with the offence of conspiracy to rob contrary to common law. Particulars of the offence are that between the 1st day of March 1962 and 31st day of December 1962 you did conspire with Kenneth Lyall, Peter Simons, Raymond Papier and persons unknown to rob the South African Gem Corporation of a quantity of diamonds worth £945,000. How do you plead, guilty or not guilty?'

'Guilty.'

'Well, I'll be damned,' muttered Pullman to himself. He peered over his bench to the shorthand writer. 'Did you catch that?' he asked in a stage whisper.

'Yes, my Lord, but I didn't record it.'

'Good. I mean, thank you.'

•

'Harold Joseph Robeson. You have decided, albeit late in the day, to plead guilty to this offence. Notwithstanding your wish not to be represented further, I appointed Mr Holborne to act as *amicus* so as to assist the court, and I have been greatly helped by what he has said. You owe him a debt of gratitude. I take into account the fact that, as Mr Holborne rightly says, you had every chance of acquittal, and that to plead guilty at this stage of the trial took much courage. I also take into account the fact that it was your reluctance to commit perjury that persuaded you, at the last, to change your plea. For those reasons I think I am, unusually, entitled to give you credit for pleading guilty as if you had done so at a much earlier stage.

'I also take into account that you had an unimpeachable record of service to the community and charitable work that spanned many decades before this matter, and that however long a period you serve, your career as a solicitor of the Supreme Court is finished. Nonetheless, this was a professional robbery, made all the more so by your assistance. In the course of the robbery, one man was disabled for life, and even though you took no part in the execution of it, you knew that firearms were to be used and you allied yourself to the plan to use violence to steal those diamonds.

'In all the circumstances, the very least sentence I can pass, bearing in mind your plea, your previous good character and your age, is one of eight years' imprisonment. Take him down.'

Robeson was led away. 'Mr Holborne,' said Pullman,

smiling like a shark, but with a genuine attempt at warmth, 'I would like to thank you for the extremely professional and able way in which you have conducted this matter. The court is grateful. And I owe you an apology.' Charles bowed low to the judge. 'I shall rise now.'

There was the usual scuffle and hubbub as those in the press bench fought to get out and those in the public gallery stood to leave. In the well of the court the prosecution solicitor congratulated Stafford on securing the conviction and the police officers busied themselves with slapping one another on the back. Stafford leant towards Charles and spoke quietly him, his lips barely moving.

'I think, Holborne, that I too owe you an apology.'

Charles turned his head towards the other barrister. He was about to tell him to go to hell, but he suddenly felt enormously weary. Instead, he dragged his wig off his curly black hair, threw it onto the bench before him, and sat down heavily in his seat, his elbows on the bench. He bent his head and began rubbing the back of his neck. He thought momentarily of Sally and her delicate hands massaging away the stiffness in his shoulders after a long day in court and then, with an effort, put her firmly out of his mind.

'Forget it,' he said, not looking up.

'I don't think I shall forget this case in a long while,' replied Stafford. 'Will you take my hand, Holborne, and accept my apology?'

Charles turned to see a pudgy hand extended towards him. He looked up at the face of the barrister and could see that he was genuine.

'Why not?' said Charles, and shook the proffered hand briefly.

'I admit it: I was wrong about you,' said Stafford. 'And I'll do all I can to put people straight. You couldn't have disproven more effectively the rumours circulating about you.'

'So people thought I was bent, did they?'

Stafford paused. 'You know what the Temple's like.'

'Yes. I do. So I've saved my reputation at the cost of eight years of Robeson's life and my father's health. Wonderful.'

'Your father? What *are* you on about?'

'Nothing,' replied Charles bitterly. 'Forget it,' he repeated.

Charles started piling up the case papers. He heard someone call his name and he turned round. Sally stood in the aisle next to him. Her eyes were red and her mascara smudged.

'Did you hear?' asked Charles.

'I heard,' she answered calmly.

'I'm sorry, Sally. I don't know what to say.'

Stafford extricated himself from the barristers' bench and herded out of court the police officers who were still standing around congratulating one another.

'You don't have to say anything. It's me who has to talk to you, Charlie, if you'll let me.'

He shrugged. 'There's no need. Your father told me everything.'

'No, he didn't. I have to speak to you. I know what you're thinking, and you're wrong.'

'Am I?' he asked. 'You and your father make quite a team.'

'No,' she said, shaking her head violently, like a little girl, 'it's not true. Please let me explain.'

Charles looked hard at her. She returned his gaze, her eyes pleading, her lower lip trembling. 'Well,' he replied finally, 'I'm going down to see Robes ... your father. You can wait for me in the Great Hall if you want. I shan't be long.'

She nodded silently and bit her lip, on the verge of more tears. 'Do you think they'll let me see him?' she asked.

'I don't know. Maybe. I'll ask if you like. Perhaps you'd better come down to the cells with me.'

'No, I couldn't speak to him with you there.'

'I didn't mean that. They may let you see him when I've finished.'

'Okay. Then I'll come.'

They went together to the basement and Charles rang the bell. When the door was opened Charles asked if Sally could see Robeson after he was finished.

'No, sir, I'm sorry,' replied the prison officer. 'No social visits.'

'Look, no one expected him to change his plea, and we weren't anticipating a verdict today. He's now got eight years. Can't you allow her even two minutes? She's his daughter.'

'I'm really sorry –'

'But she's a barrister's clerk. Can't you put her down as a professional visit? She can come in with me and wait by your desk until I've finished. Then I'll wait for her and take her back up again.'

The prison officer wavered. 'Please?' begged Sally.

'Alright. Come on then. But you'll both have to be signed in together.'

He took their names, left Sally by his desk, and escorted Charles to another interview room.

Robeson joined him a few minutes later. The solicitor entered without speaking and sat down at the tiny table, his hands clasped before him. As a convicted prisoner he'd had his cigars taken away from him and he fiddled with his fingers nervously.

'Well, Charles. What can I do for you?'

'Nothing. I came down to see how you were, and if there's anything I could do for you. Anyone I can contact, anything like that.'

'Still the conscientious professional man, eh?' He said it without bitterness.

'Harry, I'm sorry. Believe me, I'm very sorry. I didn't want things to turn out this way, particularly as it's hurt Sally so much. But you left me no choice.'

'I know. I've only myself to blame. I misjudged you. Funnily enough, although you fear the worst, now it's actually happened, it doesn't feel so bad. It's a relief in a way.'

'I hope that feeling lasts,' said Charles, doubting that it would. Robeson was still in shock. It would take some weeks before he realised what had happened to him.

'No, you misunderstand me. I have no illusions about

what eight years means to a man of my age, especially one who's never been to prison before. What I mean is: by the time I come out – *if* I come out – the Krays'll no longer be interested in me. As you might imagine, they've been … demanding clients. For some years I've been wondering how to manufacture an exit strategy, and you've done it for me.'

'I see. Still, eight years is not that – '

'Please, Charles,' interrupted Robeson, 'don't tell me I've had a good result. That really would be too much. And I don't want to hear about remission and parole either.'

Charles shrugged. 'Very well. If there's nothing you'd like me to do, I'll go now. Sally's here to see you.' Robeson nodded.

Charles transferred his books and papers to his left hand and held out his right. Robeson hesitated, and then shook Charles's hand.

'Now, Charles, my boy, bugger off and let me see my daughter.'

Sally was no more than five minutes and when she returned, Charles was surprised to see that she was composed.

As the outer door banged shut after them, she faced Charles. 'I need to wash my face and tidy myself up a bit. You've got to get changed. There's a pub almost opposite, down that little side street, under the arch. Can I meet you there in fifteen minutes?'

'Yes, I know it. I'll see you there.'

Charles went back to the top of the building to get out of

his court robes. It was not quite four o'clock and the robing room was almost empty, most cases still being in progress. He fixed his day collar to his shirt and knotted his tie. As he stood looking in the mirror someone came up behind him.

'Hello, Charles. I hear you've had quite an afternoon.'

It was Sebastian Campbell-Smythe, a member of Charles's former chambers. Charles and Sebastian had never been very close, but Sebastian had been one of the more approachable members at Chancery Court. Notwithstanding that, they'd not spoken once in the year since Charles left.

Charles's first reaction was to tell the other barrister to piss off but then, he thought, what the hell? So he smiled with as much sincerity as he could command, and replied.

'Yes. Things have been a little ... unusual.'

'I hear Pullman gave you a public acknowledgment. That's something of a rarity, if not unprecedented. We must have a drink some time and you can tell me all about it. I'd be interested to hear the inside story of Harry Robeson.'

'Yes, let's do that.'

Sebastian patted Charles on the shoulder as he left. 'See you soon, then. And well done.'

Charles descended to the ground floor and left the building. He crossed the road and began to walk towards the pub but, the nearer he got, the slower and more hesitant became his footsteps. He stood before the door, reached to push it open, and stopped. Then he turned and walked away towards Ludgate Circus, and Chambers.

chapter 24

The two boys kept lookout, one at each end of Tuskar Street, Greenwich, throughout the morning, but with nothing to report. Then, just after 2:30 in the afternoon, one of them saw a front door open in one of the neat terraced houses just at the bend in the road. A man bearing the description they had been given stepped out and shut the door behind him. The man was tall and powerfully-built, with long lank black hair that reached his shoulders and a scar down one side of his face.

The boy positioned closest to the house began dribbling a football along the pavement towards the approaching man. At that signal the second boy, a skinny runt still in short trousers which revealed his grubby scabbed knees, turned and sprinted in the opposite direction and round the corner into Frobisher Street, a tiny cul-de-sac opening off Tuskar Street, in which a black Buick was parked. The boy tapped twice on the window and ran off.

The occupants of the American car, both wearing suits and hats, sat up, suddenly alert. The front-seat passenger reached under his seat and took out a heavy black revolver. He checked the cylinder and placed the revolver on his lap, covering it with a raincoat. The driver got out of the car and crouched on the corner just behind the line of buildings so that he was invisible to anyone approaching down Tuskar Street. The sound of a football bouncing and skidding across the pavement could be heard, and a few seconds later the older boy ran past, kicking the ball diagonally with the outside of his foot against the gardens' dwarf walls, collecting it again as it rebounded, and repeating the trick every few steps. Half a dozen paces behind the boy strode the man with the long black hair. The man on the pavement bent down to tie his shoelaces, his hat obscuring his face, just as the man with the long black hair passed him, and then stood up swiftly.

'Kenny!' he called, and Kenny Lyall whirled round. 'Can I have a word?'

Before Lyall had an opportunity to move he became aware of the other man standing a few feet off to one side. His raincoat was draped over his forearm but the muzzle of the revolver could clearly be seen protruding from the end.

'Ronnie and Reggie would like a word with you, if you don't mind,' said the man with the gun. 'We've been asked to come and get you.' Lyall looked from one man to the other, sizing up his chances of running and wondering if the man would actually shoot. 'We've been told to bring you back home afterwards.'

The two men closed in on him and the one with the gun took Lyall's elbow and guided him back to the Buick. One of the rear doors was opened and Lyall got in.

'Slide across,' ordered the man with the gun. Lyall did so, and the man with the gun slid in next to him. The other man got into the driver's seat, and the car moved off.

'Where are we going?' asked Lyall.

'Just to the Regal. Reggie's got a run of meetings this afternoon, but he promises he won't keep you long.'

'Is this about the brief, Robeson?'

'No idea. We're just chauffeurs.'

'Yeah, right. Why the gun, then?'

'You know Ronnie. It's more'n my life's worth not to bring you back. Just making sure you was gonna come as asked.'

The Buick turned onto the A102 and headed towards the Blackwall Tunnel. The two men ignored Lyall and chatted about the previous night's entertainment at the Regal, although the gun remained trained, nonchalantly, on Lyall's midriff.

'I ain't never seen anything as funny in my entire life,' said the driver. 'A donkey! A fucking donkey!'

'Fuckin' 'ell,' replied the one on the backseat. 'Of all the fuckin' nights to miss! What did 'e do wiv it?'

'Nuffing. Just sat in his chair and chatted to it. Said he was teaching it to speak English!'

'I wish I'd seen it.'

'Well, you might tonight. It'll be the one in the straw boater!'

The journey took twenty-five minutes. As the Buick pulled up outside the billiard hall the driver tooted the horn and a young man who had been standing outside by the doors went inside. The car pulled up on the wide pavement and was parked between two other American cars with "For

Sale" signs and prices displayed in their windscreens. Lyall was escorted inside.

The Regal Billiard Hall on Eric Street, Mile End, had been the Krays' headquarters for some years. It was the East End villains' principal meeting place, labour and information exchange, and watering hole rolled into one dimly-lit, smoky venue. A genuine billiard hall with fourteen tables and a bar that remained open all day and all night, it also offered lockable recesses under the seats for thieves' tools, space for stolen goods and useful cover for stolen vehicles. It was also neutral territory for any of its regulars. The Krays would not tolerate fights or internecine warfare by anyone else while on their premises.

Lyall squinted as he entered the darkened hall. The lights from the half dozen billiard tables in use cast rhomboidal planes of light through the thick fog of cigarette smoke. With one man at each elbow Lyall was walked past the tables towards a corner of the hall. Ronnie Kray sat in his accustomed chair from where he could see everyone entering and leaving, an Alsatian dog panting on the floor by his side. He was in shirt sleeves, the arms held up by silver elasticated sleeves garters, as if he was a card dealer. He wore a blue and red silk tie which matched the pinstripes in his shirt, large gold cufflinks and a tiepin.

'Thanks for coming, Kenny,' he said.

'Didn't have much choice, did I?'

'Really? Well, thanks in any case. Reggie and I wanted a word about the trial.' He rose. 'It's a bit noisy in here. Shall we go out the back?'

Ronnie Kray led the way past the billiard tables and out through some swing doors at the back of the hall. Lyall followed, his minders on either side of him. They passed the toilets and a storeroom and came to a wooden door. Lyall followed Ronnie outside into a small yard. Reggie Kray was waiting for them with two other men. In Reggie's hand was a cutlass. Lyall looked round at the others. One had a sharpened sword; another an implement that looked like a bayonet. They were all armed with something sharp. Lyall turned and spoke to Ronnie who, he now saw, had a butcher's meat cleaver in his hand.

'Look Ronnie, I had to do it! He was threatening me, you know, with that old girl what died in Coulsdon.'

'I told you, Kenny, it was all under control. But you didn't listen to me, and now look what's happened.'

'But he's just a bent brief, for Chrissakes!'

'Exactly,' said Reggie from the other side of the circle now closing in on Lyall. 'He was *our* bent brief, and now he's no fucking use to us at all. No shooters,' ordered Reggie to the others.

'Hold on, hold on! Please Reggie! I want a trial!'

Reggie Kray stopped and the others in the circle followed suit. Reggie looked at Ronnie.

As far as Lyall could see nothing passed between them, no words and no facial expressions, and not for the first time he wondered at the telepathy they so often displayed and for which they were renowned.

'Sorry, Kenny,' said Reggie, 'but this ain't an occasion

for a trial. There's no doubt what you did, and no doubt about the penalty.'

The first blow came from behind, and from Ronnie. It struck Lyall's right shoulder and more or less severed his right arm. The second came from Ronnie who slashed at his leg, causing Lyall to fall to the ground. Thirty seconds of frenetic stabbing and slashing later, and Lyall lay still in a widening pool of blood that spread outwards in zigzag trickles, following the depressions between the cobbles covering the yard. He had made almost no sound since the first slash.

'Pick up all the pieces,' directed Reggie, 'and put them on the tarpaulin. It's in the back of the van. Wrap him up and take him out to Canvey. They know he's coming. Alberto – get the hose and wash down the yard.'

'Bollocks,' said Ronnie, examining his shirt. 'These garters are no fuckin' use. I've still managed to get blood all over me fucking cuffs…'

chapter 25

1963 was drawing to a close. In Britain a new Prime Minister was appointed and in America the assassinated American president was buried. Towards Christmas Charles found himself suddenly much more popular at the Bar. He didn't know whether it was the publicity from the Robeson case or the long-awaited upturn in his practice, but the diary filled up well into the New Year and the pile of briefs on his desk grew. Christmas celebrations began and the Temple began again to feel like the friendly place it once had been.

Charles had heard nothing from Rachel, who he assumed was still in America, for nearly a month, when he received a brief note from her in the post asking him to admit two of her friends to her flat in Dalston. He met a rather embarrassed young Jewish couple on the pavement outside the flat in which he had sheltered when on the run from the police. He escorted them upstairs and watched, with some sadness, as they cleared the rest of Rachel's clothes and personal belongings, avoiding his gaze. As they left Charles handed them his keys to Rachel's flat. Two days later, by arrangement, they arrived at Charles's flat on Fetter Lane with a cat basket to collect Philomena. And that was that.

Charles was not looking forward to Christmas. Harry

and Millie Horowitz were planning to go to Bournemouth as soon as Harry was discharged from hospital. They were going to spend a few weeks with old friends while Harry recuperated. David and Sonia had invited Charles to spend the holiday period with them but, sincere as the invitation was, Charles knew that the newlyweds would rather be alone.

He thought often about Sally, her urchin smile, soft skin and small agile hands, but he couldn't bring himself to call her. One Friday night however, a couple of days before Christmas, he was about to go home after a few drinks with colleagues in the Witness Box when he saw a familiar figure at a table at the far side of the bar. Charles excused himself and went over, pushing through the boisterous crowd of young lawyers and journalists.

'Hello, Sally.'

She sat alone at a small table, almost surrounded by a loud Christmas party group from the Daily Express, mostly young men. There was an empty glass before her. She didn't look up, but her cheeks flushed.

'Do you mind if I sit down?' he shouted, looking about for a second chair.

'I've been watching you and wondering if you'd see me,' she said. 'I'm surprised you want to talk to me at all.'

'I wouldn't have come over otherwise.'

She neither answered nor looked up. Charles stood by the table looking at her bowed head, waiting, the party-goers' raucous noise ringing round him.

'OK,' he said, buttoning his overcoat, 'perhaps you're

right. I'll go. I just … felt I owed you an apology. For not turning up at the pub after … the case. I … I just couldn't face it. I'm sorry.'

He turned, but before he could find a space in the crowd to negotiate his way towards the door, he felt a tug on the back of his coat. He turned. Sally was standing, and there were tears in her eyes.

'Wait,' she asked, sitting down again immediately.

'Of course,' he replied, and he pulled a chair from an adjoining table and sat down. Sally bent over the table again, her hands clasped tightly in front of. Charles watched her nails digging into the skin and, hesitantly, he reached across and placed his big paw on top of her tiny white hands.

'You don't want to do that,' she said, her voice catching in his throat, 'people'll see.'

Charles left his hand where it was and she made no attempt to remove it. Two fat tears ran down her cheeks and plopped onto the shiny surface in front of her. Charles reached into his pocket with his other hand and pulled out what was, thankfully, a clean handkerchief. He offered it to her and she took it from him and dabbed at her eyes, smearing mascara all over it. She offered it back to Charles, and he waved it away.

'Keep it,' he said.

Her crying gradually subsided. 'I didn't expect you to understand,' she said at last, occasional sobs still punctuating her breathing. 'But I thought at least you'd listen.'

'I didn't think there was anything to say. I'm sure you did what you thought was right to protect your father.'

'You're wrong.'

'Am I?' he asked, disbelieving.

Sally took her hand from underneath his and reached into her handbag. She drew out a plastic season-ticket holder. Slipped into the back, behind her ticket, was a piece of card. She extricated it from the plastic holder and handed it to Charles. He frowned and turned it over. It was a photograph.

'I was three. Michelle must've been a few months old. Tracey hadn't been born yet.'

Charles had to hold up the dog-eared photograph to examine it in the poor light. It was black and white and showed a young couple on a windswept pier. In the woman's arms, entirely swathed in a shawl, was an infant. The man stood beside her, squinting slightly into the sun, holding a child by the hand. The child was small and dark and was frowning, also perhaps because of the light that shone in her eyes. The family stood in front of an amusement arcade behind which Charles could make out a huge expanse of grey sand and, in the distance, the sea.

'It was taken at Southend. The little girl's me. And that's Dad,' she said, pointing to the man. It was unmistakably Harry Robeson, then, Charles guessed, in his thirties. Charles studied the slice of life he held in his hand. He peered into the grainy photograph, trying to see into Robeson's eyes, looking for any glimpse of the man he would become or the fate that would await him twenty-five years later.

'He left about a year and a half after that. Mum never

remarried. When she took up with Frank – I was about twelve – she changed all our names to his, but only to stop the neighbours talking. I don't know if she ever loved him, but they stayed together long enough. I'd forgotten almost everything about Dad by then anyway. But I kept the photo, and I'd look at it and try to picture what had happened before and after it. It was my one bit of certainty; do you understand? At least I had proof that I had a father, even if only for that day, even if only at that very moment.'

Charles nodded.

'And from that I would extend it outwards, like I was reclaiming land, until I could pretend I remembered the whole day, all of it, like I had a film. I'd try and picture a whole week, a whole month, to try and imagine him as part of my life. I'd try to guess what he'd have thought or said in any situation. I even used to have imaginary conversations with him in bed when I was lonely.

'Then, after I left college and I was looking for a job, I saw an advert in *The Standard* for a barrister's clerk. I went to the interview and I didn't get it, but the idea stuck. I tried for months, and then Mum said that she knew someone who might be able to help. She never said who or nothing, just an old friend. I didn't meet him. Mum just told me an interview had been set up at a place called Chancery Court, and I should go. And I got the job. It wasn't until a couple of months had gone by that Stanley let slip that a Mr Robeson had got me the interview.

'Course I knew immediately who it must've been. I looked Dad up in the Solicitors' List. Turns out he had an office less than a mile from where we lived. So I just called in one day, on my way home, just to thank him. I didn't tell Mum. And a few weeks later he phoned me and said he was finishing a case at Southwark, and did I want to meet for lunch? So I said yes, and we got on really well. We started meeting every couple of months, just for a sandwich or maybe a quick half after work.'

'Why are you telling me all this, Sally?'

'Cos I want you to understand.'

'This isn't helping me understand.'

'I love him.'

'Yes; so what? What're you saying? Because you love him, you agreed to sleep with me? Okay, I can understand that. But I can't believe you seriously thought that having sex with me would affect how I represented him, did you?'

'No, of course not. Dad may have, but I knew how professional you were. I knew it wouldn't make any difference to you.'

'I don't see how that can be true. We had that first kiss in the pub – remember? – and within two days Robeson and Co briefs start rolling in?'

'I'm not saying that was a coincidence. I *did* speak to Dad to see if he'd help out. I was worried about you, Charlie; you said you were going to leave the Bar. I wasn't even sure you'd take the work – I knew it'd look odd. But I asked, and I was over the moon when he did actually help. That's all there was to it, Charlie, I swear.'

'If that's true, then why didn't you just tell me? Why

didn't you say: "My father's Harry Robeson, and he's agreed to send you some work"?'

'I thought you'd stop seeing me – or stop taking the work. I didn't want either. Everyone knew he was a villains' solicitor, and most people thought he was bent and in the Krays' pocket. Turns out, he was. But so what if he decided to instruct you in his own case? You needed the work and I knew you'd do a fantastic job for him, so why not?'

'And you had no idea he'd use our relationship as a lever if he had to?' asked Charles, his voice heavy with sarcasm.

Sally hung her head and nodded. 'Oh, yeah, I've no illusions. But by then what was I supposed to do? Deprive my father of his chance of acquittal? Or stop seeing you?' She looked away from him again at the backs of the besuited drinkers.

'Oh, come on Sally. We'd only been seeing one another for a couple of weeks. Don't try to tell me …'

Charles stopped in mid-sentence. Her head was bent low and she was crying in earnest now, tears rolling unchecked, one after another, down her cheeks, splashing onto the table and leaving two small puddles which slowly merged.

'I knew it, you see?' she sobbed. 'I saw it coming and I knew that, whatever I did, I was going to lose both of you.'

'I just don't see – '

'No you don't see, do you? Why are you so fucking blind?' Sally almost shouted the last words, causing some of the people standing about them to look down at the two of them and grin at one another. She didn't appear to care, but stared up at Charles almost defiantly, her mascara smudged afresh, her eyes red and her cheeks wet. He felt a wave of tenderness for her sweep over him.

'I'm in love with you, you fucking idiot,' she said softly, still staring into his eyes. 'I've been in love with you for years. Since long before you saved my doubtful virtue from that smelly old man! But I never thought for a second anything could come of it. I was just the junior clerk, and you were married to the daughter of the head of Chambers, a Viscount no less! And then it happened... and... it was wonderful. Sort of, like my father, you know? No, don't laugh. For years I'd imagined what he was like, and when I got to know him, it turned out I was right. He was great; he was my Dad, funny, and caring, and a laugh to be with. So, just the same, I'd imagined what it would be like with you. I'd run that first time over in my mind a thousand times before it actually happened. And when it did...it was... unbelievable.' She paused, and spoke more quietly still, more to herself than to him. 'Like coming home.'

'Oh, Sally.' Charles reached out and took her hand again.

'You do believe me, don't you, Charlie? I saw all this coming ... I just didn't know how to get out of it. Please say you believe me.'

'I do. I believe you.'

Her nose was running and she sniffed, to little effect. She laughed, embarrassed. 'Sorry,' she apologised. She delved again into her handbag, found Charles's wet handkerchief, and blew her nose noisily.

'Well?' she asked, her voice muffled.

'Well, what?'

'I don't know. Just … now what?' She tried, and failed, to wipe away some of the black tracks that had coursed down her face.

'You do look a state,' he said with a grin.

'I bet.'

'Look, the flat's just over the road. D'you want to come over and tidy up? I think you even left some makeup there.'

'There's a mirror in the loo here,' she pointed out. 'I wouldn't want to disrupt your evening.'

'You won't. I had nothing planned. I was going to watch TV and have an early night.'

'On your own?'

Charles smiled. 'Not necessarily.'

'Well, I ain't got nuffin' better to do,' said Sally, deliberately reverting to the Cockney urchin.

Charles reached out and grabbed one of her wrists in each of his hands, pulling the handkerchief away from her face. Then he half-stood, leaned forward and brought his face close to hers.

'I'm all runny,' she protested.

'Don't care,' he replied, and kissed her wet lips.

chapter 26

The following day Charles ran up the steps of Marble Arch underground station two at a time and emerged onto the corner of Oxford Street and Great Cumberland Place. He prepared to unfold his umbrella again but the rain had stopped. Fluffy white clouds now scudded across a blue sky, but it was cold and Charles realised that he'd missed the whole of the summer.

He turned the corner and checked his watch. He was late, so he jogged down Great Cumberland Place the two hundred yards or so to the hospital.

His father was ready to leave when Charles arrived at the private room on the second floor. Harry Horovitz sat in the armchair reading a newspaper, already wearing his sports jacket and trilby, with his holdall, containing his pyjamas, toiletries and books, zipped and ready to go by his feet.

Charles bent to kiss his father on the cheek. 'Sorry I'm late, Dad. Where's Davie?'

'He went to find matron to give her the chocolates your mother bought for the nurses. He should be back any – '

And the door opened and David entered. 'Charles,' he said, and he embraced his older brother warmly.

'All done?' asked Harry Horovitz.

'All done. She says thanks, but she's involved in a handover right now.' He patted his inside pocket. 'I've got the discharge letter for the GP.' David checked his watch. 'The cab should arrive in five minutes. Shall we go?' He picked up his father's bag and held out his hand to assist Harry to his feet.

'Hang on,' said Charles. 'I need to go to the administration office on the ground floor.'

'Why?'

'I spoke to a Mr Bloomfield last week, who told me to pop in and discuss payment terms. They don't normally …' Charles tailed off as he saw his father and brother turn to one another and share a smile. 'What?' he asked.

'Shall we tell him?' asked Harry.

'Tell me what?'

'I think you should, don't you?' responded David.

Instead of replying Harry reached across to the holdall at David's side and unzipped a side pocket. He drew out an envelope and handed it to Charles. Charles opened it. It was a letter to his father from Robeson, headed "Wandsworth Gaol."

Dear Harry,

I hope I can address you by your first name, as one Harry to another. I wanted you to know how much I appreciated the expert assistance Charles gave to me over the last few months. The fact that, as you will see from the head of this letter, I am now in prison is in no way due to him. I'm here because of decisions I personally made, and no advocate could possibly have done more for me than did Charles. You should be very proud of him. He is a brilliant barrister but, more importantly, he is utterly incorruptible. If I had a son, I could do no better than one like Charles.

Please don't worry about the hospital invoice. I've given instructions to my office to pay it directly and by the time you leave hospital it will already have been settled in full. For obvious reasons I have no immediate use of the money and it's much better spent on you! I suspect Charles will insist that the money is treated as a loan. I can't prevent him from repaying me if that's his wish, but as far as I'm concerned it's a gift from one Harry to another.

Please tell Charles to look out for himself – he'll know what I mean – and I wish you personally a gezunt ahf dein kop!

Harry Robeson

'What does that last bit mean?' asked Charles, showing the letter to David and pointing at the last line.

David looked again at the letter over his brother's shoulder. 'I wish you good health; literally "Good health on your head". What does he mean by that bit about you looking out for yourself?'

Charles shrugged and shook his head. 'No idea. Just wishing me well, I suppose.' Charles looked down at his father and found himself being scrutinised. 'Now what?' he asked.

Again Harry didn't answer directly, but instead opened the newspaper folded on his lap. He leafed through to the second or third page, folded the newspaper carefully so that a particular article was uppermost and handed it up to Charles. There, under yet another report concerning the resignation of Prime Minister Harold Macmillan, was the headline: *"Missing person enquiry: More gangland violence?"* Underneath a smiling photograph of Lyall was a short report to the effect that the police were still seeking the whereabouts of Mr Kenneth Lyall, the man acquitted in the summer of the Coulsdon Diamond Robbery. Lyall had been reported missing several weeks earlier and, despite extensive enquiries, appeared to have disappeared without trace. Police investigations were continuing but the continuing turf war between gangland criminals was thought to be responsible for his disappearance.

Charles handed the newspaper back to his father. 'So, Charles, should I be worried?' asked Harry.

Charles considered lying. Harry's surgery had taken place only a fortnight before and he was still convalescing; he'd been given strict orders to avoid stress. But although Harry Horowitz said little, he missed nothing. He wouldn't believe Charles's reassurances and would worry just as much as if he knew the truth.

'I hope not. But I do need to square things with a few rather unsavoury people whose noses I may have put out of place.'

Harry sat back in the armchair, and indicated that his sons should sit down too. 'Sit,' he ordered.

'The cab – ' said David, pointing out of the window. 'Will wait,' said Harry.

The brothers sat side by side on the bed. 'So: the Krays?' asked Harry.

Charles nodded. 'I think so, yes. Harry Robeson told me

that he was ... associated with them ... and that they'd be unhappy if he was convicted.'

'I did wonder,' commented Harry. 'Be careful, Charles. They're dangerous boys – Ronnie in particular. There's something wrong with that one.'

'How do you know so much about them?' asked David sceptically.

'Because, Davie, I used to know their Dad, Charles Kray. He was a "pesterer" before the war, and started by working the streets round where we lived.'

'"Pesterer?"' asked David.

'Yes; he knocked on people's doors and pestered them for old clothing, furniture and jewellery. He made a decent living. And he used to sell the gold to your mother's brother, Ephraim, when he had his shop in Black Lion Yard.'

'Ephraim? Isn't that the uncle who boxed?'

'Kid Carter he was called. English welterweight champion for two years – before he emigrated. Fastest hands I've ever seen. Your stance reminds me of his, Charles. So, the Krays' father and Ephraim became friends.'

'Is Charles Kray still alive?' asked Charles, suddenly more interested.

'Wait. Let me tell you the story.'

'Don't tire yourself out, Dad,' warned David. 'You're supposed to be taking things easy for at least three weeks.'

'So, this is not taking things easy? Sitting and talking to my sons? Shuh – let me finish already. So, I got to know Charles Kray too, and because we were always down the gym, we got to know his kids.'

'The twins?' concluded Charles.

'Yes, the twins when they started but, before then, their older brother, Charlie Kray. They were all boxers.'

'Dad,' Charles insisted. 'Is Charles Kray senior, the pesterer, still alive?'

Harry turned to Charles. 'I don't know. I haven't heard of him for years. But I do know where you can find the twins' older brother. Charlie Kray.'

•

Charles stood on the pavement of Wilton Place, Knightsbridge, opposite the door to Esmerelda's Barn, wearing his dinner jacket under his overcoat. For half an hour he had watched an apparently never-ending stream of taxis and chauffeur-driven limousines delivering and collecting members of the haute monde to the club cum casino.

Finally, he looked both ways and trotted across the road. An enormous doorman wearing a tuxedo and carrying a clipboard barred his way.

'My name's Holborne,' said Charles. 'Mr Charles Kray is expecting me.'

But the doorman didn't check his clipboard for Charles's name. Instead his eyes narrowed and he regarded Charles carefully for a second. Then: 'Wait there.'

The doorman stepped back into the lobby where he picked up a telephone. He spoke for a few seconds, hung up and returned to Charles.

'Mr Kray says you're on the list. He's sorry, but there ain't nothing he can do.'

Charles frowned, not understanding. 'Are you saying I can come in?'

'No. Not this list,' the doorman said, jabbing at the clipboard with his finger.

'Then…?'

'The Colonel's List.'

'"The Colonel"?'

The huge doorman laughed shortly. 'You serious? Ronnie's the Colonel.'

'And his "List"?' asked Charles.

The queue held up behind Charles began to get restive. He felt someone tap him on the shoulder. 'Come on chum,' said a male voice. 'Get out the way if you're not going in.'

'What do you mean, the "List"?' insisted Charles, holding his ground.

The bouncer's right hand flashed forward with astonishing speed and grabbed Charles's lapel. He dragged Charles's face towards him, lifting him to his tiptoes, and leaned forward. Charles's nose was assailed by a blend of alcohol fumes, aftershave and sweat.

'It means you're dead,' whispered the doorman. 'Got it? Once you're on Ronnie's List it's just a matter of time.'

The doorman dropped Charles back to the ground and dismissed him with a sweep of his arm. Charles found himself shoved out of the queue. The doorman pointed at a well-dressed couple in evening wear waiting to get in. 'Next!'

Acknowledgements

Huge thanks to Emma Riddell, the best unpublished writer I know, whose thoughtful analysis is always invaluable.

And of course thanks to my long-suffering family, who imagined that retirement from the Bar would see me finally emerge from my study, and have been sadly disappointed.

Thanks also to Tony McDaid, Martin Hulbert, Paul Bleasdale QC and all at No 5 Chambers, England's outstanding barristers' Chambers, for unfailing support.

Simon Michael was called to the Bar by the Honourable Society of the Middle Temple in 1978. In his many years of prosecuting and defending criminal cases he has dealt with a wide selection of murderers, armed robbers, con artists and other assorted villainy.

A storyteller all his life, Simon started writing short stories at school. His first novel (co-written) was published by Grafton in 1988 and was followed in 1989 by his first solo novel, *The Cut Throat*, the first of the Charles Holborne series, based on Simon's own experiences at the criminal Bar. *The Cut Throat* was successful in the UK (WH Allen) and in the USA (St Martin's Press) and the next in the series, *The Long Lie*, was published in 1992. Between the two, in 1991, Simon's short story "Split" was shortlisted for the Cosmopolitan/Perrier Short Story Award. He was also commissioned to write two feature screenplays.

Simon then put writing aside to concentrate on his career at the Bar. After a further 25 years' experience he now has sufficient plots based on real cases for another dozen legal thrillers. The first, *The Brief* was published in the autumn of 2015 to widespread aclaim and 5-star reviews.

Simon retired from the Bar in 2016 to concentrate on writing. He lives with his wife and youngest child in Bedfordshire. He is a founder member of the Ampthill Literary Festival.

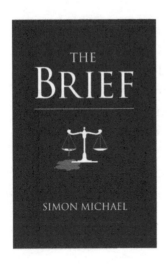

THE
BRIEF

SIMON MICHAEL

ISBN 978-1910692004, £8.99, 288pp, paperback

1960s London – gang wars, corrupt police, vice and pornography – ex-boxer, Charles Holborne, has plenty of opportunities to build his reputation with the criminal classes as a barrister who delivers. But Charles, an East End boy made good, is not all he seems, and his past is snapping at his heels. When his philandering wife has her throat slashed, Holborne finds himself on the wrong side of the law and on the run. Can he discover the truth of the brutal slaying and escape the hangman's noose? Based upon real Old Bailey cases and genuine court documents, **The Brief** is the first in barrister Simon Michael's series of compelling criminal dramas, an evocative slice of sleazy glamour from the Swinging Sixties. Simon Michael delivers an authentic and addictive read for any crime fan.